THE BANDIT TRAIL

WILLIAM MACLEOD RAINE

THORNDIKE
CHIVERS

This Large Print edition is published by Thorndike Press, Waterville, Maine, USA and by AudioGO Ltd, Bath, England.
Copyright © 1949 by William MacLeod Raine.
Copyright © renewed 1977 by the Estate of William Macleod Raine.
Thorndike Press, a part of Gale, Cengage Learning.
The moral right of the author has been asserted.

LIBRARY OF CONGRESS CATALOGING-IN-PUBLICATION DATA

Raine, William MacLeod, 1871–1954.
   The bandit trail / by William MacLeod Raine.
      p. cm. — (Thorndike Press large print western)
   ISBN-13: 978-1-4104-3545-3 (hardcover)
   ISBN-10: 1-4104-3545-8 (hardcover)
   1. Large type books. I. Title.
PS3535.A385B36 2011
813'.52—dc22   2010049327

BRITISH LIBRARY CATALOGUING-IN-PUBLICATION DATA AVAILABLE
Published in 2011 in the U.S. by arrangement with Golden West Literary Agency.
Published in 2011 in the U.K. by arrangement with Golden West Literary Agency.

U.K. Hardcover: 978 1 445 83690 4 (Chivers Large Print)
U.K. Softcover: 978 1 445 83691 1 (Camden Large Print)

Printed and bound in Great Britain by the MPG Books Group.
1 2 3 4 5 6 7 14 13 12 11 10

LIST OF CHAPTERS —

CHAPTER ONE:
LIVE OAKS WAKES UP

Jack Lovell drew up at the crest of the rise and looked down into the cup where Live Oaks lay huddled at the entrance to the canyon. This was strange terrain to him, but he had heard his uncle Chad tell about it often enough. The street that followed the rambling creek must be Rincon, the one crossing it at right angles, Blaine. From the defile that should be Dead Man's Gulch the latter emerged, a brown ribbon that passed over the bridge and wound up Millionaire Hill to the log and adobe houses scattered on its slope.

The place looked forlorn enough, though in the heyday of its mining boom it had reveled in an hour of glamorous dream. That had been before the gold veins pinched out. Now the fabulous Crescent was only a hole in the ground. Live Oaks remained on the map only because it was a convenient center for the surrounding cattle ranches as a supply point.

Lovell moved down the steep road into the sunlit bowl. The village seemed peaceful as old age. Except for the horses drowsing at the hitch bars in front of stores and saloons, Rincon appeared almost empty of life. It was the noon hour, and there was a drowsy warmth in the atmosphere.

At the end of the street, cut off from the other buildings by several vacant lots, were the livery stable and its connecting corral. Lovell turned into the yard through a wide gate above which was a sign: *Jim Roberts, Prop.*

Since the traveler's call brought no answer, he concluded that Jim Roberts, Prop., was absent for the moment. Lovell unsaddled and tied his mount in a stall. From the grain bin he took a measure of oats and emptied it into the feed box. The horse had been watered at a creek a mile back.

Lovell walked back through the stable to wash his hands and face at the pump in the yard. His glance picked up a man lying in one of the stalls face down. Past observation told him what that meant. A man had stumbled into the stable to sleep off a drunk. On the way back, after washing up, his eyes fell on the prone figure again. Something stiff and unnatural in its attitude held his gaze. He stared at the back of the head, trying not to believe what he saw. The hair was clotted with blood.

He stepped closer, to see a bullet hole above the base of the brain. The victim had been shot from behind. Probably the assassin had dragged the body into the stall for temporary concealment.

Jack Lovell thought fast. He knew the way of Western towns — to look upon a stranger with suspicion until he had proved himself. Just now he could not afford to be arrested, even though later he might be able to win clear. A man on the dodge is not in a position to stand investigation. Better get out of here while there was still time.

He took a step toward the stall where Keno was munching oats. Too late. A man walked whistling into the stable. He was tall and lanky, with tiny crow's-feet radiating from shrewd, friendly eyes. In age he was between thirty-five and forty.

Lovell said, "You Mr. Roberts?"

"That's right."

"I didn't see you around and fed my horse. That all right?"

"Sure. You staying long?"

"Don't know yet. Might be two-three days. Might be longer."

"Be four bits a day for the horse."

11

"Fair enough. What's the best place in town for me to eat?"

"The Tip Top. Run by a Chink; the grub's good." The lank man's eyes fixed on something back of the stranger. He craned his head sideways to see better. "What's *he* doing here?"

Lovell turned, not too fast, not too slow, to take a look at the man lying on the straw. "Oh, him! He was here when I came. Sleeping off a jag, wouldn't you say?" His voice was light and casual.

The owner of the stable showed a little annoyance as he stepped forward to identify his self-invited guest. "Third man in ten days who has come here to —" He cut off his sentence with a cry of amazement. "Good God! He's been shot." A moment later words of shocked recognition broke from his throat. "It's Zach Young."

Jack Lovell was as much surprised as the livery-stable man. He had never met the big cattleman, but everybody in the West had heard his name and knew him for an old-timer, predatory, forceful, and ruthless. Chad Lovell had been one of many he had crushed.

The local man turned on his customer, eyes already quick with suspicion. "I didn't get yore name," he said.

12

The stranger was ready for that question. He told the truth in part: "John Fremont." His surname he omitted.

Roberts sized him up quickly. He saw a man neither tall nor large, with chill gray eyes set in a hard, tanned face, one that showed no apprehension or disturbance. The newcomer stood at careless ease, but with a certain poised vigilance that might be released instantly as the power of a coiled spring. Packed muscles flowed down from the brown neck to the strong shoulders. He wore corduroy trousers stuffed into the tops of high-heeled boots, a polka-dot cotton shirt with blue bandanna knotted loosely around the neck, a low-crowned wide hat just a little tilted. The stamp of the outdoor West was written all over him, its audacity, self-reliance, and freedom from restraint. He might be a cowboy on the chuck line, but probably not. More likely he was one of the gentry infesting Brown's Hole or Robbers' Roost, a scamp very much wanted by the law.

"Someone shot him from behind," Roberts said.

"Correct."

"He was lying there when you came in?" Roberts went on, feeling his way.

"Like I told you before, yes." Lovell's

voice was quiet and sure. He had given up the idea of making an immediate getaway. It was not feasible. "Better get the sheriff, hadn't you?"

"That's right — and Doc White."

The livery-stable keeper hurried out of the building. The slap of his running feet could be heard and the sound of his shouting voice.

Lovell walked to the door and looked up the street. Live Oaks had wakened from its siesta. Men were pouring out of stores and saloons like pips squirting from a squeezed lemon, all headed for the corral. Excited shouts drifted down the street. Out of an office popped a plump little man, bag in hand. That would be Doc White.

The tide swept past Lovell into the stable. He found himself shoved to the wall against the bridles and harness hanging from pegs. A way through the crowd was made for the doctor. There was a babel of voices. Out of the confusion came the doctor's verdict.

"Nothing I can do. He's dead — shot in the head from behind."

A heavy-set man running to fat pushed to the front. He was the sheriff, Peter Houck. "Who knows anything about this?" he demanded. "Were you here when he was killed, Roberts?"

"No, Pete, I wasn't," the owner of the place answered. "I was eating dinner at the Tip Top. When I got back, Young was lying there dead. A stranger was here — claimed he had just reached town." Roberts's glance swept the crowd and fell on Lovell. "There he is."

Lovell shouldered into the open space near the stall and faced the officer.

"Who are you and what are you doing here?" demanded Houck.

"The name is Fremont — John Fremont," Lovell answered. "I'm looking for a job."

"Where you from?"

"Lubbock, Texas."

"How did you happen to hit Live Oaks?"

"Man named Chad Lovell gave me a letter to Bedford Rudholt. Seeing that I'm on the loose I drifted in here. Figured he might take me on."

A silence followed; significant it seemed to the man who had just come to the town, as if he had said something that they understood the importance of better than he did.

"So you brought a letter to Ford Rudholt — from Chad Lovell," Houck repeated, his voice falsely suave. "Sure that was all you brought?"

The stranger measured the sheriff with eyes cold and hard as frosted granite. This officer was a politician, he judged, a town man who rustled around with a glad hand and got votes. Naturally he would pick an outsider upon whom to fasten this crime rather than stir up the resentment of anybody he knew.

"If you're claiming I killed this man Young — if that is his name — why, you can get that out of yore nut right now. I never saw him alive. For what reason would I want to kill him?"

A short bandy-legged man with a dish face and a thin-lipped, cruel mouth edged to the front. "Why, you lunk-headed fool, you've told us the reason yoreself. You admit you are a go-between from Chad Lovell to Ford Rudholt."

"Lemme see that letter," ordered Houck.

Lovell took a letter from his pocket and handed it to the sheriff. Under the circumstances he knew that it was not going to do him any good. He had mentioned it only because he had thought it better to speak of it before he was searched. What already stood out like a bandaged thumb was the fact that both his uncle Chad and Bedford Rudholt were enemies of Zach Young, though Chad had been out of the picture for a good many years. Fortunately Jack had picked his alias before the letter was written.

The sheriff grunted and handed the letter to the dish-faced man. "I reckon you'll say you've never seen Rudholt either," he jeered, his gaze hard on the suspect.

"If I knew him I wouldn't need a letter of introduction to him, and if I'd met him since I got here he would have the letter and not me," Lovell replied.

The bandy-legged man passed the letter to a man with a fine head of silvery hair. "You read it, Colonel. The fellow is guilty as hell. He's jest trying to alibi himself."

Colonel Krock's title was political. He had once been on a governor's staff. Despite his white hair he was not much past fifty. His ruddy face looked young and the blue eyes in it friendly and benevolent.

"Let us make haste slowly, Ben," he said. "This young man may be innocent, as he claims. I've no doubt if we give our good sheriff time he'll lay hold of the guilty party." He turned to Houck. "Don't you think, Peter, you had better have a more private hearing to discuss this? Doctor White will want to remove the body. Perhaps you would like to take this young man and any witnesses there may be to the courthouse."

"Just what I was going to suggest, Colonel," Houck agreed. "I'll take yore gun, young man. You are my prisoner."

Lovell handed his revolver to the sheriff. "You're barking up the wrong tree," he said.

Ben Ringold showed his bad teeth in a grin. "Talking about trees," he suggested, "after Pete gets through with Mr. John Fremont, if that's what he calls himself, we can take him up Dead Man's Gulch and hang him nice to a live oak."

The colonel shook his head reproachfully. "That's no way to talk, Ben. As foreman of the Bar Z Y outfit you ought to show more respect for the law. We must consider this young man innocent unless there is proof that he committed this crime. All good citizens of Live Oaks will want to be sure that justice is done."

"Sure thing," Ringold gibed. "I want to have hold of the rope while we're doing it."

CHAPTER TWO: A FINGER OF SUSPICION

A dozen men trooped into the office of the sheriff. Houck took the armchair back of the desk. He did not offer his prisoner a chair, but that did not bother Lovell. With a sweep of the hand the stranger brushed

18

papers away from the corner of the desk and sat there, one foot on the floor, the other dangling negligently.

The sheriff flushed angrily, annoyed at the fellow's almost insolent insouciance. He thought of telling him to get up, but did not quite bring himself to it. There was something forceful, almost dangerous, about the man. He was not a run-of-the-range cowpuncher. It was easy to see in him the capacity for murder.

"How long were you in the stable before Jim Roberts got there?" Houck asked.

"Just long enough to unsaddle and feed."

"It takes less than a second to shoot a guy," Ringold interposed.

Lovell looked the foreman over carefully, appraisingly. "That's right," he agreed.

"If you'd let me run this, Ben, we'd get along faster," the sheriff said irritably.

He fiddled with the letter of introduction, rereading it.

DEAR FORD:
Meet John Fremont. I think you could use him in your business. He is thorough.
CHAD LOVELL.

"This reads funny to me," Houck said. "That stuff about Rudholt needing you in

19

his business." He jabbed a finger at the words. "Cover-up talk."

"You're certainly going to earn yore pay, Sheriff," Lovell told him derisively. "Not every officer can dig up a plot out of plain English. I thought Rudholt's business was cattle. And you'd better buy you a pair of spectacles. Chad doesn't say Rudholt needs me. It says he thinks he could use me."

"You're thorough, are you?" Houck snapped.

"I wouldn't want to brag on myself, Sheriff."

"What's the use of beefin'?" interrupted a rawboned puncher in shiny chaps. "It's plain as a bear track on a muddy trail. This fellow bumped off Mr. Young. Gimme his gun, and I'll prove it."

"You Bar Z Y boys are in too big a hurry, Sid," Colonel Krock said in mild but firm reproof. "A man's life is important. We don't want to jump at conclusions."

"Some folks think Zach's life was important too, Colonel," Ringold flung back. "I don't aim to sit here and let a hired killer talk himself out of the rope. Twenty years I worked for Zach Young. Best boss I ever had."

"Take it easy, Ben," urged Houck. "He ain't talkin' himself out of a thing."

"Lemme have that gun," the big cowboy repeated. "Betcha six bits a cartridge has been fired."

Houck broke the gun and examined it. The chamber upon which the hammer rested was empty, as was customary. The others had shells in them.

"Doesn't prove a thing," Ringold explained. "He had plenty of time to get rid of the cartridge."

Jim Roberts said, "Looks like someone would of heard a shot."

"There was no shot after I reached town," Lovell mentioned. "Young must have been dead before I got here."

The sheriff turned to the doctor. "How about that? Could you tell how long ago he had been shot?"

Doctor White considered. "No. I would say he hadn't been killed within thirty minutes of the time I got there, judging by the heat of the body."

"Which lets me out, since I hadn't reached town then," cut in Lovell.

"Says you and who else?" sneered Ringold. "We don't know when you got in here."

The arrested man ignored Ringold but spoke to the sheriff. "A woman rode down from the summit two-three hundred yards

21

back of me. Find out who she is. That ought to be easy. She'll tell you someone was just ahead of her."

A middle-aged man in town clothes made a suggestion. "Might have been Miss Esther Young. She was in and got her mail a little while ago."

"Have someone get her, Nat," Houck replied. "We'll see what she has to say."

Nat Holbrook left the room. He was owner of the store where the post office was housed. A man entering passed him on the way out.

The newcomer's light-blue, flinty eyes swept over those present, in them a mocking, unfriendly derision. From the broad, deep shoulders down he was powerfully built. The flesh on his thighs was packed like ropes of steel. His arrival, Lovell noticed, was a disturbing surprise to the sheriff. To others it was a challenge that brought them to wary attention.

"What's this I've heard about my name being mentioned in this business?" he demanded, his voice like the crack of a whip.

Houck was embarrassed. He was a man of sinuous ways who did not like to have hidden hates brought into the open to force him to decisions. "Glad you drapped in, Ford," he said with affected heartiness.

22

"We're trying to clear up this killing. Fact is
—"

He hesitated, searching for words to make his answer smooth and without offense. The cowboy who had been called Sid helped him out.

"Fact is, Mr. Rudholt, this dirty killer here was toting a letter to you from some bird in Texas," he said harshly.

Rudholt's gaze rested on the prisoner. "Who is this man?"

The sheriff gave him the note of introduction. Rudholt read it swiftly. "Any proof he killed Young?" the cattleman asked.

"Yore friend is guilty as hell," Ringold snarled. "He was caught on the spot before he could make a getaway."

Very steadily Rudholt looked at the foreman. "Be careful, you fool," he said in a low, clear voice that dripped menace.

The eyes of Ringold slid away. "He had a letter to you."

Lovell slipped in a word, his voice light and cool. "May it please the court, I wasn't trying to make a getaway."

"Looks like he might of done it," Houck said to Rudholt. "We think so. But seeing as you don't know him, why —" He left the sentence unfinished, with a gesture that acquitted Rudholt.

"A minority opinion claims he didn't," Lovell differed. "The chief evidence seems to be that I had a letter of introduction to you." He grinned at Rudholt, unabashed by the agate-hard eyes of the cattleman fastened on him.

The salient jaw of Bedford Rudholt clamped tightly. His searching gaze left Lovell and swept the room. Most of those here were unfriendly to him, a few were active enemies. The four Bar Z Y riders present were no doubt ready to fight at the drop of a hostile word. The sheriff had been hand-picked for election by Zach Young. Even Colonel Krock owed his position as judge to the support of the Bar Z Y owner. But Rudholt was a masterful man, iron-willed, and arrogance rode hot in him.

He said, deliberately, dragging out the words, "Maybe some of you would like to make comments on this letter."

Nobody picked up the challenge. Colonel Krock broke the long moment of silence. "Let us not have any bitterness we might later regret. A sad tragedy has occurred in our midst this morning. Our friend has been snatched from us by the weapon of an assassin. It is natural that those close to him should be incensed at the foul crime. But as yet we have no proof whatever as to who the guilty party is. We must act with restraint and coolness."

Rudholt's cynical eyes were cold as the ice on a mountain lake. "You have certainly buttered it up nice, Colonel, the way a lawyer *would* do. But me, I don't hold with this bouquets-for-the-dead stuff. Maybe Zach was your dear friend. He wasn't mine. To me he was plain wolf, and I won't be wearing any mourning for him. But I don't shoot men in the back, and it won't be safe for anybody to hint that I do."

The colonel's smile was still warm and urbane. "I am sure that nobody could harbor such a thought," he said.

But Ringold would not sit still like a whipped schoolboy. His anger flared out. "Don't try to run on us, Rudholt. We don't have to take it. You're not the czar of Rooshia. Nobody claims you killed Zach. This guy here did. But when he shows a letter to you from an old enemy of Zach, we got a right to ask what's doing."

"Don't ask out loud, for if I hear you I'll tell you to go to hell," the cattleman flung at the foreman.

The door opened. A young woman came into the office, followed by Nat Holbrook. Her face was pale and disturbed. She glanced at Ringold and then at Rudholt,

25

aware that she was interrupting a scene. At her entrance the sheriff heaved himself up from his chair.

Holbrook said, "I found Miss Esther at Medford's store."

"I had been at the hotel and hadn't heard about my uncle," she said to the sheriff. "It's true — that he has been killed?"

Houck nodded. "Yes, Miss Esther, it's true. He was shot from behind. We've caught the man we think did it. This fellow." He gave a lift of his hand toward Lovell.

Esther Young looked at the stranger. "Aren't you the man I saw coming down from the pass ahead of me?"

"That's right," Lovell said. "To murder a man I had never seen, and then to stick around till I get arrested."

"Did you hear the sound of a shot as you passed the corral?" Houck asked Miss Young.

"No," the young woman answered.

"Any idea how long ago it was when you reached town?"

"I know exactly when I got in, by the courthouse clock — twelve-fifteen."

Colonel Krock took out his watch. "I set it by the town clock an hour ago. It is now twelve-forty-six. But I can tie up the time

26

closer than that. It was just twelve-twenty-three when I heard Jim Roberts shouting that Zach had been killed."

"Which cuts the time I had been in town to about eight minutes — and Doctor White said Mr. Young had been shot at least a half an hour before," Lovell told the sheriff.

"I still think he did it," Ringold snarled.

Esther Young differed and said so. "How could he when he wasn't here till after Uncle Zach was killed?"

She was long-limbed, with pliant lines. A faint rose flush had beat up through the brown coloring of the skin. The girl was not beautiful, Lovell thought. The jaw was a little too square and the lips too firmly set. But she had an interesting face, alive and decisive, in keeping with the fine animal vigor of the body.

"I think we'll have to count Mr. Fremont out," Colonel Krock said. "Miss Esther's testimony gives him an alibi."

The sheriff took that sourly. He did not want to accept the stranger's innocence. To do so would be to posit a more unpleasant situation. For if Fremont had not shot Zach Young, some local person had killed him. It might be somebody in the room at the present moment. In the course of a long, hard life old Zach had trod on the toes of

27

scores of people roughly. Moreover, Houck was not sure about the credibility of the witness furnishing the alibi for the accused man. Esther Young had quarreled bitterly with her uncle, and had left his ranch to live on a small adjoining one owned by her, a brother, and a younger sister.

"Have you ever seen this man Fremont before today, Miss Esther?" he asked.

She looked at the prisoner carefully. "I don't think so."

"When was the last time you saw yore uncle?"

"Early this morning, when he passed in his buckboard on the way to town."

"Did you talk with him?"

The color flushed her cheeks more definitely. The answer came curtly, "No."

Houck frowned down at the blotting-paper on the desk and made small circles on it with the stub of a lead pencil.

"If this Fremont didn't kill Zach, who did?" demanded Ringold.

"Zach must of gone down to the corral to hitch up his buckboard and start for home," the sheriff said. "Any of you know when he went there?"

"He was in the post office about half-past eleven," Holbrook volunteered. "Said he was leaving right away for the ranch."

Another man said he had seen the cattle-man passing down the street on the way to the corral about that time.

"Must have been right after I went into the Tip Top for dinner," Roberts suggested.

"If any of you saw another man headed that way before or after Zach went down, now is the time to tell me," Houck said.

Nobody offered information on that point.

From a tight throat and dry mouth Jim Roberts spoke. "Might as well bring it into the open. Some of you are thinking I could of done it before I went to the Tip Top for dinner. You're wrong. Zach hadn't come down to the corral yet. Besides, I had no reason, even if I was a killer — which I ain't."

One of the men leaning against the wall gave a scoffing snort. "Owned the mortgage on yore outfit, didn't he? And was pressing for payment, I hear."

"That's silly," Esther Young protested indignantly. "It's no reason at all. Jim would still owe the money to the estate. Besides, he just isn't the kind to shoot a man in the back."

Roberts said, color beating up into his face through the tan, "Much obliged, Miss Esther."

Colonel Krock agreed with the girl. "If we

29

are going to suspect every man who owes your uncle money, we shall have to include half the town," he said with a smile. "After all, he owns the bank, or did."

"Somebody shot Zach," the sheriff insisted doggedly. "And I don't mean Jim either. There are men in this room who know more than they are telling. We've got to work together if we're going to pin this on the murderer. This town can't let its most prominent citizen get shot from behind and just say, 'Well, ain't that too bad!' If any of you know or suspicion evidence you're keeping back, it's yore duty to come through with it." He waited for a response, and when none came, snapped an irritable dismissal. "That will be all for right now. I'm getting nowhere with so big a group. But don't think for a minute that I've quit on this case. I aim to find who killed Zach. All of you keep yore eyes peeled, and if you see or hear anything I ought to know, tell me."

Those in the room began to troop out. Lovell asked the officer if he had decided not to arrest him.

"Not right now," Houck answered sourly.

"Then I'd like to have my gun back."

"You don't get it. That gun may have killed Zach Young. In spite of what Miss Young says, I think myself it did. Anyhow, it stays with me for a while."

"I wouldn't feel dressed, Mr. Sheriff, without a forty-five on my hip — not with this town as hostile to me as it is just now," Lovell said, dragging the words a little. "You wouldn't want two men murdered the same day, would you?"

"I'm keeping the gun," Houck told him obstinately.

Lovell accepted the decision with a lift of his shoulders. He decided he had probably better buy a revolver.

CHAPTER THREE:
DAD CANTRELL OFFERS ADVICE

Lovell sauntered across the street from the courthouse. Since he had no particular place to go and was in no hurry, he leaned against the plastered adobe wall of a store and watched the life of the town float past him. Esther Young came out of the courthouse with Colonel Krock on one side of her and Rudholt on the other. As they moved down the walk and across the street, it struck Lovell that she was devoting her remarks to Krock to the pointed exclusion of the cattleman. Evidently this did not disturb Rudholt. His cynical smile suggested amusement.

As they reached the sidewalk he swept his big hat off and bowed. "No use asking me to stay longer, Miss Young," he mocked. "I really must be going."

The only good-by she gave him was a look of complete disdain. Still smiling, he walked past Lovell into the store without noticing him. The man anchored to the wall watched the girl as she went down the street. She moved lightly and firmly, with untamed freedom, rhythm in every step. He had liked her low-pitched, husky voice. He guessed she was an imperious young vixen. But unless his judgment was wrong, she belonged to herself, would go her own way in life and not be driven by outward pressure.

Rudholt came out of the store, flicking at a bootleg with the lash of a quirt. At the sight of Lovell he stopped.

"Sorry you got in a jam before you met me," he said. "I'd like to oblige Chad, but I couldn't use you now. Can't afford to have people think I framed it with you to knock off Young." He added, carelessly, "I don't suppose you did kill him, eh? Or did you?"

The cool insolence of Lovell matched the arrogance of the other. "No, did *you?*" he drawled evenly, meeting him eye to eye.

The cattleman gripped the handle of the quirt so hard his knuckles stood out white. Lovell believed for a moment the man was going to use the whip. It was clearly in Rudholt's mind. He stood glaring at the Texan, then turned abruptly and walked away. He had thought better of it.

With a hint of amusement on his lean, reckless face, Lovell observed the reaching strides of the cattleman take him down the walk. Rudholt was tall, well-built, and coldly handsome, one who would get what he wanted out of life and not be too particular as to the method. Lovell felt sure he could name one of the man's objectives. When Esther Young had come into the sheriff's office, he had noted the expression in Rudholt's eyes, a greedy possessiveness blotted out almost instantly. It was possible she was attracted to him, though she certainly did not approve of him, perhaps because of the long, bitter antagonism between him and her uncle. She had a spirit keen and tempered as a fine blade. It would be interesting to learn — since he would probably not be around to see for himself — whether Rudholt's overbearing force could make him a welcome suitor in spite of accumulated resentments.

As Lovell sauntered down the sidewalk,

he knew that he was a focal point of attention. The stores and saloons on Rincon Street were crowded with people, brought downtown by the news of Zach Young's murder. Those who had been at the barn were identifying him to later arrivals as the man found in the stable beside the dead body.

He strolled as far as the crossroad that ran out of Dead Man's Gulch and over the creek to ramble crooked as a snake's trail up Millionaire Hill. Leaning on the railing of the bridge, he looked up at the gray dumps of the mines long since deserted. One of these must have come from the Crescent, over which his father and uncle had fought with Zach Young. On the shoulder to the left was the residence district, a good many of the houses log cabins or one-story frames. In a grove of live oaks running up from a draw, the roofs of more pretentious houses stood out, built no doubt by men who in the boom days thought they were on the road to fortune.

The sound of footsteps on the bridge caused Lovell to look up quickly. They reminded him that he had not yet bought the revolver he had promised himself to get. A man no longer young but still spry was moving toward him. He wore a battered old

Stetson, a checked shirt and open vest, and Levis which climbed up the legs of dusty, high-heeled boots. His face was tanned and wrinkled. On the back of his leathery neck was a pattern of crisscross lines. He stopped in front of Lovell and flung an abrupt question at him.

"You aimin' to be a permanent resident, young fellow?" he barked.

Jack Lovell turned, his forearms resting back of him on the railing of the bridge. "So you're a committee of welcome," he drawled.

"I ain't no sich a thing," the old-timer retorted in a high-pitched falsetto. His forefinger pointed to a graveyard on an adjoining slope. "That there is Boot Hill. Look at it good. That's where you'll be planted if you stick around here — in the boneyard."

"You a messenger for some other gent?" asked the young man lightly. "Or do you expect to rub me out yoreself?"

"Neither. I'm jest tellin' you. My name is Don Cantrell. Used to know Chad Lovell. Him and me were side-kicks. Where's the old vinegaroon at now?"

"Living on a ranch on the Green River. Who is so anxious to plant flowers on my grave? It has been proved I didn't kill Zach Young."

35

"Hmp!" Cantrell snorted. "So *you* think." Though nobody was in sight except for two men lounging on the hotel porch fifty yards away, the old man lowered his voice. "There's an open season on you, fellow. Those who are sore because Zach was killed are liable to bump you off. But the ones you want to be most scared of are the guys who killed him. You drapped in right convenient. If they fill you full of slugs, folks will be satisfied that justice has been done. Houck will be real happy because he won't have to start making enemies of important people. Case closed."

"So it's that way," Lovell said.

"That's whatever. Fool around till night and you won't ever leave. Understand, you're jest a two-spot in this game. Jest the sucker some guy can use to cover up what he did down at the corral."

"I'd better be careful not to let him get me too from behind," the young man said carelessly. He could not quite believe that Cantrell had sized the situation up right.

"You're figuring it wrong, fellow. This won't be a one-man job done on the quiet." Cantrell slammed a fist into the open palm of the other hand. "Get wise. They're tankin' up down at the Blue Moon right now. Have you ever been at a lynching? It

36

ain't nice."

"Oh, come, Mr. Cantrell," the younger man said pleasantly. "You're loading me or yoreself one. This is America — the land of the free, you know, where all men are equal if not more so. The boys may let off steam a little at the Blue Moon, but they're not going to take an innocent stranger and strangle him. It wouldn't be reasonable."

"Reasonable!" The sun-bleached eyes of Cantrell flamed with excitement. "Dod gast it, who claimed it would be reasonable? This here town is sitting on a keg of dynamite. Any time it's liable to blow up. Chances are the fellow who shot Zach Young has started a war. You're in it, whether you want to be or not."

"First time I ever saw Young was when he was lying dead in the stable. Until this morning I had never met anybody who lives in this town or neighborhood. I'm an outsider not drawing cards in the game."

"So *you* think." Cantrell glared at him with the impotent irritation the old often feel toward the jaunty confidence of the young. "Did Ben Ringold act like he thought you were only eye-ballin' [kibitzing] when he talked about stringin' you to a live oak? Thing for you to do is high-tail it back to Texas right damn now."

Jack Lovell intended to leave when he got ready, but there was no point in arguing with Cantrell about it. "I've got to rest my saddle awhile," he said amiably. "But I'm certainly obliged for your advice."

The old man threw up his loose-skinned hands. "All right. Go to hell on a shutter if you like. It's none of my doggoned business anyhow. I came to bring a message. Young lady wants you to come see her at the hotel — Miss Esther Young."

Lovell was surprised. He did not know what she could want with him, but he did not raise that point. Presently she would tell him herself.

"Now?" he asked.

"Right off. She's starting back to the ranch soon."

The men walked back toward the hotel together. Three cowboys were coming down the street. Lovell recognized two of them, the foreman of the Bar Z Y and next to him the big puncher in shiny chaps who had been called Sid.

Don Cantrell said hurriedly, "Talk soft, fellow, and don't go shootin' off yore mouth, or hell will break loose in Georgia."

The Bar Z Y men were still twenty yards away when Cantrell dragged open the gate in front of the hotel yard and tried to shove his companion through.

Light flickered in the shifty eyes of the foreman. The teeth back of his tight, cruel lips showed. "Look who's here?" he jeered. "If it ain't the killer himself."

"Now, boys," the old man implored, "let's not have any trouble."

"Get outa the way, Dad," ordered Sid. "You ain't in this."

"He ain't armed," Cantrell cried. "Houck kept his gun."

"The gun he used to shoot Zach from behind," Ringold retorted. "Come into the open and take yore medicine, you damned yellow-belly."

Lovell knew there was no way of escape. If he made a break for the house, he would be cut down before he got five steps along the path. He could not back off and use the old man as a shield, not and live with himself afterward. Since he was without a weapon, he could not even go down fighting.

With a sweep of the arm he flung Cantrell to one side and stood back of the fence facing his enemies. A door slammed behind him as Ringold swung up his forty-five. He heard the slap of feet coming swiftly from the house. His eyes were on Ringold's trigger finger, his body braced for the shock of the lead that would tear the life out of him. But the foreman did not fire. He glared with frustrated fury at somebody running up the path toward them. From his ugly mouth an oath ripped.

"Can't you ever mind yore own business?" he snarled.

Esther Young pushed down the barrel of his revolver, the eyes in her white face hot with anger. "You blundering fool!" she flung out. "Haven't you a lick of sense? He didn't kill Uncle Zach. He couldn't have."

"That's yore story." There was black temper back of Ringold's insolent sneer.

"It wouldn't make sense," she added. "He had no motive."

"You don't know a thing about him," the ZY foreman exploded. "His name is Lovell. He's a nephew of old Chad, who had the big fight with Zach over the Crescent Mine. His father was Gabe Lovell, killed up there on Millionaire Hill. Bill Sommers knew him soon as he set eyes on the fellow. He lied about his name. He lied when he said he was from Texas. He's one of those scalawags roostin' in Brown's Hole, and he's got a rep as a bad man."

Miss Young brushed that aside. "I don't care who he is. He didn't get here till after

Uncle Zach was dead. Nothing else matters."

"He's in it somehow." Ringold's shallow eyes smoldered with spleen. For the moment he had to choke back the urge to kill. This meddling woman had saved Lovell. "You can't tell me different. He gets here right spang when Zach is shot. That didn't just happen."

"We'll clear this up later," the girl told him imperiously. "I'm not going to have you murder him. Put up that gun."

The third cowboy, a black-haired graceful young fellow, caught hold of Ringold's wrist and pinned it to his side. "Take it easy, Ben," he said cheerfully. "No use pushing on the reins. You hear our new boss give orders. She's right too. This idea of bumping off an unarmed guy on suspicion is cockeyed. He's Jack Lovell all right, like I told you. But what of that? It may not mean a thing."

"Turn me loose, fellow," Ringold growled viciously.

"All right, Ben," Sommers said. "Let's not go crazy. Shove that hogleg back in its holster. You can chew the fat without fireworks." He loosened his grip watchfully, pretty sure that Ringold was past the point of immediate danger.

41

Lovell had not spoken a word since Ringold had drawn on him. He was a man who knew when to be silent, and he was aware that anything he might say would enrage the infuriated foreman. It was better just now to let others fight his battle. He had been quietly non-aggressive, but nothing in his bearing had suggested fear.

Ringold pushed the revolver into its holster and said hoarsely to his companions, "Let's go." He turned and went down the sidewalk in the direction from which he had come.

The big puncher Sid followed him, but Sommers stopped for a minute to make a less hostile exit.

"Sorry he blew the coop, Miss Esther," he said with a grin. "I don't know what the heck got into him. He must of been drinking, I reckon."

"Then he'd better let liquor alone," the girl said curtly.

"That's right," he agreed, then ducked his curly head in a bow and wheeled to rejoin his companions.

CHAPTER FOUR:
THE CIRCLE 72 HIRES A RIDER

Dad Cantrell sputtered like an uncorked bottle of pop. "Great jumpin' Jehosaphat, ain't you got no sense a-tall, girl? You got some fool idea you are bullet-proof? That yellow wolf might of — might of —" He took his weather-beaten old hat and flung it to the sidewalk in exasperation, entirely unable to put into words the fear that had paralyzed him and the relief that could find vent only in vexation.

"Don't excite yourself, Dad," Esther told him. "You know he wouldn't dare run the risk of hitting me."

"He could of plugged you before he had time to check himself. Lordy, I ain't been so scared since Hector was a pup." The old man's eyes still blazed wrath at her.

Lovell said, with an ironic, whimsical smile, "Don't you know it's bad form to walk into a loaded forty-five in the hand of a crazy man?"

The girl did not respond to his smile. Her cold eyes told him he was at the bar of judgment. "Is your name Jack Lovell?" she asked.

"Since I've been smoked out — yes," he told her airily.

"Knew you reminded me of somebody," Cantrell cried. "You're the spittin' image of Gabe." He shook hands warmly.

"What are you doing here?" Esther demanded.

"Just recovering from being rescued by Miss Young," he told her. "And none too soon. In two seconds it would have been too late. I'm certainly grateful."

She would have none of his thanks. "You haven't answered my question, sir."

His obligation was too great for him to tell her that he did not intend to answer it. "Since I was on the chuck line, I thought I would drift around to the old stamping ground of my family and maybe tie up with some cattle outfit," he explained.

"Strange you got here just when my uncle was killed."

"Just after, you mean," he corrected.

"Before or after," she insisted.

Colonel Krock came out of the hotel and joined them at the gate. "Good God, Miss Esther, what do you mean by interfering with men when they have guns out?" he reproved.

"I saw only one gun out, Colonel," she replied.

"Hell's bells!" exploded Cantrell. "One gun could kill you just the same as twenty."

"Right," Lovell agreed.

Krock appeared shocked at the danger she had run. "You must not take such risks, my dear. You were in the direct line of fire. Of course you didn't think of that, but you must not be so impetuous. I was so frightened for you that I dared not even follow for fear of exciting Ringold more."

Lovell told him, a slurring drawl in his low speech, "Miss Young thought of nothing, sir, except that she could not stand there and see murder done without lifting a hand to stop it." He added, a gleam in his eyes, "It sure was no ladylike way to act."

She rejected his gratitude, if that was what he implied, almost with indignation, the more readily because there was in his personality something vital that struck a spark from her imagination. She would have known the kind he must be, even if Bill Sommers had not certified him as a bad man. It was written in his cool and mocking eyes, in the muscular co-ordination of his lean, whipcord body, in the almost jaunty indifference with which he offered a dubious explanation of himself. The bone conformation of his face showed strength. If he was one of the desperadoes who infested

Brown's Hole, he had not slipped into crime by reason of weakness. It was the way of life he had chosen, and no doubt he followed it with cynical disregard of public opinion.

"Do you know who this man is, Colonel?" the girl asked. "His name is Lovell. He is the son and nephew of the men who tried to jump Uncle Zach's Crescent."

The stranger said grimly, "That's not the way I have heard it told."

"He says he is here looking for a ranch job," she continued. "That's too pat. I just don't believe it."

Colonel Krock said gently, "My dear, the young man's story may be true, since sometimes coincidences do happen."

"He lives in Brown's Hole, not in Texas as he claimed. At least Ben Ringold says so."

"I did not say I live in Texas," Lovell interrupted. "What I said was that I came from there. I was born at Lubbock. As for Brown's Hole, even though it has a bad name a few honest settlers live there."

"And a lot of ruffians wanted by the law," the girl threw at him scornfully. "An honest man does not come under an assumed name, unless he has done something to be ashamed of his own."

"Unless he is afraid he will be murdered if

he uses his own," he amended with a thin smile.

Cantrell bristled up to support Lovell. "Now don't you jump the gun, Miss Esther. I knew this boy's father and uncle. Slept under a tarp with them many's the night. They would do to ride the river with. I'll bet this young fellow's all right too."

Miss Young looked at him coldly. "I thought you worked for the Circle 72," she said.

The old-timer's eyes of washed-out blue met those of the young woman steadily. "You buy my time, Miss Esther, but not my opinions," he said, and added in reproof, "It ain't like you to talk thataway."

The girl knew he was in the right and did not resent his independence. She had known him all her life, a man honest, blunt, devoted to her family. He had taught her to ride when she had been scarcely more than a baby. When she broke with her uncle he had gone with her. But he was his own man and always would be.

"All right, Uncle Don," she replied, and her smile was warm with friendliness. "We won't quarrel about that."

"Suits me down to the ground," he agreed, and turned a frowning face on Lovell. "Young fellow, come clean," he snapped.

47

"You're holdin' back on us. Like Miss Esther says, you didn't come here hunting any thirty-dollars-a-month job."

"A fellow likes to ramble over the hill once in a while," Lovell said. "What's queer about that?"

"Would you care to mention where you worked last?" the colonel asked courteously.

"On my uncle's ranch in the Green River Valley." He smiled. "The old man is just a little bossy. I thought if I was away a couple of months, he might discover how much he needs me."

"Sounds reasonable," the colonel admitted.

Esther's dark eyes rested searchingly on Lovell. She had a feeling that all his explanations were evasive — that they covered sinister practices he wanted to keep concealed.

"Doctor White might have made a mistake," she ventured. "Uncle Zach may not have been dead as long as he thought. If that's so —"

Lovell picked up the sentence where she dropped it, a sardonic smile on his lips. "If that's so, Sheriff Houck can lay this killing right in my lap, where he wants it, and everybody will be satisfied."

Her frowning regard still rested on Lovell

disapprovingly. She was affronted at his cynical acceptance of her suggestion. An honest man would have defended himself indignantly. Yet it was strong in her mind that, no matter how far he had trodden forbidden trails, he was not guilty of the murder of her uncle. Character etches itself on the faces of frontiersmen. She read in the countenance of this lean, brown stranger a recklessness that might be ruthless, a self-sufficiency that could have carried him far outside the law. But unless she was mistaken there burned in him a spark of self-respect that would not let him shoot even an enemy in the back.

"Are you going to work for Mr. Rudholt?" she asked.

He shook his head, the flash of a whimsical smile in his eyes. "I don't qualify," he answered. "Mr. Rudholt wants his riders like his stock, stuff that grades A 1. A nice clean outfit with no cut-backs in it."

"You've talked with him, then?"

"He talked with me," Lovell corrected. "Long as I'm a suspicious character, nothing doing."

He told it casually, as one stating a fact, but Esther knew there was an ironic background to his words. During the years while Bedford Rudholt had been at war with Zach

Young, he had been as unscrupulous as his opponent. His riders had been tough hombres and the title to many of the cattle on his range very dubious, though recently he had put on a cover of respectability with the increase of his holdings.

"You quarreled with Mr. Rudholt," she said.

"We disagreed," he answered dryly. "Mr. Rudholt is good at handing out insults, but he doesn't like to take them."

When Esther thought about it later, she could not understand the impulse that found expression in her next words.

"I could use you on the Circle 72," she said.

He was astonished at the offer, but perhaps not more than she was.

"You've hired a rider, ma'am," he said.

CHAPTER FIVE:
DAD CANTRELL TALKS

Jack Lovell was saddling when Esther Young and Cantrell came out of the white house and walked across to the barn. The girl was in boots, Levis, checked shirt, and white Stetson. Even in that garb she was a picture that held the eye. It was one that stirred in the new Circle 72 rider an amused resentment. He was ashamed of it, for she had saved his life at some risk. But there it was in the back of his mind — a feeling that a young woman, so slim and gracefully built and vitally feminine, ought not to be so sure and so competent in affairs usually handled by men. She treated him with a touch of unstudied insolence, as if he were a ranch property instead of an individual in his own right. He responded with a studiedly polite indifference.

She said to Cantrell, almost ignoring the younger man, "Better take Lovell with you to push back any strays drifting into the brush."

The two men jiggled up the dusty road between the wire fences.

"Will you tell me why she hired me?" Lovell asked presently. "After laying herself out to show me what a no-account scalawag I am."

"I raised Cain with her for taking on a man she didn't know a thing about," the old-timer explained. "She can be doggoned impulsive. I'd say she hired you partly because you were getting a bad break and partly because Rudholt had turned you down."

The new rider tossed a bomb at the foreman. "Think she will marry Rudholt?"

Cantrell pulled up and glared at his companion angrily. "Marry him, you jugheaded chump! Whyfor would she marry that ornery skunk? She hates him good."

"Yeah, I noticed that. And she thinks about him a lot. He's a handsome devil, impudent and aggressive. Not the kind to wait at the gate but to push right into the house. He's aiming to marry her."

"You're crazy with the heat," Cantrell snapped, the excitement of hot denial in his high, falsetto voice. "How come you to get such a fool idea? Hell's bells! They don't hardly speak."

"I happened to be watching him when Miss Young came into the sheriff's office. His eyes gave him away. She knows it too. Right now she is fighting against it."

"You know so blamed much, don't you?" Dad yelped. "That fellow's not good enough to be a doormat for her. She wouldn't look at him. Not in a million years." He slammed his fist down on the horn of his saddle, eyes flaming with resentment at the indignity such a suggestion offered to his mistress. "You ride herd on what you say, fellow, and pay no mind to notions like that. They don't make any sense."

"You don't like Rudholt," Jack said, prodding him on. He had been gathering facts about the set-up in the district, but he still had a lot to learn. The easiest way to get persons and their relations to one another into a proper focus was to provoke people into talk they did not know he had got going.

"Like him! The same way I do a sidewinder. He started in here as a homesteader with a few cows. You never saw a herd grow like his. Every cow must have had about three calves a year. He picked up a piece of land here and there along the creek from busted nesters. How he got it God knows. First we knew he was the leader of all the starved outfits in the country. When he did not need them any longer, he kicked all his old friends in the face. Mr. Rudholt was going to be a big cattleman come hell or high water, and he hadn't any more time for the lowdown cow thieves who had helped make him what he is."

"If he built up his herd by rustling, he must have branded a good many Bar Z Y calves," Lovell said. "Why didn't Zach Young stop him?"

"Rudholt is as slick as a greased shote, and we never could quite get the proof. I grant you that he has plenty of gravel in his craw. Any time Zach wanted a fight, the fellow was there both ways from the ace. In those days he elected the county officers. We couldn't get anywhere in court. Once we found three Bar Z Y calves in a waddy's barn. He claimed we trained our stock to break in to get his feed, and I'm dunged if the judge didn't let him get away with it. Rudholt sat there in the room laughing."

"Must have hurt good old Zach, who was so simon-pure honest, to have such a sink of iniquity as Rudholt's Flying R for a close neighbor," Jack said innocently.

Cantrell rubbed with his open hand the crisscross wrinkles that made a diamond-shaped pattern on the back of his neck. Massage at the base of the brain helped him to clarify his thoughts. He was willing to admit to himself that Zach's predatory instincts had disturbed him at times, just as they had his niece Esther, but that was all in the family and the less said the better. Yet he could not blame Jack Lovell for not liking the man who had been responsible for his father's death.

"I ate at Zach's table for a good many years," the old man said gently.

"And you left it, just like his niece did, when you couldn't stand for his crooked ways any longer," Lovell reminded him.

"You hold yore opinion about him and I'll hold mine," Cantrell said stiffly.

54

The young man nodded agreement. "Why not? Live and let live is a good motto, though it wasn't Zach's. But I will say the old fellow was smart as a whip. After he had beaten us out of the Crescent and saw it was petering out, he sold it to an English syndicate for two hundred thousand dollars and let it hold the empty sack. I reckon that was the money which started him on his way to be a cattle king."

"That's right. The Bar Z Y was a small outfit till then, but he started building it up right away."

"I gather that Miss Esther, her young brother, and her sister, Miss Lucy, inherit their uncle's estate."

"There's a fourth heir, their cousin, a little older than Miss Esther. The will was made four years ago. They say Zach meant to change it, after the fuss with his niece, leaving her out, but he never got round to it."

"I haven't heard of this cousin," Jack said. "Did he live with Zach?"

"Yes. Name is Nick Haley."

"What's he like?"

"Between you an' me an' the gatepost he don't amount to a hill of beans. Good-looking, wild, nothing in him you can tie to."

"Who is going to run the Bar Z Y?"

"You'll have to ask someone that knows. I don't. The will says Haley, Miss Esther, and Colonel Krock are to have joint control of the estate until ten years after Zach's death. Krock is the lawyer for the outfit."

"How can he practice law and be a judge too?"

"The colonel is the only lawyer in town. When he ran for judge, it was agreed he need not give up his private work if it didn't come into his court. Nobody had any objections. So that's the way it is."

They rode beyond the fences to a rough brush country, back of which lay a tangle of rock pinnacles concealing canyons and gorges where nomadic night riders skulked on nefarious errands.

"That's where the cattle bootleggers hole up before and after their raids. They come down the outlaw trail from Brown's Hole — the whole cussed caboodle of scoundrels that nest there, train and bank robbers, horse thieves, rustlers, and killers." The old foreman turned on his companion angrily. "Hell, I don't need to tell you, seeing you're from that district yoreself. I reckon you've met Butch Cassidy and Kid Curry and the rest of the Wild Bunch that stick up banks and trains."

"I know Cassidy, and once at Casper, Kid

Curry and his brother Loney were pointed out to me. None of them live in the Green River country, though they pass through coming and going. The Hole-in-the-Wall, far up in Wyoming, is supposed to be their chief hang-out. I'm told they wander over the wilder parts of half a dozen states."

"There is a regular trade in stolen cattle that the Wild Bunch get the credit for," Cantrell said. "They run the stuff north by trails honest folks don't travel much, through mountain-walled valleys to Robbers' Roost and Brown's Hole. Later they push the herds to wherever there is a market. Of course I'm telling you what you already know."

"Everybody who lives along the outlaw trail, or within a hundred miles of it, knows what is going on, but most of us don't know for sure who the rustlers are," Lovell said. "My opinion is that Cassidy and Kid Curry and the crowd closest to them don't fool much with cattle any more. They prefer big hold-ups where they can make quick getaways. But there are a lot of desperate fellows — some of them hangers-on of the Wild Bunch — nesters in the mountain parks back of the long trail, who make a living from other men's stock. It is a wild country of deep defiles and cross-canyons,

57

unknown to anybody except themselves."

"Whoever they are, they have confederates right here in some of these ranches." Cantrell slapped irritably at a horsefly on his mount's neck. "Someone tips them off when and where to make their raids. Maybe some of the nesters along the creeks, or maybe some son of a gun right on the Circle 72. *Quien sabe?*"

"Any guess who?" Lovell asked.

"Hell, no!" exploded the old foreman. "I could guess plenty it might be, but guesses don't buy us anything. If we knew, we would string him up quick. Some day we'll find out."

Lovell agreed that spies would be hard to trap except by chance. "I might be one myself," he added with a grin.

The old-timer did not think that was funny. His faded eyes rested a long time on the other's face. "That's what I told Miss Esther," he answered bluntly. "I said it was plumb foolish to hire you without a recommend from someone she knew."

"And what did she say to that?"

"She said if you were planted here to give rustlers tips, we had better have you right under our eyes all the time."

Lovell laughed dryly. "I'm sure much

obliged for the good opinion my bosses have of me."

"Whose fault is it?" Dad wanted to know, his voice rising sharply. "We done give you a chance to come clean and you wouldn't take it."

That was true, Lovell admitted to himself. But he had a conviction that neither Miss Young nor Cantrell believed him to be a spy or he would not have been employed.

They rode up from a hollow in the low hills by a backbone ridge that brought them to a brake of thick underbrush stretching across the mesa to the rimrock bounding it. Dad pointed out cattle browsing in the tangled growth. He swung the head of his horse to ride down and turn the stock back to the Circle 72 range.

The ping of a rifle bullet whistled across the ridge. Lovell felt the shock of a blow. A slug of lead had torn the leather from his saddle horn.

His reaction was instant. He sent his mount plunging into the chaparral, straight toward the spot from which a thin drift of smoke was rising. Branches whipped at his face and limbs as he plowed through the dense growth. He heard but did not heed the sound of a bullet zipping past him. The rifleman could not see him now. The shot had been flung out wildly as a threat to stop his charge.

His horse slid down a three-foot bank into a dry wash, raced across the sandy floor, and scrambled up the opposite bank. Lovell heard the slap of bushes violently disturbed. He knew what that meant. The fellow who had bushwhacked him was scudding for safety.

The brush thinned as he drew closer to the rimrock. He caught a glimpse of a rider on a sorrel horse disappearing into a break that cut the sandstone wall like a sword cleft. Lovell dragged his pony to a halt. He was not going to ride across that open stretch, an easy mark for an assassin sheltered in the rocks ahead. Nor was he going to follow into a canyon where an enemy could shoot him down from a point of his own choosing.

The noise of Dad Cantrell thrashing through the high bushes drifted to him on the light breeze. He turned back into the thicket and moved toward the sound. Presently he lifted his voice in a shout. The flogging of the horse's progress through the chaparral stopped. Cantrell had pulled up to listen, to find whether he was friend or foe. Jack gave his name and rode forward.

Cantrell snapped a question at him when

they were close. "Aren't you the lunkhead I heard telling a girl the other day how crazy it is to head slam-bang at a gun in a killer's hand?"

Lovell pleaded guilty, but added an explanation. "If I'd tried to gallop back down the ridge he could have picked me off sure. He would have had a couple more cracks at me in the open. Down in the brush he couldn't see me. And I've noticed a drygulcher wants the breaks. I reckoned his nerve would weaken when he heard me heading for him. Like it did."

"Hmp! You went for him hell-for-leather because you were plumb scared. That it?"

"Right. I hunted the nearest cover."

"You're the doggonedest liar I ever met up with. Don't you ever run out of them and tell the truth?"

"I'm peculiar," Jack said. "I don't like a fellow with a Winchester to make a target of me. So I skedaddle *muy pronto*."

"If you'd lit out like I told you, nobody would be shooting at you. No need of you stickin' around that I can see."

"I don't like to be crowded. When I find out who has an open season on me and why, maybe I'll hit the trail."

Lovell had been living on the border of a district which was entirely outside the law, one settled by rustlers and frequented by bandits. This was an entirely different set-up. Its inhabitants were supposed to be respectable citizens upholding law and order. But underneath the surface he sensed here crosscurrents of hatred both concealed and open. He was beginning to understand what Dad had meant when he said Live Oaks was sitting on a keg of dynamite. A hundred men had resented the dominance of old Zach. He had quarreled with his own family. Rudholt was at odds with his old friends and his old enemies. Thieves made for distrust between neighbors. Evil was not bold and rampant here as in Robbers' Roost and Brown's Hole. It was smoldering and hidden. Therefore more explosive. The only wise, tolerant man he had met here was Colonel Krock.

CHAPTER SIX:
BILL SOMMERS SITS IN

A lean, brown man with a hardbitten face sat in the office facing Houck. He was a deputy United States Marshal, and he had explained he had come south looking for a fugitive who had lit out.

The sheriff hammered the desk with his fist. "Knew it. Knew from the first he was a bad egg. Hadn't hardly lit from his saddle before he had shot Zach Young from behind. I've seen too many of these birds who come down the outlaws' trail not to know one right off. They're ear-marked, Mr. Parker, if you can read what's written on them."

"Some of them," Lloyd Parker agreed. "Not all. One of the worst killers I ever met is a pint-size, smiling little fellow as mild as skim milk. You may have heard of him — Nate Winters. He's still around. We think he was one of the fellows with Lovell when he robbed the U.P. express at Wilcox. Far as Lovell himself goes, he was just a reckless cowboy who went bad. He still has a lot of friends. One of the gang killed Sheriff Hazen, when he was crowding them after they had reached Castle Creek above Casper, but we don't know Lovell was the one. Might have been Kid Curry. He's quick on the shoot."

"So is Lovell," the sheriff said. "He had a letter to Ford Rudholt from old Chad Lovell, both enemies of Young. I'm not saying who, but someone hired him to get Zach."

"Know where he is now?" the marshal asked.

"Working on the Circle 72 for Miss Esther Young, I've been told." Houck added, significance in his voice, "Maybe it ties in and maybe it doesn't, but she heirs a big slice of Zach's property — and not two weeks before the old man was killed she had had a quarrel with him and left the ranch."

Parker shook his head. "I wouldn't think Jack Lovell is that kind of a killer."

"Different here," Houck disagreed. "Zach was responsible for his father's death, folks say. He comes down the hill the very hour Zach is bumped off. We find him tied up to three of the old man's enemies. Jim Roberts walks into the stable and finds him there with the dead body. What more do you want?"

"I've talked with Doctor White and Colonel Krock, and it looks as if Lovell has an ironclad alibi. But he hasn't one for the Wilcox train robbery. That's where we cinch him."

Houck grumbled assent. That might be the best out for him. If Lovell was a train robber, it ought not to be hard to convince people that he was also a hired assassin. By taking the fellow back up the trail, Lloyd Parker would relieve the sheriff of responsibility. Even with evidence enough to convict Lovell of the Zach Young murder — which he certainly had not got yet — one never knew what would come out at a trial. Any

64

testimony that slipped from a witness implicating any of Houck's allies might be very embarrassing.

"Want me to help you arrest him?" Houck asked.

"I might need help. He's a tough guy, and he may light out before I reach him."

"I'll take a couple of deputies with us," the sheriff said. "They might come in handy."

The lean, brown man said, a gleam of sardonic mirth in his gray eyes, "Do you think two will be enough?"

"For all we know he's got friends ready to help him," Houck explained. "Better have too many in the posse than too few."

Bill Sommers was lounging in front of the Blue Moon when the posse was ready to start. The sheriff called to him and he strolled up to the hitching bar where the men were mounting.

"You ride for the Bar Z Y, don't you?" Houck asked.

"That's correct," the curly-headed youth answered.

"I've been told that fellow Jack Lovell is working for Miss Young at the Circle 72. Do you know if that's so?"

"How would I know?" inquired the black-haired youth coldly.

"The ranches join, don't they?"

"Sure. But we don't play marbles with the Circle 72 boys."

"Thought you might have heard some talk."

"No information," Sommers said bluntly.

The four riders jogged up Rincon Street, stirring up a cloud of hot yellow dust. The cowpuncher watched them disappear around the bend in the road. They must be going to collect Lovell. Probably some new evidence had come out that tied him to the killing of Zach Young. From the first Houck had been set on hanging it on the stranger if he could. He was the kind of schemer who would look out for himself every time.

Sommers was not a friend of Lovell. He had never spoken a dozen words to him. But he liked the nonchalant way the fellow had stood up to his accusers in the sheriff's office and later had faced Ringold's gun. Bill had been at outs with the law himself more than once, and he was temperamentally against man-hunters, especially those of Houck's stripe.

He considered the situation, while he leaned against an adobe wall and rolled a cigarette. He had been sent to town for some ranch supplies and on his way back to the Bar Z Y could detour by way of the

Circle 72. If he got a hustle on him and went over the notch gap, he could arrive before the posse. His hunch was that Lovell had not been implicated in the Young killing: In any case he was ready to give him the benefit of the doubt.

The young fellow grinned wryly. Why go out of his way to hunt trouble? He had enough of his own. A picture of a girl flying from the hotel to slap down a pistol pointed at a man's heart flashed to his mind. It brought him to an impulsive decision.

"Damfidon't," he said aloud, and half a second later was jerking free the slipknot that tied his mount to a hitch bar.

He deflected from Rincon to take the canyon trail starting just back of Roberts's corral. It wound up through a grove of live oaks, narrowing to a steep rocky trough few cared to travel. A hundred feet from the summit Sommers dismounted. He was at the foot of a sandstone rim that marched almost straight up.

The mustang could climb like a cat, but it had to be urged to try the precipitous ascent.

"Let's go, Blaze," the man cajoled. "Hang on by yore eyebrows. You cain't get killed but once anyhow."

Blaze eyed the boulder-strewn precipice,

dug in his front hoofs, bunched ropelike muscles, and plunged forward.

The rider stopped at the top for a breathing space. No need to hurry. The sheriff's posse was not going to founder any horses to get to the Circle 72.

Above the gulch a draw bisected the plateau, deep enough so that a rider following it could not be seen from the road well off to the right. The notch gap bounded the mesa, a gateway in the crotch between two peaks.

Emerging from the gap, Sommers could see far below a line fence of the Circle 72. Beyond that a windmill's blades caught the sun rays and flashed signals at him. The house, in a valley back of a hill, could not be seen yet.

He dropped down the slope, crossed a sage flat, and came to the ranch steading from the rear.

There was activity in a corral. Two men were trying to saddle an unbroken colt and a third watched from the top of the fence. Sommers rode to the corral. He discovered that the observer perched on the rail was Esther Young. She wore dusty boots, chaps, and cotton shirt. One of the men working with the colt was her young brother Jerry. The other was Jack Lovell.

CHAPTER SEVEN: ESTHER BLOWS HOT AND COLD

Esther Young turned her head and looked at Sommers as he drew close to the corral. She had seen him once before, beside Ben Ringold in front of the Live Oaks Hotel. Her eyes asked him silently what he was doing here. Already she had learned the wisdom of few words.

Sommers took the hat from his curly head and smiled. "Good mornin'," he said. "Like to speak to Lovell, ma'am."

The young woman called to the horse-breaker, "Someone to see you, Lovell." To her brother she added, "Just leave the saddle on Chips a while and let him get used to it, Jerry. That will be enough for today."

Jerry was a gangling, seventeen-year-old with brindle hair. "All right, sis," he said. "I might fork him after dinner."

Lovell walked to the fence and laid a strong brown hand on the top rail. He nodded at the Bar Z Y rider, an inquiring gaze fixed on him. Sommers was a little embarrassed. He would have preferred warning Lovell while his employer was not present.

"Houck heading this way with a posse,"

he blurted out.

"Looking for me?" the man in the corral asked quietly.

"He asked me if you worked here. Stranger with him."

"Know the stranger's name?"

"The story about town is that he's a United States Marshal from Utah. Registered at the hotel as Lloyd Parker."

The cool, steady eyes of Lovell told nothing. They looked at the saddled pony, but they were seeing something else.

A pulse beat in Esther's throat. "Does the Government want you?" she asked, her gaze full on the lean, sun-tanned face of her employee.

"It has not mentioned so to me," he replied, his ironic smile mocking her anger.

The hot blood crept up into her face. "If you are a criminal, don't look to me for help," she warned, the sting of a small lash in her low voice.

"The law can make a mistake and pick on the wrong man," Lovell pointed out to her, his manner light and casual.

She interpreted it as impudent effrontery. "I knew all the time there was something wrong about you," the girl cried, a repressed violence almost breaking through the words.

"So you hired me to reform me," he said.

"I was a fool," she answered bitterly.

Sommers murmured advice to the fugitive. "Better dust, fellow."

"So I had," Lovell agreed. "Much obliged, Sommers." To his employer he said, "If you're a fool, Miss Young, it's a fine kind of folly. I take my hat off to it. What you have done for me I'll never forget."

He turned away, leaving her surprised and disturbed. There had been no trace of levity in his manner. She wished he would be one or the other — an impudent scoundrel or an honest man unjustly accused — and not keep her in a swither of doubt.

He walked to the stable, then ran up and saddled his buckskin. From the open window of the living-room she watched him ride down the lane at a road gait. He showed no sign of hurry and no concern for his safety. The raffish side of him was in the ascendant again. He was singing a Negro song, and the words drifted back to her on the breeze:

Oh, de boll weevil am a little black bug.
  Come from Mexico, they say,
Come all de way to Texas, jus' a-lookin'
    foh a place to stay,
  Jus' a-lookin' foh a home, jus' a-lookin'
    foh a home.

The anger hardened in her heart. What was the sense in fighting the evident truth — that he was a desperado dyed in the wool? Any nincompoop knew that a bad man could have an engaging manner and an honest face.

The sheriff's posse arrived five minutes after the dust stirred by the buckskin's hoofs had settled.

"Sorry to bother you, Miss Esther," Houck explained apologetically, "but the fact is we have come to pick up an outlaw who has just started riding for you, fellow by the name of Lovell."

Esther stood on the porch facing the men on horseback. "What has he done?" she asked.

"He's one of the fellows who robbed the U.P. train at Wilcox, Wyoming, and later killed Sheriff Hazen." Houck broke off to introduce the Utah officer. "This is Mr. Lloyd Parker, a United States Deputy Marshal, who has come to pick up Lovell."

"You are sure this man Lovell is guilty?" Esther asked the marshal.

"It looks like he's the man we want," Parker answered. "He answers the description of one of the bandits. This was a Butch Cassidy job, and Lovell was seen riding with Butch a few hours after the hold-up while they were in the hills making their getaway. Before we could arrest Lovell, he lit out from his uncle's place on Green River, where he had just got back after being away more than three weeks."

"I knew he was an outlaw soon as I laid eyes on him," Houck put in smugly. "Don't be scared, Miss Esther. We'll arrest him without any trouble, unless he's fool enough to resist."

"He isn't here," Esther told him.

"Not here? Why, I got it straight that he's riding for yore outfit."

"He was, until ten minutes ago," she said evenly. "I suppose he got to worrying and thought he had better leave, so he saddled up and rode away."

"Did he tell you where he was going?" Parker asked.

"No, just said he thought he would be on his way again."

"Which way did he go?" demanded the sheriff.

Esther pointed to the north — to the faraway rock pinnacles where fugitives from justice were supposed to find safe refuge.

"Riding like the heel flies were after him, I reckon," Houck growled.

"Not at all," Esther answered, her eyes bright with mocking lights. Even though anger at Lovell was still burning in her, she was glad to see the sheriff frustrated. "He left at a road gait singing a song."

Houck just managed to cut off the oath that almost slipped out. He was annoyed, at Esther Young as much as at the fugtive who had for the time just escaped him. The impudent little devil was laughing at him. His mind was full of suspicion. From the first she had thrown in with Lovell. Her testimony had freed him from arrest for the murder of her uncle. She had saved his life at the hotel and had taken him on as a rider for the Circle 72. Likely enough she had the fellow holed up on the ranch within a mile of the house. But it was his settled policy not to make important enemies. He had to swallow his mistrust and lump if not like it. It would not do to have against him the young woman who was now part owner and one of the directors of the big Zach Young holdings.

"We can probably pick him up jogging along the road not far from here," Parker told the sheriff. "He won't be expecting us."

Esther watched the posse canter down the lane, a tumult in her breast.

"I hope they don't get him," Jerry said. "Jack's all right."

His sister turned on him hotly. "What do

you mean he's all right? He's a train robber and a bandit."

Her anger was at herself and not at Jerry, at the traitorous emotion that betrayed her judgment. She too hoped the scoundrel would escape, and she despised herself for the softness that flooded her and vitiated her integrity.

CHAPTER EIGHT:
NICK DECIDES NOT TO BE A TWO-SPOT

Nick Haley and Colonel Krock drove over from the Bar Z Y just in time for dinner. Though they had come to talk business, that waited until after they had eaten. Nick was a slim, dark, good-looking youth with a line of brash talk that went well among girls. Mirth came easily to him, and when he smiled his coffee-brown face broke to flash two rows of fine white teeth.

Lucy reached the table a little late, and at sight of her Nick brightened at once. She was seventeen, and decidedly the beauty of the family. In her there was none of Esther's toughness of fiber. She looked as soft and cuddly as a kitten. Her brown eyes had amber lights in them, and in the sunlight her hair showed a tawny gold shot through with copper. The lower lip was full and sometimes sulky.

The talk centered on Jack Lovell. Not ten minutes ago Dad Cantrell had got back from the south pasture and he wanted to know all about what had occurred. Esther said very little, but Jerry talked enough for two. He had an attentive audience, for both Krock and Haley were interested.

"I don't care whether he's a train robber or not," Lucy said, excitement in her face. "I hope he gets away." That made it unanimous in the family, though Lucy would not have guessed it from her sister's reproving look.

"And I hope they get him," Nick differed. "I'm not satisfied that he didn't kill Uncle Zach."

Colonel Krock shook his head. "You're wrong there, Nick. Miss Esther's testimony clears him of that. But I'm afraid he is guilty of this train robbery. It's too bad. I liked him." Regretfully, he asked, "Why do so many young men who might have useful happy lives blast their futures by wild folly?"

"Betcha he didn't rob that train," Cantrell piped up shrilly. "Betcha he ain't a bandit any more than I am."

Esther was grateful to her foreman for his

sharp defense of the accused man, none the less because she knew he was not as confident as he sounded, but had rapped out his protest out of loyalty to the friends of his youth and partly from friendship to Jack.

"The fellow certainly threw a big shadow at the Circle 72," Haley said with a sour laugh.

"You would like him if you knew him, Nick," Lucy told him.

His eyes rested on the girl's soft blond loveliness. He did not feel more disposed to like Lovell because she was his champion.

With their two guests Esther moved to the small room that had been her father's office years ago and now was hers. They had some decisions to make in regard to the Bar Z Y.

Nick rolled a cigarette. With the permission of their hostess the colonel smoked a cigar.

"We've been talking to Ringold about buying that bunch of whiteface stuff your uncle was negotiating for before he was killed," Krock said. "He thinks we should go through with the deal."

"Does it matter what Ringold thinks?" Esther asked. "He is only an employee."

"That's right," Nick agreed.

"He's a good stockman," the colonel suggested. "Knows cattle."

"I don't like him," Esther said. "Never have. He's a bad-hearted man, too quick with a gun."

Colonel Krock agreed that he did not very much like him, but he felt that personal feeling ought not to enter too much into business relations. Zach Young would not have kept him if he had not been competent.

Esther thought that a good point. She did not press her opinion further. For the present at least Ringold would do as foreman.

A minute later she had come to a flat difference of opinion with her cousin. He wanted to be manager of the Bar Z Y, and she did not approve of that at all. To her surprise Colonel Krock backed the claim of young Haley.

"I'm the oldest of the heirs and the only man," Nick urged. "What's the matter with me running the ranch?"

"I don't want to be personal, Nick, but you've never done anything but spend. You just haven't earned the right to have charge of other people's money." Esther spoke quietly, without heat.

"I suppose you'd like to run it yoreself," he gibed.

"Yes, I would. I represent three fourths of the heirs, and for years I have done all the

78

bookkeeping for Uncle Zach. You have never taken any real interest in the place."

"A boy grows into a man," the colonel suggested gently. "And if necessary we can advise him. Of course Nick would be willing to consult us. I think he ought to have his chance. It might be the making of him."

"Sure — sure," Nick promised glibly. "I'll ask your advice."

"It wouldn't work," Esther said flatly.

Unfortunately by the terms of the will the ranch could not be divided until ten years after the death of Zach. The heirs had to work in harmony. If they disagreed, some compromise would have to be evolved. Esther knew that her cousin was both weak and headstrong. It would not be easy to cooperate with him. She thought it strange that the colonel did not realize Nick's unfitness for so much responsibility.

"You were always Uncle Zach's favorite — before you fussed with him," Haley charged. "I was only a two-spot and you were ace-high. But you're not going to boss the show now. I'm going to have my rights."

The colonel reproved the young man mildly. "You are going at this the wrong way, Nick. That hotheaded kind of talk isn't helping you any. It takes a reasonable man, one with balance, to handle a ranch like the

Bar Z Y. It's because I think that at bottom you are sound I want you to have your chance. But you have a lot to learn. Unless you realize this and live up to your responsibilities, you will not succeed." He turned to the girl. "There is no hurry, Miss Esther. Let us all think this over carefully and prayerfully."

Esther agreed that this did not have to be settled now. Her opinion had not changed, but she was one of three administrators, and knew she could not impose her will against a majority vote. Later in the day she was going into town to order some spools of barbwire. She could have a private talk with Colonel Krock then and tell him very plainly her objections to Nick as ranch manager. Her cousin was slack, indolent, and at times dissipated. He lapped up flattery, and would be very easily imposed upon. Most of his time would be spent in town instead of at the Bar Z Y. The organization would begin to break down very quickly.

CHAPTER NINE: THE BAD PENNY RETURNS

As soon as Jack Lovell was no longer within sight of the house he put his pony to a canter. The sun streamed across the desert, tipping the mesquite with a silvery sheen. Fine dust drifting in the air gave the atmosphere a yellowish haze.

When the road dipped to cross a water run, he left it and followed the arroyo. A long-legged killdeer ran ahead of him protesting noisily his approach. His glance picked up two antelope flitting through the brush. Across the sand a whirling dust devil moved. Far away rose papier-mâché mountains, a thin, broken-edged silhouette in the untempered light. Except for one small bank of fleecy clouds the sky was a deep, unbroken blue.

His pony fell into a road gait. Jack had ridden the animal hard during the forenoon and it showed signs of weariness. He patted its neck gently.

"Soon as we find grass, Chipmunk, I'll throw off and give you a rest," he promised.

The country grew more hilly, less dry. He turned into a draw carpeted with alfilerillo and swung to the ground. After unsaddling, he picketed the pony in the grass.

In the shadow of a mesquite he lay down and looked up into the arch above him. There was a smile on his lips. He was thinking of Esther Young, so young and hard and inflexible, proud, with a banner of courage in her eyes. Now that she had inherited from her uncle, she would soon be known as a cattle queen all over this part of the country. And the man who married her — unless it turned out that Bedford Rudholt, who aimed to be a cattle king in his own right, was the winner of the lady — the man who married her would be Esther Young's husband, a two-spot in the land. A prince consort to that cattle queen would wear not a crown but a yoke.

Jack's eyes drooped — half-opened — closed again. His shoulders settled into a more comfortable position. He fell asleep and dreamed that a dark-eyed lady wearing a crown was pursuing him with a horsewhip while he dodged behind the palace furniture and back of marble pillars. Ducking into an alcove, he found himself trapped. She said, triumphantly, "I've got you now."

Her voice was such a surprisingly heavy bass that he awoke, to discover that Sheriff Houck was the speaker, and that in his hand was a forty-five pointed directly at his midriff.

Lovell drawled, reproachfully, "Did you have to wake me, Mr. Sheriff?"

A lean, brown man standing beside Houck said, "I've come quite a ways to get you, Lovell."

"Hope I didn't put you to any inconvenience, Mr. Parker," the awakened man answered. "If you'd only dropped me a postcard, I could have come to where you were at."

One of the deputies laughed, which annoyed Houck. "You're going back to Utah to be hanged, fellow," he snapped.

"Unpleasant, if true." Lovell smiled cheerfully at the officer. "Want to make a little bet on that, Sheriff?"

"Stay where you're at," the sheriff ordered gruffly. "Try any funny business, and I'll blast a hole in yore belly. Williams, put the cuffs on him."

A bowlegged deputy came forward and fastened handcuffs over the prisoner's wrists.

"Not necessary," Lovell mentioned. "I'd rather have that slug in Mr. Houck's gun than in my belly."

They saddled Chipmunk and gave the captured man a leg up into the seat. After an hour's travel, Lovell discovered that they were headed back to the Circle 72. He guessed that Houck, who did not like Esther Young but was too politic to show it openly, was glad of a chance to annoy her by humiliating the man she had helped.

"Nice of you to take me back to the

ranch," Lovell said, light sarcasm in his gentle voice, "I've got a week's time coming to me and I hit the trail too sudden to collect."

A dull flush beat into the sheriff's heavily fleshed face. "She'll be glad to see her pet again," he growled. "But I don't reckon she can talk you outa this jam."

"Afraid she won't try," Lovell said, and grinned ruefully. "Miss Esther has as much use for me as she has for a hydrophobia skunk. She called me down plenty this mo'ning before she handed me my walking orders. You don't savvy the lady. She's tough as a ten-year-old bull's hide, but she wouldn't kick out a mangy yellow dog without giving him a chance. I got mine, but she figured me an ornery cull and cut me out of the Circle 72 herd."

Houck slid a suspicious look at him. "Funny you lit out ten minutes before I came to arrest you," he suggested craftily. "Looks like you might have had a warning."

"When a waddy gets his time he hits the trail," Lovell replied. "No use sticking around where you're not wanted."

"Miss Esther didn't say anything about canning you. She told us you quit."

"Did she?" The prisoner laughed, as if considering some inner source of amusement. "Ain't that like a woman? When one gets through talkin', you got no idea what she's really thinking."

When they reached the ranch house, Colonel Krock and Nick Haley were just getting into the buckboard to leave. Esther and Lucy were on the porch to wave their guests a good-by.

As Esther looked at the handcuffed man, a tight, hard ball bunched inside her stomach. His cool, sardonic gaze swept the group and came to rest on her.

"The bad penny you flung away shows up again, ma'am," he told her smilingly.

It was strange, she thought, how his impudence could carry off even this situation. They had caught him and were taking him away, perhaps to his death, and he was still not only a man unafraid and unashamed, but one who found in his plight a mocking zest.

"We're taking him away for good, Miss Esther; he'll never bother you again," Houck promised. "It's the end of his crooked trail."

Esther's eyes, resting on the sheriff, did not reflect his jubilation. A sour, crossgrained man, mean-spirited, with no warmth in him despite his surface heartiness, she decided.

"I can take care of myself," she said coldly.

From his seat in the buckboard Colonel Krock said gravely, "I'm sorry you got into this trouble, young man."

"Man is born unto trouble, as the sparks fly upward, Colonel," Lovell tossed back at him airily.

"It would be well if you would use your Bible for instruction and not for levity," Krock reproved.

"He'll have plenty of time to read it from cover to cover where they're going to put him," Haley said with obvious malice.

"You ought to be ashamed of yourself, Nick," Lucy told him. "Talking that way to a man when he is down."

Haley turned on the girl irritably. "You want me to talk nice and friendly to a train and bank robber?" he demanded.

She flared up. "I don't care how you talk to him. He isn't a train robber to me until he's been proved guilty. Or a bank robber either."

"You're tootin', Lucy," Dad Cantrell said, approval on his homely, wrinkled face. "Mebbe he's guilty, but Pete Houck's calling him so don't settle it with me."

"Long as I can remember you always were a cantankerous old vinegaroon, Dad, taking the wrong side of every question," Houck charged. "Mr. Parker here will tell you

86

there's evidence enough against this bird to convince any jury in the land."

Nick Haley said, with a derisive, angry laugh, his gaze on Lucy, "Beats all how a woman falls for a crook if he's halfway good-looking."

Lucy flushed. "If you'd only mind your own business, Nick Haley!" she cried.

"That's too much to expect, Lucy," her sister said dryly. "Nick hasn't any business. He's a gentleman of leisure."

Jerry flung a question at the prisoner. "Why don't you tell them you didn't hold up that train — if you didn't?" he asked sharply.

A cynical smile broke the set lines of Lovell's lean, brown face. "Looks like I can't *talk* myself out of these bracelets, boy." He lowered his voice and said, plain enough for all to hear, "But I never did like jewelry, and I'll not be wearing them long."

The sheriff snorted, "That's what *you* think." He turned to the United States Marshal. "Let's get going and put this two-cent bad man in a cell where he belongs."

The posse headed for Live Oaks.

While Dad Cantrell discussed with Esther the advisability of throwing a bunch of beef stuff into the south pasture for a few days, Nick maneuvered Lucy to one side.

"How about the dance at Doble's Saturday night?"

She pretended not to understand this was an invitation. "What about it?" she asked innocently.

"Come off it," he told her. "You're going with me."

Her long-lashed eyes slanted a doubtful look at him. "I don't think I like you very well."

"Don't make me ride off into the chaparral and shoot myself," he said, turning his white be-toothed grin on her.

She fell back to a second line of defense. "Esther doesn't let me go to dances alone with men. Jerry will have to go along."

"And Esther particularly doesn't want you to go with Nick Haley, who is yore cousin," he said resentfully. "What has she got against me?"

"Better ask her," Lucy suggested, a smile dimpling her cheeks. "She would love to tell you."

"Esther acts like I've got smallpox," he protested. "Well, Saturday night. And wear that pink dress, kid."

"I'll tell Jerry you're yearning to take him to the dance," she said.

Despite her persiflage Lucy thought of Nick often.

CHAPTER TEN:
LOVELL SUSPECTS

On the way to town the sheriff's posse stopped at the Four Roads store to drink at the pump. Lovell took the dipper which the marshal handed him and raised it with both manacled hands to his mouth. Since the day was a sizzler, he found the cool water refreshing to his parched throat. Jack thanked Parker. He was of opinion that if the marshal had not been there he would have gone thirsty.

Two horses drowsed lazily at the hitch rack in front of the store. One of them was a sorrel gelding. Lovell could not be positive, but he was fairly sure that less than a week ago he had seen that big-barreled body and the white-stockinged legs vanishing up a canyon a few minutes after an assassin had tried to drill him from the brush.

Two men in shiny chaps jingled out of the store. The one who started to untie the sorrel was Ben Ringold, his companion the cowboy called Sid. At sight of the posse, the bowlegged man left the hitch rack and strutted forward, a grin on his crooked, thin-lipped mouth.

"So you woke up and arrested the killer, Pete," he jeered.

In the sheriff's reply was offended dignity. "I don't arrest a man till I have enough evidence, Ben. We've rounded up this fellow for a crime we can make stick. He's one of the guys who held up the U.P. express at Wilcox, Wyoming, and later killed Sheriff Hazen."

Ringold's face showed for an instant not only surprise but disappointment. It set stirring in Lovell a faint premonition. He remembered Dad Cantrell's warning, that the men whom he should most fear were the ones who had killed Zach Young and wanted to divert suspicion. But Ringold was the Bar Z Y foreman, a trusted employee of old Zach. Surely he would be the last man in the world to kill the man who had promoted him to a responsible position. Unless there was in the evil underdrifts of this community a hidden, urgent reason why he must destroy his boss.

Jack thought of the motives that lead men to murder. A sudden passion must be left out, for this had been deliberate assassination. Greed — fear — revenge — love — hate. There was no use guessing until he had the key to the explanation. He had to admit to himself that the probable simple truth was that Ringold had nothing to do with the crime.

"You can't make me believe he didn't kill Zach Young too," the foreman cried harshly.

"I won't try to make you believe it, Ben," the sheriff said. "I'm of that opinion myself."

"Do you figure that the Bar Z Y boys will sit with their hands folded while some guy from outside slips the killer away and maybe turns him loose among his Brown's Hole friends?" Ringold demanded angrily.

"No, Ben, keep yore shirt on," the sheriff advised him suavely. "Mr. Parker is a deputy United States Marshal. He claims they have got the goods on Lovell. This scalawag is a pal of Nate Winters, a sure-enough bad man. Lovell and Butch Cassidy are thick as thieves. He's a friend of Kid Curry. The least the Government will do is sock this fellow for twenty years in a federal prison."

"That's what *you* think. My idea is different." The thin-lipped, cruel mouth of the bandy-legged man tightened. "We don't aim to let some slick lawyer get free the fellow that killed our boss. He ain't going up the trail."

The hard eyes in the lean, tanned face of Parker fastened on the foreman. "If you or anybody else tries to take my prisoner from me, somebody is going to get hurt," the marshal said quietly. "Don't make any mistake about that."

The lids of the Bar Z Y man narrowed to slits. "You talk a good fight," he snarled.

Parker gathered his bridle reins. "If you're all ready, we'll go, boys," he said.

As they rode townward, renewed doubts of Ringold crawled through the mind of the prisoner. The fellow had been so eager from the first to persuade others of Lovell's guilt. It was hard to accept his attempt to shoot down an unarmed man on the street as due to anger based solely on loyalty. Lovell was a stranger against whom he could have no personal animosity. Yet he had tried to bushwhack him from the chaparral. Why? To convince people that the murderer of Young had met a just fate through the vengeance of the cattleman's friends?

Lovell decided he would like to know more about Ringold's relation to Zach Young. It was possible that Dad Cantrell or Esther Young might know of some trouble between them. Or, more likely still, Colonel Krock, who was the old cattleman's associate in business and his legal adviser.

They drew up in front of an adobe jail, a structure that did not promise much resistance to an attack from without. Lovell mentioned as much to the United States Marshal.

"I'll be around," Parker said. "None of

yore friends or yore enemies want you out badly enough to try to break in, I reckon, but if they do they'll find me waiting at the gate."

Lovell was glad to hear this. He had been put in an iron cage inside the adobe walls. To break out would not be possible, but it would be easy for determined men to get in and shoot him down. If Ringold was bullheaded enough he could bring a bunch of riders to town, round up some loafers, prime them with drink, and tear a hole in the crumbling walls. Jack Lovell was glad to be a prisoner of Lloyd Parker rather than of Sheriff Houck. The deputy marshal was a tough, fighting officer who had dragged many a criminal out of the brush to justice. He was not the kind to let a drunken mob take from him a man he had arrested.

Through the window of the cell Lovell watched the life of the town move up and down Rincon Street. He caught a glimpse of Colonel Krock standing on the courthouse steps. The distance was too far to recognize his face, but he knew Krock was the only man in Live Oaks who wore a Prince Albert coat. People drifted in and out of Holbrook's store. One of them was Rudholt. He stood on the sidewalk reading a letter he had apparently just received.

Five cowboys on horseback came down the street at a road gait and tied in front of the Blue Moon. They pushed through the swing doors into the saloon. A short, bow-legged man led the way — Ben Ringold.

The man looking down from the barred window found this disturbing. He guessed that the foreman of the Bar Z Y had ridden in to make trouble. There was something about this Lovell did not understand. Ringold's animosity was too persistent, too keen-edged. Even if he had rubbed out Zach Young, no suspicion seemed to point toward him. Was it possible that there might be another urge driving him — some hangover from earlier days? He had been one of Young's men for a long time. He was credited, so Dad Cantrell had told Jack, with having done a lot of dirty work for Zach. A startling thought jumped to Lovell's mind. The man might be Gabe Lovell's assassin, and the fear might be riding him that Gabe's son had come to exact vengeance.

Chapter Eleven:
Esther Takes a Hand

When Esther drove the buggy into the corral, Jim Roberts was perturbed. He wished she had chosen some other day to come to

94

Live Oaks.

"Gonna be in town long?" he asked.

"You needn't bother feeding the horse. I'll be leaving right after supper."

"I wouldn't stay too long, Miss Esther," he advised. "The town is a little excited. The sheriff just brought that fellow Lovell in, and some of the boys have got notions."

Her dark eyes fastened to his. "What do you mean?"

"Crazy talk about breaking into the jail and hanging him."

A cold wind blew through her. "Who is doing this talking?"

"Some of the Bar Z Y riders started it. There's a lot of drinking going on."

"We'd better go see the sheriff, Jim," she said, much troubled.

As they walked up Rincon Street, Esther knew that Roberts had not exaggerated the danger. More people were on the streets than usual. They stood in small groups talking earnestly, sometimes angrily, she thought, and as she approached, the talk broke off abruptly. Out of the saloons came the sound of many voices.

In front of the post office they saw Bedford Rudholt reading a letter. His hat swept off at sight of the girl.

"My lucky day," he said.

"Have you heard what they mean to do?" she cried. "Break into the jail and murder that man Lovell."

"Probably just whisky chatter." A thin satiric smile etched itself on the cattleman's face. "Funny how much more popular a man can be dead than alive. A month ago half the people in the district were cussin' Zach Young. Now they want to lynch the guy who got rid of him for them."

"But he didn't," Esther protested. "He couldn't possibly have done it. We've got to save him."

"Why have we?" Rudholt asked. "He's one of the Hole-in-the-Wall gang. If the noose has caught up with him, why should we worry? What the Bar Z Y boys do is strictly none of my business."

"It's some of mine," she answered unhappily. "I'm responsible for what my riders do."

"My advice to you is to go home and forget it," Rudholt replied. "Nobody with any sense can blame you for what drunken ruffians do."

"The man hasn't had a trial," she flung back, angry at his callousness. "I'm going to save him if I can. No good citizen can refuse to help."

Not waiting to hear any defense he might

have to make, she turned and walked away. Emotion choked her throat.

"Don't mind what he said," Roberts comforted her gently. "I never liked him. He's got ice water in his veins for blood."

They found the door of the sheriff's office locked and on it tacked a notice that he had been called out of town on business. A man standing near said that Houck had left a few minutes earlier.

"A convenient call," Roberts said. "Pete is ducking trouble."

Colonel Krock was in his courtroom looking over some legal papers when they entered. He rose at once, suavely courteous. "An unexpected pleasure," he told Esther.

After hearing what she had to say, he was inclined to think that the situation was less serious than they believed. The cowboys and the town riffraff with them were probably just blowing off steam. It was a long way from loose whisky talk to a lynching.

Esther was not satisfied and asked the colonel to go see for himself.

"Perhaps I had better," he agreed. "If you'll go to the hotel, I'll meet you there, my dear."

She wanted to go with him and said so, but he refused firmly. If her fears had any foundation, the streets would be no place for a young lady. He promised to report to her very soon, either in person or through Jim Roberts.

There were more people on Rincon Street than there had been when the corral owner had passed down it fifteen minutes earlier. A merchant drew the judge aside and told him he was afraid there was going to be trouble. The Bar Z Y cowboys were in town and were inflaming others. Just now they were at the Blue Moon.

"I'll see Ringold and try to talk some sense into his head," Colonel Krock answered.

He asked Roberts to go into the saloon and bring the Bar Z Y foreman out. "Don't let him wave you off. Tell him it is imperative I see him."

The barroom was filled with men, most of them heated with liquor. Roberts was seized by the big puncher, Sid.

"Come and have a drink, Jim. It's gonna be a big night in the old town. We don't aim to let them take this killer Lovell up the trail and turn him loose. Not none. He shot Zach from behind without giving him a chance. The guy is a bad egg. So we stop his clock."

"But, Sid, he couldn't of done it," Roberts cried, making himself heard over a babel of voices. "The evidence showed —"

"Blast the evidence," Sid interrupted. "It was cooked up to save him. Lovell has come to the end of his crooked trail."

"I've got to see Ben," Roberts said, and broke away.

Ringold listened sourly to the message. It seemed both to annoy and disturb him. "Tell the colonel I got no time to see him now," he growled. "I'm gonna be too busy for a while. Later I'll drop around to his house."

"Colonel Krock said he had to see you now," Roberts insisted. "Said this was mighty important. He's waiting outside."

The foreman gave way reluctantly. "All right," he snapped. "Let's get it over with quick."

Through the side door Roberts led the way to the alley back of the saloon. Out of the shadows the colonel came to meet them.

"Have you gone crazy, Ben?" he demanded sharply. "Do you know what you are doing?"

Though Ringold had poured down a good many drinks, he was still steady on his feet. He flushed angrily, shallow eyes hot with defiance. "Sure I know. We're bumpin' off a dirty killer who will be better dead." He added, dragging the words for emphasis,

"Better for you and me both."

In Krock's steady gaze there was a warning. "The man is a dangerous criminal of course," he said. "As you say, it is better for society that he be put away where he can do no more harm. But let the law take its course. Individuals have no right to be judge and jury."

"You're damned legal," exploded Ringold. "Well, I'm not. I aim to finish this now."

"Not unless you are a brainless fool," Krock answered, a challenge in his icy voice and cold eyes. "Go through with this and you are finished with the Bar Z Y. Have you thought of that?"

Ringold glared at him. "Why am I? The ranch ought to give me a bonus for stringing up this fellow."

Their hard looks clashed. Roberts had a puzzled feeling of something secret and hidden behind their words.

"Esther Young won't stand for this," Krock said, all the urbanity gone from his usually smooth voice. "I just left her. She's furious. If you go on with this lynching, you'll get your time and be kicked off the ranch at once."

"She can't do it. You've got some say, haven't you?"

The bleak eyes of the judge were hard as

topaz. "I won't lift a hand for you. Don't expect it. Finish this business and you'll be booting yourself out of the best job that you ever had or ever will have."

Ringold's ugly mouth set. "If you think you're gonna throw me down —"

The older man interrupted sharply. "I'm not throwing you down. I've got Miss Esther to agree to keep you on as foreman. But I can't protect a fool against his folly. You're making the choice, not I."

A man had come out of the darkness silently and swiftly. He stood close to Ringold, on the fellow's right, with the barrel of a forty-five pressed against his ribs. A quiet voice said, "Don't make a mistake, Ringold."

The foreman's face tightened. "What the hell!" he demanded, swinging his head to face Lloyd Parker.

"You're under arrest for inciting riot. I'm taking you to jail."

For a long second Ringold hesitated, then made his choice. The eyes of this lean, brown man were slits of shining menace. He would go through to a finish. The foreman knew that.

"You can't do this to me," he protested angrily. "Tell him so, Krock."

The marshal spoke to Roberts. "Slip his

gun out of the holster."

Roberts did as he was told, and obeying a second order tossed the weapon over a fence into a vacant lot.

"We're going across the street nice and friendly to the jail," Parker explained. "The four of us. You and Roberts side by side, Colonel. We'll be right behind you. Take it easy. No hurry."

The marshal shifted to his prisoner's left side. He tucked his arm under Ringold's, the six-shooter partially concealed. A good many men were in the street moving to and fro or standing in small knots talking. If any of them were curious about this group moving toward the jail, they gave no sign of it.

Still under instruction from the marshal, Roberts knocked on the jail door. A head appeared in an upstairs window.

"I've brought a prisoner, Hogan," the marshal said.

The door was presently opened, to admit Parker and Ringold.

"This is an outrage!" the foreman shouted. "I haven't done a thing. He's got no warrant for me."

"We'll lock him up where he'll be safe, Hogan," the marshal mentioned, entirely disregarding Ringold's rage. "If he was footloose, I would probably have to kill him."

After Ringold had been disposed of, the jailer unlocked the room containing the cell holding Lovell. The prisoner had been looking out of the window.

He said, lightly, "Looks like it's Live Oaks' night to howl."

"Some scalawags have notions in their heads," Parker replied. "I don't reckon they will push them too far, but you never can tell. I've just arrested the wolf howling the loudest. Fellow named Ringold. You've met him."

Lovell smiled thinly. "So I have. First time we met he wanted to hang me to a live oak. Next time I missed by the skin of my teeth being shot down when I didn't have a gun. Third time he sent a blue whistler at me from the brush. You were present at meeting number four." He was silent for a space, letting his mind run over all this. "I wonder what there is about me crowding Mr. Ringold to be so urgent," he added dryly.

"He thinks you killed his boss."

"Does he? I have a different idea. He knows who killed Zach Young. Unless I'm guessing wrong, he knows who killed my father."

"I've heard yore father was killed. That

103

was before my time."

"Yes." Lovell put his reaching thoughts into words. "And maybe the same man rubbed out both my father and Young. Maybe he wants me bumped off because he's scared I have come to square accounts."

Hogan's startled eyes stared at the prisoner. "Jumpin' Jehosaphat!" he cried. "You don't think Ben Ringold shot Young."

From the street below someone barked an annoyed question. "Where's Ben Ringold at?" Those inside could tell from the sounds of shuffling feet and lifted voices that the pack was pouring out of the saloons for the kill.

Parker handed to Lovell through the bars the revolver he had taken from him earlier in the day. "There's an off chance you'll need this," he said. "I don't reckon so. If you don't, I'll collect it when the fuss is over. I'm going to have a powwow with the boys."

They could hear a voice exhorting the mob. Lovell looked down and reported grimly. "That big Bar Z Y rider Sid making war talk."

The roar from many throats lifted into the air.

"What we waiting for?" someone yelped,

and again somebody flung out a demand: "Where's Ringold?"

Lovell said, "Much obliged for giving me back old tried and true." With a not too hopeful glance at the marshal he made a suggestion. "How about letting me side you down there? Three men can talk peace to those wolves better than two."

Parker vetoed this, as Lovell had expected he would. "No, I'm going alone. Hogan will have to watch the back of the building."

"You're not going outside," the jailer protested.

"Yes. With my sawed-off shotgun. It won't make them feel comfortable."

The marshal waved a careless hand at the prisoner. "Be seeing you later," he promised.

Jack Lovell was worried. He was not sure that was a promise the marshal would be able to keep. Some drunken fool might shoot down Parker.

Chapter Twelve:
Parker Makes Peace Talk

Hogan was an old pioneer who had fought the Apaches in the early days. He still limped from a badly healed arrow wound.

"If they rush us, we won't last any longer than a snowball in hell," he told the marshal, chewing calmly his cud of tobacco.

"Point is not to let the rush get started," Parker said. "I've got to talk them out of any gunplay."

He opened the door leading to a small second-story porch facing the road and moved out.

"You be mighty careful," the jailer warned. "I still think I ought to side you."

Parker closed the door behind him and sat down on the railing of the porch, the barrel of the sawed-off shotgun resting across his thigh. His glance swept coolly and deliberately the excited faces upturned to his. The roar that had greeted his appearance died away.

"We want Lovell!" a pockmarked cowboy shouted.

"You can't have him," the officer said, his quiet voice clear and strong. "I'm a United States Marshal and he is my prisoner."

Sid pushed to the front, a jeering grin on his face. "For how long?" he asked.

"Till I turn him over for trial in Wyoming," the marshal answered.

"We're gonna save you the trouble of taking him there, Mr. Marshal. We aim to hang him from the limb of a live oak in the canyon."

There were shouts of approval. "That's

106

right!" . . . "Bet yore boots!" . . . "We'll learn hired killers to keep away from here!"

The voice of the man with the pitted face rose above the others: "We're telling you, Parker, not asking. What we say goes."

The marshal waited again for silence. His face had as much pliability as that of a wooden Indian. When he spoke, it was in a gentle, persuasive tone, without a trace of anger in it. "Let's understand each other right from the chunk, boys." He patted the shotgun resting on his leg. "Both barrels of old Nancy here are loaded with buckshot. When I fire her she spatters all over Arizona. I'd hate to turn her loose on you, but I'm going to keep my prisoner. You boys are starting something it ain't worth finishing. Before you rub me out, I can get five or six of you." He raised his hand to check the yell rising in the lifted throats. "Might as well hear me through. I gave Lovell back his forty-five, and when you bust into the room where he is he'll start smoking. He's one tough hombre, and he totes six lives in that gun. Hogan will be right there with him doing his darndest." Parker smiled amiably on the packed faces. "Fact is, boys, it's too smoky round the edges for you. The game isn't worth the candle. You might get Lovell, but there aren't coffins enough in Live Oaks to take care of all the dead men there will be in the next twenty minutes."

"Bluff!" Sid flung up at him. "You wouldn't have a chance, and you know it."

"No mob can take a prisoner from me long as I can stand and pull a trigger," the marshal replied quietly. "I'm going to do my job no matter how many get hurt."

Sid rubbed his unshaven chin with the palm of a hand. He could not back down and quit, but he was not happy about the situation. This lean, brown, hard-eyed marshal might be just dumb enough to go through to a finish.

"Let's mill this over," Sid said. "Yore big talk don't fool us any, but there's no sense in you getting hurt. We got nothing against you. You've said yore little piece. Nobody can blame you if we've got bull in the neck and won't listen. It would be plumb crazy for you to get killed off for an ornery bad man not worth a hill of beans, especially seeing you can't save him anyhow."

The marshal's gaze ranged over the crowd. "I don't see friend Ringold with you, after he took so much trouble working you-all into a lather," he said, with amiable derision. "Do you reckon he slipped away so as not to be here when the fireworks begin?

You wouldn't be cat's-paws for him, would you?"

"He went into the jail with you a while ago," someone cried.

"So he did." Parker smiled pleasantly. "We had a little talk and he saw the light. Mr. Ringold has a good job he doesn't want to lose any more than he wants to go to the pen for interfering with a United States officer doing his duty. Slick as a greased pig, Mr. Ringold is."

"Ben is still in the jail!" the pockmarked man cried. "He never came out of that door."

"You think he's hiding there while there's a back entrance for him to slip out?" Parker asked, grinning. "Wouldn't surprise me if he was halfway to the Bar ZY by this time."

Sid spit out angrily the frontier fighting epithet. "If he has walked out on us, I'll sure fix him right," he threatened.

"If you claim he's not in the jail, let one of us go see," the bartender of the Blue Moon shouted.

Parker shook his head, still smiling. "This isn't visiting day," he said.

A big hulk of a fellow in the background ripped out an oath. "What are we wasting time for? Talk doesn't buy us anything. Let's go get Lovell."

"If you want him so much, why hug that wall so close?" Parker drawled. "I'm not going to bring him to you way back there."

This brought a laugh. A fat man said, "Pick yore coffin and right up to the front, Brad. A few buckshot won't hurt you — much."

Several men seized the big fellow and began to push him forward. Parker hoped he had got the break he wanted, a comedy touch that would deflect them from the urge to kill. But a redheaded puncher in chaps interrupted the horseplay.

"Thought we came here to get us a killer. I'm tired of letting that bird on the balcony buffalo us. Where I come from, one bully-puss saddle bum doesn't ride herd on fifty. How big odds do you rabbits want?"

Gun in hand, the redhead bowlegged across the road. As he came out of the crowd, Parker's scatter gun covered him.

"When yore foot touches the sidewalk, I'll cut loose," the marshal said.

"I don't have to reach the sidewalk," the redhead answered. "This six-shooter carries more than two yards. I'm talking turkey, fellow. Yore bluff is called. Pull that trigger, and we'll fling forty slugs into you."

There was a long moment of tense silence. The nerve of one man in the crowd broke.

He cried, "For God's sake, don't start anything."

The showdown had come. More than one stomach twisted into a hard, icy knot. The firing of a single shot might be the signal for the death of many.

A whiplike voice snapped, "Hold everything." Jack Lovell had stepped onto the porch and joined the marshal. "If there's a gun fired, I'll empty this forty-five into the crowd," he warned.

On his heels came Hogan carrying a Winchester.

At sight of Lovell no roar of rage came from the mob. The danger was too imminent for that. Two or three of those on the fringes of the crowd slipped away. They had not enlisted for a battle. Ringold and Sid had talked them into thinking that by reason of their number the marshal would have to turn his prisoner over to them after a formal protest, but with three determined men facing them it was clear Lovell could be taken only after a desperate struggle.

CHAPTER THIRTEEN: RUDHOLT THINKS FAST

Esther could not sit quietly in the hotel parlor and wait for a report from Colonel

Krock. A sense of imminent danger oppressed her. That his enemies could stir up such a fury against this graceless scamp did not make sense, but she remembered that her uncle had once told her that an inflamed mob was beyond reason.

She walked out of the house to the gate, and presently opened it to move down the sidewalk toward the business section. It was growing dark and the lights were beginning to come on in front of the saloons. As she saw the unusual number of people on Rincon, not drifting casually to and fro but driven by some restless excitement within them, the agitation in her breast increased. There must be something she could do to stop this tragic folly. In the town were scores of good people and none of them were lifting a hand to interfere. She knew why they were holding aloof. This man was an outlaw, one of the bad men from Brown's Hole. If he was in trouble, it was his own fault. Before he took up his evil way of life, he had known that a bandit could not expect to escape a sudden violent end.

But Esther could not just accept the fact that Jack Lovell was a villain and forget him. He was not merely a criminal who had chanced to cross her path, but a man as near and close as breathing. She could reproach herself for her folly, but she could not feel any sense of shame in it. Though she could not justify herself by logic, she knew there was in him a clean and wholesome strain.

On the breeze there came to her the full roar of voices, and she trembled at the sound. There was no more mercy in it than there was in the howl of a wolf pack.

She had been opening the gate to return to the hotel, but she closed it without going into the yard. Hesitation was at an end. She could not wait any longer to find out what was going on.

Before she had walked thirty yards she met Jim Roberts. He brought her no good news. The mob was already moving toward the jail. Roberts gave her what crumbs of comfort he could. Parker had arrested Ringold and had him locked up. The deputy was a stout-hearted officer and would do all he could for his prisoner. But it was clear to Esther that Jim had little hope.

She choked down the tightness in her throat. It would not do to play the baby now. A way must be found to save him.

"I've got to stop this horrible thing, Jim," she said.

He shook his head. "They're hell bent on it, Miss Esther."

"I'll talk to the Bar Z Y boys. They can't

do this and work for us." Already she was walking swiftly down the street.

Roberts felt that he ought to stop her, but he did not know how. The beauty and vitality of her supple body were wholly feminine, but she had the direct force of a man. He tried to explain that the scene of a mob lynching was no place for a lady, and she either did not hear a word he was saying or paid no attention to it. Her mind was searching for a way to make an impact on this mass hysteria.

She and Roberts rounded the curve in the street and came in sight of the jail just as Jack Lovell stepped out on the porch to join the marshal. A man standing in the doorway of a butcher shop spoke curtly to Esther.

"What are you doing here?" he demanded.

She turned, and saw Rudholt. "I'm going to stop this, since you men are afraid to do anything," she said, her contemptuous eyes scorning him.

"And how are you going to do it?" he asked.

Esther did not answer. She turned, heading straight for the mob. Before she had gone two steps he caught her arm.

"Don't act like a fool," he ordered.

"Turn me loose," she flamed.

His fingers tightened. "Get out of here!"

he told her harshly. "Inside of two minutes twenty guns will be smoking."

"Let me alone!" she cried, and tried to twist free.

"I tell you hell is going to break loose."

Her breath came deep and ragged. "Don't be afraid," she taunted. "You're out of the line of fire and safe here." Almost with a sob, she added, "You coward."

Rudholt's lids narrowed. Swift stabbing thoughts raced through his mind. This was his chance. He could put her under such a debt of gratitude that she would be unable to escape from it, and at the same time he would be showing her what kind of man he was. Quickly his mind made a right-about face.

With a twist of his strong fingers he flung Esther back against Roberts. "Take her into the shop and keep her there," he snarled.

He moved rapidly, at first skirting the crowd. His heavy broad shoulders plowed forward, as his powerful arms flung men aside. "Out of my way!" he cried, and fought through to the steps of the jail.

The marshal's scatter gun covered him.

Lovell spoke fast. "Wait. His gun isn't out."

The cattleman stood on the top step, arrogant and masterful, his salient jaw thrust out, cold, hard eyes sweeping over the mob scornfully. His steel-trap lips opened, and he poured scabrous, mocking words down on them. He made it clear that he did not give a tinker's damn whether Lovell lived or died, but he was not going to let a bunch of drunken bums ruin the town's reputation. If they wanted to get themselves killed, they could pick some other way. Half of them were not worth the powder to blow them up. There was a driving force in his vitriolic attack, and before he had finished telling them off, the men on the porch above knew that the danger was over. The shouts of resentment from some of the crowd rose from the whipped anger of defeat. They had been shaken by the cool determination of the three on the porch. When Rudholt joined them as an ally, they were through.

The mob began to melt. Some moved down the street, others returned to the saloons. Many felt a sense of relief that the lynching had been frustrated.

Colonel Krock had come out of a store and moved to the jail steps. He lifted a hand for silence.

"Friends, this is a happy ending to what might have been a tragic mistake," he said. "The law is going to take care of this young man Lovell. It is going to put him away

116

where he will never bother us again. He will pay the penalty of his crime. You and I cannot protect society by breaking the law. When we have had time to cool, we shall all realize that we have escaped blotting the fair name of our community with a sad error. I am sure you will all depart peaceably to your homes."

Rudholt told the colonel, not taking the trouble to conceal his sarcasm, that Krock's few well-chosen words had certainly saved the day. The marshal also thanked him, a little dryly, for his timely assistance.

"The liquor talking in the boys made them pretty rambunctious," Parker added. "I've never seen a necktie party yet that couldn't be broken up if the right fellow stepped in at the right time. We're much obliged to you, Mr. Rudholt — and the judge, of course — for reading the riot act to the gents on the prod."

The cattleman said curtly that they didn't owe him a thing. He had not interfered to help the prisoner.

Lovell watched him pass through the crowd to join a young woman standing in the doorway of the butcher shop. He wondered what Esther Young was doing here, certainly no place for a young woman to be. A corollary to the thought was a guess that

Rudholt's activity had some connection with the girl's presence.

"What about Ringold?" the colonel asked. "Would you care to turn him over to me?"

The marshal thought not. "He can do that cooling off you mentioned better in jail than in a saloon. I'll have him held till I have started up the trail with Lovell. He might get ideas again."

Lovell said, "Like to talk with you a few minutes, Colonel."

Krock wondered what the man had to say to him.

Chapter Fourteen: Masks Off

Hogan went down to let the judge into the jail.

"I reckon I couldn't tell you all the thanks I owe you, Lloyd," the prisoner said.

"We'll never know how much we owe Rudholt," the marshal replied. "I think he got us out of a tight spot."

"You're right. We'll never know. I've a notion you had them whipped before Rudholt took a hand, but some fool might have upset the apple cart." Jack's mind jumped to another angle of the adventure. "Did you see Miss Young standing across the street?"

"Yes. After the rumpus. Why in Mexico was she there?"

"That girl is always where trouble breaks. I never saw the beat of it." Lovell's eyes narrowed in thought. "My notion is that we can thank Miss Young and not Rudholt for what he did. She needled him into it somehow."

Colonel Krock came into the room and shook hands with Parker. "You handled a difficult situation very well," he said. "I congratulate you, sir, for the efficiency with which you upheld the law."

"It's what I'm paid for," the deputy answered shortly. He thought the colonel a trifle effusive.

Krock turned to Lovell, his manner dignified and aloof. "You wanted to see me, young man?" he asked.

"Yes. I'm a bit puzzled about some things. I thought perhaps you could make them clearer to me."

Parker walked out of the room and left them alone, after relieving the prisoner of his six-shooter.

"I understand you knew Mr. Zach Young well, that you were his lawyer and a partner in some of his enterprises," Lovell said.

"That is correct, sir."

"Do you know whether there had been

any trouble between Mr. Young and Ben Ringold just before his death?"

The judge regarded Lovell a long moment before he answered. A change had come into the benevolent eyes, one that left them hard and wary. "I don't know what you mean. Ben was a trusted employee — had been ranch foreman for years."

Jack saw that he was not going to get any help from Krock. But the swiftness with which the man had gone on the defensive alert interested him. He was concealing something he did not want uncovered. For an instant there had been a flash of fear on the bland face.

"You have lived here a long time, Colonel," Lovell said.

"For a considerable period," Krock answered cautiously. He did not know where this was leading and he did not intend to be trapped into any damaging admissions.

"Who killed my father?" the prisoner demanded abruptly, his gaze fast on the eyes of the older man.

It was not the question Krock had expected. There was, Jack thought, a flicker of relief on the suave front that masked the real man.

"Nobody knows," the colonel replied. "He was shot one night in his cabin by an unknown assassin."

"A hired killer paid by Zach Young."

"That is a presumption unbacked by evidence."

"He was the only man who profited by my father's death — except the actual murderer." Lovell added, a challenge in the quiet, deliberate words, "I must except too the lawyer who stole the proofs of the Crescent ownership from the records and forged others."

There was no suggestion now in Krock's face of the warm friendliness, made vivid by the ruddy cheeks framed with the fine shock of silvery hair, that had been the man's advertisement for years. Bone and muscle had tightened, and the eyes held a wolfish fierceness. His mouth had become an ugly crooked line.

"Too bad I didn't let them kill you," he said.

"Don't blame yoreself," Lovell told him with dry contempt. "All you did was spout words that didn't mean a thing — after you were sure the necktie party was fizzling out. Just one of yore tricks for building up importance."

The lawyer's face was stiff with anger. He glared at Lovell, tight-lipped, then turned and walked out of the room. Jack knew he had made a bitter enemy and he was glad of it. A pulse of heady excitement throbbed in his throat. He had brought the hypocrite into the open. It would be war between them now.

Hogan came into the room. "What's eatin' Colonel Krock?" the jailer inquired. "He walked past us like he didn't see us."

The young man smiled. His reply was an understatement. "I think he is a little annoyed with me."

In spite of his cavalier brush-off of Krock, the young man did not make the mistake of thinking him unimportant. The man was deadly as a rattlesnake and crafty as a fox. Jack had very likely made a mistake in throwing down a challenge to him. He had let anger override prudence. The charge that the colonel had manipulated the steal of the Crescent had been a shot in the dark, but Lovell knew now that it had scored a bull's-eye, though he would never be able to prove it.

"Parker tells me he aims to start up the trail with you in two-three hours," Hogan said. "Good idea, I think. The lads who were anxious to string you up won't start any more funny business of that kind, but some of them are sore enough to take a crack at you from the brush."

"Maybe so." Jack's warm smile thanked the jailer. "You've treated me nice at yore hotel, Mr. Hogan. I'll recommend it to any other train robbers I meet."

"Why in hell does a fellow like you want to fool around with robbing trains?" Hogan asked hotly. He was irritated with himself for feeling sympathetic toward this young reprobate. "You'll finish up like all bad men do — laid out on a slab with a lot of bullets in you."

Lovell told him with a grin that if so he would be very dead.

Chapter Fifteen: The Hole-in-the-Wall Gang

Chad Lovell rode the brush on Pot Creek looking for a stray. He was a small weathered man in his sixties, deeply tanned, with sky-blue eyes from the corners of which radiated tiny wrinkles. The boots he wore were scuffed and dusty, and the Levis thrust into the tops of them faded from many washings. His disreputable Stetson had not been new for many years, but he wore it tilted jauntily. Though life had taken its toll of Chad, he still faced it with indomitable gaiety.

His ranch nestled in the angle formed by the junction of Pot Creek and Green River. Diamond Mountain backed it up. Behind the terraces rising from the valley high ranges enclosed the park on all sides. For Brown's Hole lies in an almost inaccessible corner of three states, a terrain well-watered by the Green and its tributaries as they wind through the Uintah Mountains to the Lodore Canyon.

Chad was that rarity, an honest man who lived among thieves and held their respect. He tolerated them because he had either to do so or to get out. Until the past few months they had not molested his stock. He was a neighbor, and they recognized his right of ownership. But of late new men were sifting in — criminals from outside wanted by the law, bandits seeking refuge after train and bank hold-ups, and bands of organized rustlers. A bunch of his stuff had been picked up, added to a herd stolen in Arizona, and driven to Craig for disposal in Routt County. Chad had announced bluntly that if he could find out who the thieves were, he would shoot it out with them. The arm of the law did not reach as far as Brown's Hole. One had to protect his own.

He was working his way through a plum thicket when his nostrils picked up the pungent tang of piñon smoke. That meant a campfire, which indicated strangers. Chad pulled up his mustang and started to draw the Winchester from the holster beside the saddle.

"Leave it lay, fellow," a harsh voice ordered. "Put yore hands on yore saddle horn."

A dark thick-set man with a heavy drooping black mustache pushed through the thicket toward him. The sawed-off shotgun in his hands was held close to the hip and pointed at the ranchman.

Chad's gaze ranged over the gunman and he did as he was told. He knew better than to argue with a man who had the drop on him.

"Shove along slowly," directed the owner of the scatter gun. "Start anything, and I'll cut you down."

They moved out of the brush into a meadow of native grasses strewn with wild flowers. At the far end was a small lake, and behind it a grove of white-trunked quaking aspen marching up a small hill that stemmed from a pine-covered mountain back of it.

Near the lake was a campfire around which lounged four men. Chad recognized two of them, Butch Cassidy and Harry Longabaugh. Butch was the leader of the notorious Hole-in-the-Wall gang, members of which were suspected of having robbed the express at Wilcox. Longabaugh, usually called the Sundance Kid, was reputed to be one of the outlaw bunch. It was known that the train robbers had been hard pressed. From the time of the hold-up, posses had hung close to their heels. Very likely they had cut down by the Rock Springs Trail to find a temporary refuge in the Hole.

A small man who had been hammering down a nail in the inside of his boot asked mildly, "Who's yore friend, Harve?"

The quick mind of Lovell seized on the name. His captor must be Harvey Logan, alias Kid Curry, a desperado over-quick on the trigger, one who had left behind him on his evil path a trail of victims, including the famous Pike Landusky, a pioneer of northern Montana.

"Search me," growled Curry. "Found him starting to drag out his Winchester, so I asked him would he come along with me."

Lovell nodded at Cassidy. " 'Lo, Butch," he said casually. "How are cases?"

Cassidy grinned at the old-timer. "You don't need that gun for Chad. He's okay."

The ranchman answered dryly, "Much obliged. Nice to know I have yore permission to ride my own range."

Kid Curry bristled up. "Hell! He was lugging out his rifle, like I said. Why for?"

"Probably saw a rattler," the little man with the boot said ironically. He was smiling, his manner suave, his voice gentle as the purr of a kitten.

Lovell looked the pint-sized outlaw over coolly. "I'm hunting a muley cow if it interests you. Maybe she has a young calf with her. She's due any day. The dadgummed critter always hides out in the brush when her time comes."

The little man still clung to the fact that their visitor had been uncasing his weapon. "Some annoyed at the muley, I reckon, or maybe scared it would attack him."

"I told you Chad was all right, Nate," Cassidy said.

Chad guessed this must be Nate Winters, whose homicidal tendencies were known all over the bandit belt.

"Do I have to explain why I ride my own range?" Lovell demanded. "I smelt the smoke of yore fire. Rustlers ran off a bunch of my stuff three months ago. I don't aim to have it happen again."

The Sundance Kid said amiably, "Don't blame you a bit, old-timer. Rustlers are a pesky lot." He laughed. Now and again he

127

had been one. "Where's Jack?"

"His feet got fidgety and he rambled down the trail a month or so ago."

"Haven't seen him since we were raising Cain in Rock Springs two years ago come Fourth of July," Longabaugh said.

"This old man Jack's dad?" Kid Curry asked morosely.

"His uncle." Cassidy spoke briskly, pushing into the discard doubts any of his companions may have had. "We're here only for a short time, Chad. You haven't seen us, if anybody asks you."

Cassidy was tanned as a cowboy, but better dressed than most punchers. His boots were custom-made and his Stetson an expensive one. In build he was stocky and of medium height. When he smiled, two rows of small even teeth showed. Though he had served a term in the penitentiary at Laramie, the story current was that he had never killed a man. He was popular and good company.

"All right," Lovell replied stiffly. "I haven't seen you. If I couldn't keep my lip buttoned, I wouldn't be alive now — not in a place as full of thieves as Brown's Hole. All I ask is that rustlers leave my stuff alone. When they don't, I get on the prod."

The Sundance Kid laughed. "All right,

Dad. We don't want any of yore mossy-horns. Keep yore shirt on."

For the first time the fifth member of the party spoke. He was a tall, slim, good-looking man. "If we stick around for two-three days we'll need to beef somebody's critter," he drawled. "How about buying one from Mr. Lovell?"

"That's right, Elza." Butch Cassidy peeled a bill from a roll and handed it to Lovell. "Will it be all right if we butcher one of yours?"

Chad looked at the bill and pocketed it. "I'll say yes," he snapped. "You'd take one anyhow."

"He's sure a cross-grained old vinegaroon," Curry said sourly. "Maybe I'd better learn him good manners."

"Forget it, Kid," Cassidy warned quickly. "Chad has some right to be annoyed at being brought in with a gun."

"How are you stocked with grub, Mr. Lovell?" Elza Lay asked. "We're short of coffee, flour, and salt."

"Reckon I can fix you up. Can't let you have but one pound of Arbuckle's, though. Keep right down the creek and you'll come to the ranch. If any of you run across that muley, I wish you'd let me know."

Cassidy said they would, and Lovell left

for the ranch. He heard the outlaws discussing him as he went. No fear for his own safety disturbed him. Men on the dodge had to build good will among the settlers near their hide-outs. Their policy was to propitiate them and pay well for any services received.

Elza Lay dropped into the ranch toward evening to get the provisions. In payment for them he wanted to leave with Chad a fifty-dollar bill. The old man looked him straight in the eye and shook his head.

"The price is one dollar and six bits," he said.

The outlaw tried to wave the protest aside. "That's all right. Forget the change."

"You owe me one dollar and six bits," Chad said stoutly. "No more." He might keep quiet about having seen the bandits, but if so it would not be by reason of a bribe.

Next morning Chad found fresh tracks of horses pointed for Hill Creek. The Wild Bunch, as the gang was often called, had headed for Green River, Utah, and from thence for parts unknown.

Chad was making supper that evening when he heard horses' hoofs and the creak of saddle leather outside. Through the window he saw two riders dismount stiffly. Evidently they had come a long way.

He went to the door and shouted a greeting. "Hi yi, boys! I'm sure glad to see you. Git off and rest yore saddles."

The riders were Lloyd Parker and Jack Lovell. They unsaddled and fed their mounts while Chad prepared food for them.

As they sat down to eat, he dropped his surprising news. "Friends of you boys been visiting us."

"Meaning who?" asked Jack.

"Five gents from Wyoming — Butch Cassidy, Kid Curry, the Sundance Kid, and two other right nice specimens."

"Are they here now?" the marshal asked.

"Pulled out this mornin'," Chad said. "Took the Utah Trail."

The marshal looked at Jack and groaned. "No rest for the weary. We'll have to hit the road tomorrow morning," he said.

"I reckon," Jack agreed. "When I signed up to be a deputy United States Marshal, I didn't know what I was letting myself in for."

"Including being the near victim of a necktie party," Lloyd grinned.

"What's that?" asked Chad. "You loadin' me?"

"No, sir. A mob at Live Oaks was real anxious to string up yore nephew," the marshal said.

"Because they found out he is a marshal?"

"They haven't found that out yet. Because they thought he had killed Zach Young."

The old man slewed his head in quick alarm toward Jack. "You weren't so crazy as to —"

Jack interrupted. "No, I wasn't. Somebody killed him five minutes before I reached Live Oaks. He was shot from behind by some party unknown."

"Lord love a duck! Who in tophet could of done it?"

"No information on that point," Jack said. "But there's no law against a fellow guessing. Ever hear of a bird called Ben Ringold?"

"Sure I have. A fellow ugly as galvanized sin and mean as Satan. He was active in the fight against us in the days before yore father was killed." The old-timer's eyes gleamed with excitement. "You don't think he killed Zach Young?"

"I think he killed both Young and my father," Jack said. He went on to give his reasons.

Chad turned over in his mind what his nephew had told him. "Ringold sure was crowdin' you, boy. I don't reckon it was jest because he didn't like the color of yore hair. You dead sure he couldn't of got onto it

132

that you were a deputy under cover sent down to clean up this wholesale rustling?"

"Nobody knew that but the big boss, Lloyd, you and me," Jack answered. "It's a cinch none of us four talked. No, the fellow had a personal reason. A cowboy named Bill Sommers recognized me and told Ringold who I was. Ringold thought I had come down to square accounts for Father's death. So he tried to get the jump on me."

"Looks like," Chad agreed. "He figured you would get to nosing around and find out he did it."

"We got a bad break," Parker said. "If it hadn't been for Zach Young being killed right when Jack arrived, we might have pulled off our little plan. I still think the idea was good — for Jack to go down there playing he was on the dodge, for me to arrest him, and for him to escape later. He could have got in with the rustler gang mighty pretty."

"If there hadn't been a slip-up," Jack agreed. "Maybe it's just as well. We're hot on the trail of bigger game now."

"You boys want to be careful you don't have to holler for somebody to help you turn loose the bear when you get it by the tail," Chad warned. "These fellows are tough hombres. They just got through killing one sheriff."

"That's not what is worrying me," Parker replied. "Four or five posses have been running the tallow off these fellows. We're morally certain they held up that U.P. train, but we haven't evidence enough that would stand up in court to convict a louse. What's the sense in arresting them and having to turn them loose afterward?"

"They're free talkers when they are drinking, if you could get next to them," Chad said. He added, with a grin, "They're free shooters too, especially Nate Winters and Kid Curry. Soon as they suspicioned you they would start smoking."

"Might be we could pal up with them," Parker suggested dubiously.

They agreed to follow up the outlaws and take a chance on gathering the evidence they needed.

CHAPTER SIXTEEN:
KROCK LAYS THE LAW DOWN

Ben Ringold walked into Colonel Krock's office and said, "Sid tells me you want to see me."

"Shut the door," the lawyer answered. He drew a chair to the side of the desk close to his own. "Sit down."

The Bar Z Y foreman sat. His shifty, shallow eyes came to rest on Krock. "What's eatin' you?" he asked.

The colonel looked his accomplice over with critical distaste. It was a pity, he thought, that a man had to use as tools such undependable ruffians as this.

"I'm wondering whether I can get you out of this mess you've got yourself into by your folly," he said coldly.

"I dunno what you mean," Ringold retorted sourly. "I'm not in any mess."

"No?" The voice and manner of the judge were scornfully frigid. "You've lost your job. Very likely you will be flung into the penitentiary for stealing cattle from the ranch you run. The son of Gabe Lovell knows you killed his father and intends to rub you out. Maybe none of this spells trouble to you."

Ringold's mind fastened on the most dreadful of these evils. "Who told you Lovell knows?" he asked.

"He as good as told me. If it interests you, he found out because you kept ramming it down his throat. How could he miss it when you tried three or four times to kill him? You had to have a reason."

"Zach was a good enough reason," Ringold said.

"He didn't think so. I would not in his

place." Krock added more trouble to the load he was piling up on the unhappy foreman. "And it looks as if you might have trouble about the killing of Zach. Old Pud Lyman came to me this morning and told me he saw you coming up back of Roberts's corral just after Zach was killed."

Stark fear stared out of Ringold's face. "Pud Lyman. Goddlemighty! I reckon the old fool has tattled it all over town."

"Not yet. He came to ask me if he ought to go to Houck and tell him he had seen you. It's been worrying him. You were running along close to the fence and went into the Blue Moon. He was outside his old cabin digging worms to go fishing. About ten minutes later Lovell came out of the barn to the pump and washed his face. He can almost swear that only you two left the stable by the back way."

"If he blabs it —"

The colonel interrupted the worried foreman. "I told him to say nothing to anybody — that you were Zach's best friend, his faithful employee, the last man in the world who would hurt Young."

"Just the same, he might talk. You never can tell." Wrinkles of anxiety furrowed the mean face of Ringold. "Maybe I had better make sure. Maybe —" He broke off, a question in his harassed eyes.

"No," Krock vetoed sharply. "Forget about it. I have put Lyman's mind at rest. Don't stir up more trouble." He added contemptuously, "You haven't the pluck of a rabbit."

Ringold's dread flared to a snarling threat. "If they put this on me, I'll tell all I know. You can't let me be stuck and slip out yoreself. I won't have it thataway."

"Won't you?" The malignity of Krock's face was appalling. "Listen, my friend. Threaten me and I'll throw you to the wolves. You haven't even a scrap of paper to implicate me. Do you think the word of a murderous scoundrel like you would stand against mine?"

The hard confidence of the lawyer daunted Ringold. "I shot Zach because he found out we were sending Bar Z Y stock up the trail," he whined. "I had to bump him off quick. You good as told me that morning, after he talked with you, that it had to be awful fast."

"You can't prove a word of that. You shot him to save yourself. It was your own choice. Now listen. If you keep your head, you can still get out of this. But not by trying to drag me in. Make one move in that direction and I'll put a rope around your neck."

Ringold mopped from his forehead tiny beads of sweat. He did not trust this man under whose domination he had fallen. Driven by pressure, Krock would sacrifice him without an instant's hesitation. But he was helpless as a writhing snake pinned by a cleft stick. "All right," he said out of a tight, parched throat. "Tell me what to do."

"Do nothing. Let everything ride quietly. You've been in such a sweat to fasten this on Lovell that some people must have wondered. Let them forget the whole thing."

"If I'm through at the Bar Z Y, I might as well light out," Ringold said despondently.

Krock leaned back in his chair and looked steadily at the foreman for a long five seconds. "If it was worth while I might even save your job for you," he said. "But I would have to know that you would take orders. I'll not put up a fight for you on any other terms."

"I s'pose it's the girl that wants to boot me out," Ringold growled.

"Yes. I can handle Haley because he wants to be manager of the ranch. Together we have a two-thirds vote. If we override the girl, she will never forgive me. I don't know that there is enough profit in having you foreman to make an enemy of her."

"If you're aiming to milk the ranch, like you been doing, you got to have a fellow in cahoots with you that you can depend on," Ringold argued.

Krock knew this was true. With Haley manager of the Bar Z Y and Ringold foreman, the set-up would be just what he wanted, but he was not going to admit it to his tool.

"Trouble is I can't depend on you," he said contemptuously. "Men like you are a dime a dozen. No brains, no stamina. You lose your nerve and start dry-gulching when it isn't necessary."

A dull flush beat into the dish face of the foreman. "You good as told me we had to get Zach before he had us arrested," Ringold countered angrily. "He had already talked with Houck. I had to stop him *muy pronto.* You let me take the risk, then throw me down."

"Houck will keep his mouth shut," Krock said. "Don't worry about that. He has no evidence anyhow. I got out to the ranch soon as Zach was killed and got the letter the Routt County sheriff had written him about stuff with his brand being sold up there, and I wrote the sheriff an answer that will satisfy him Zach had sold the stock to the trail drivers. And I'm not throwing you down. I'm trying to keep you from doing that yourself. If you can get it into your thick head that I know better than you what to do, I'll give you another chance."

Ringold promised grumblingly to do as he was told.

They discussed the ranch personnel. The foreman thought there were two or three of the riders they ought to get rid of, men clever enough to suspect that the cattle raids on the Bar Z Y pastures might be planned from the inside. Krock told him to make some excuse for giving them their time. He had a couple of cowpunchers who had just come down the trail he wanted put on the pay roll. Their names were Grogan and Darrow. A few days later he might want to place a third, man by the name of Bullen. Ringold was to fix it up so that young Haley would agree to the discharge of those to be fired. A plausible reason must be found. Krock was going to drive across with Haley to the Circle 72 that afternoon to see Esther Young. On the way he would drop a hint that the undesirable riders were unfriendly to Haley and resented the proposed appointment of him as manager.

CHAPTER SEVENTEEN: RUDHOLT VISITS HIS NEIGHBORS

On the night of the lynching fiasco, Esther had made it clear to Colonel Krock that Ringold must be discharged at once. The next day she had driven to the Bar Z Y and told Nick Haley that she wanted the foreman and the cowboy Sid sent down the road. Both the colonel and her cousin had protested mildly, but her attitude was so firm that each of them had apparently consented.

She was so busy supervising the fencing of a new pasture that she did not see either of them for more than a week. One afternoon Jerry rode across the flat to where the men were working, bringing a message to his sister that she was wanted at the house. Colonel Krock and Nick had come to have a talk with her.

When Esther reached the house, she found Colonel Krock on the porch reading the local newspaper and Nick in the sitting-room flirting with Lucy. He had got hold of a letter the girl had been writing and she was trying to get it back from him. Giggles and laughter accompanied their romping.

Nick was wearing a well-cut riding-suit and a freshly laundered white shirt. Since Esther was in Levis, dusty boots, and a sweat-stained blouse, with a mud streak on one cheek, it did not make her any happier to see her immaculate cousin playing up to Lucy as usual. He ought to be looking after the ranch.

When she learned that Ringold was still foreman of the Bar Z Y and that both of them wanted him to retain the position, Esther let her anger rip loose. They had promised, she claimed, and now they were reneging. Ringold was a dangerous ruffian and had forfeited all right to a position of responsibility.

The colonel corrected her gently. He had not promised. He had said he would consider her request. It did not seem wise to let go one of the best cowmen in the state merely on account of an excess of zeal. He had talked with Ben, and the foreman had expressed regret and promised amendment. The man had erred chiefly because of loyalty to and affection for Zach. He ought not to be punished too severely for his mistake.

Nick was a little ashamed of himself but stubbornly determined to hold fast to the stand he had taken. He let the colonel do most of the talking. Esther was furious at him. She knew he did not care whether Ringold and Sid stayed at the Bar Z Y, that he was supporting Krock only in return for his pledge to put him in as manager. To get what he wanted Nick was willing to break with his relatives.

Her anger beat on Krock with no more effect than waves have on a great rock anchored to a cliff. He was suave, courteous, reasonable, but firm. She felt he was putting her in the position of a schoolgirl in a tantrum. He was very anxious, he said, to meet her wishes whenever he could, but the interests of all must be considered. To subordinate his considered and experienced judgment to her impetuous impulse would be weakness.

They left her both angry and disturbed, moved by a dread of impending trouble that she could not explain. Krock had always shown himself so friendly. After the quarrel with her uncle, she had gone to him and found sympathy and understanding. His words were still smooth as butter, but she felt no reality back of them.

Her visitors were hardly off the place when she caught sight of Bedford Rudholt riding down the lane. Her temper flared again. He had no right to be on their ranch.

But if she had to meet him, she must get into decent clothes. She asked Lucy to be hostess until she could take a hurried bath and get dressed.

All her life Lucy had heard of this man. Often she had seen him on the streets of Live Oaks, but she had always passed him without speaking. He was an enemy of the Youngs, first as the head and front of all the little nesters who had been nibbling at the grass, at the water holes, and at the stock of the Bar Z Y, and later as a formidable rival of the big ranch by reason of his aggressive fight for water and pasture Zach Young claimed on account of priority use. He was a kind of human Beelzebub, in her immature opinion. Though she had not expected him to have horns and hoofs, she was not prepared for a certain charm she found in his effrontery. He was in his late thirties, and around the temples the hair was slightly grizzled. But he moved lightly, and his body looked steel-strong. She tried to be cool toward him, but her stiffness melted before his warm friendliness. He could not be as bad as she had been brought up to believe.

She would have been amazed if she had known the thoughts drifting through his mind. She was so young and lovely and pliable. One could mold her into the kind of woman he chose; she had none of the stiff-willed inflexibility of her sister. A man who married her would not forever be sitting at the seat of judgment. No matter how high he climbed, he could be proud of her beauty and good taste. A wife ought to fit into her husband's plans — to let him be her conscience. It would not be that way with Esther. She had character and was self-willed. Storms would blow up and make wedded life with her gusty.

He had chosen Esther because marriage with her would be an opening wedge to control of the big Bar Z Y spread. Given this, he would be overlord of the whole district for fifty miles in every direction. Until now he had not cast a thought toward Lucy. But today he saw her with new eyes — no longer a child but an adorable girl blossoming into womanhood. Unlike Esther, she would be a rose without thorns.

His warm sympathetic manner gave the girl confidence and she expanded, even dared to make friendly fun of him as she did with other men. Though he had little sense of humor, he laughed at her quips. It was a pleasure to see the points of light sparkle in her amber eyes and the dimples

145

come and go when her face crinkled to mirth.

"Why, you're human," she told him. "I thought —"

She decided it might be safer not to tell him what she had started to say.

"The devil isn't as black as he is painted," he mentioned smilingly.

Rudholt rose, to set a chair for Esther as she joined them.

She bowed, distantly, intent on not letting him bridge lightly the gulf between them.

"I've just been finding out what a charming girl Miss Lucy is," he said.

Esther replied coldly that during the past seventeen years she had become aware of what her sister was like. Their visitor knew when to let well enough alone. He had come, he explained, to put a business proposition before her. From a noted breeder in Illinois he was buying a whiteface pedigreed bull. By taking two he could get them at a reduced price. Would Miss Young be interested in getting one of them?

Miss Young said formally that she would not. The Circle 72 was a small outfit, somewhat encumbered, and it could not afford to buy an expensive bull.

"I was thinking of the Bar Z Y," he continued. "A rumor has reached me that your

146

uncle Zach was looking around for one."

"You will have to see Colonel Krock and my cousin Nick Haley about that," she told him stiffly. "I have no say in the running of that ranch."

He was puzzled. "I thought your end of the family inherited three-fourths of yore uncle's estate."

"And one third of the control," she added tartly. "My cousin and Colonel Krock have decided to get along without my advice and regardless of my wishes. I wanted Ben Ringold discharged, but he is so valuable they mean to keep him. Nick is to be manager."

"But Nick can't handle it. He is a playboy."

"Nick thinks he can, and apparently Colonel Krock agrees with him." Esther rose, to indicate that their self-invited guest might go.

He was oblivious to the suggestion. "Nick will do wonders," he said. There was sarcasm in Rudholt's smile. "With a little help from Colonel Krock," he added dryly.

The reason for this set-up was clearer to him than to Esther. Krock was too much like himself for him not to be aware of the man's reaching ambition and his unscrupulous moral callousness. There was this difference between them, that Rudholt had

147

been in self-protection hard and lawless in the sight of all, whereas Krock covered his knavery with smiling diplomacy and a manner of unctuous good will.

The cattleman said to Esther bluntly, "Krock wants to use Nick and Ringold."

"Use them?" the young woman asked. "How?"

His hard gaze bored steadily into her eyes. "To get control of the ranch. He means ultimately to own the whole spread."

Incredulously she stared at him. "That's absurd," she flung back. "How could he possibly get it?"

"By letting the ranch run down — getting it into debt — mortgaging the stock and the property. I'll give him five years to pull it off."

The possibility of such a thing had never occurred to Esther. Krock had been her uncle's partner in at least two enterprises, one of them the bank. He had been Zach Young's trusted friend. She had known him many years, whereas Rudholt had always been an open enemy. It came to her in a wave of heat that it was a kind of treachery to listen to this man's prophecy.

"No!" she cried. "I don't believe it — not a word of it. I won't discuss it."

He shrugged his broad shoulders. "You'll

believe it before long, and when you do you'd better come to me. We'll have to join forces against him." His eyes narrowed, thinking the situation out as he talked. "It stands out like a patch of blue sky through the pines. Why else does he want Nick Haley as manager and Ringold as foreman? A weakling and a crook. For no reason except to rook the Bar Z Y."

"It can't be true!" Esther cried. "I won't listen to such talk."

The picture grew clearer in his mind each moment. "It's a cinch that Ben Ringold is a scoundrel. There's a whisper running through Live Oaks that yore uncle got the proof on him and went to town the day he died to turn the screws on Ringold."

"What was it Uncle Zach found out?" Esther asked.

"I don't know, but I can guess." Rudholt's light eyes were bright with excitement. "Somebody around here is tipping off a gang of rustlers from up the trail — somebody who can tell them when and where to round up the stock unmolested." He slammed a fist into the palm of his other hand. "Dollars to doughnuts that skunk's name is Ringold."

"Very likely," the girl agreed. "But that doesn't involve Colonel Krock. He is a leading citizen, a judge, formerly a colonel in the army. It would be silly to think he would throw in with such a man as Ben Ringold to steal cattle."

His cynical eyes mocked her defense. "Krock plays his own hand twenty-four hours of the day. Right now there is more money in wholesale rustling than there is raising the stuff. And there's mighty little risk. We have all had heavy losses, no ranch more than the Bar Z Y. I'll bet Krock is in it up to his neck."

"Colonel Krock is a friend of ours," Esther told him quietly.

"You mean that you are friends of his," he corrected. "The only friend Butler Krock has is Butler Krock."

He rose to go, aware from Esther's manner that he was outwearing his welcome.

"We must be more neighborly," he said, and offered his hand to Lucy. "In future we shall have to co-operate, and we must forget any foolish prejudices we have."

Lucy hesitated, not quite knowing what to do. She put her small hand in his large one.

"Are you making the rounds of all those who have foolish prejudices against you, Mr. Rudholt?" she asked, and giggled.

He held her fingers tightly a moment longer than was necessary. "Not all of

150

them," he conceded.

Esther was busy straightening the piano spread and did not notice his extended hand. "An opinion is not necessarily a prejudice," she said. "When based on the judgment of years, it ought not to be discarded lightly."

"It may still be wrong." His cool, bold eyes challenged her. "I'm going to change one of yours. That goes for both of you."

Lucy watched him swing to the saddle and ride away, his flat back and well-poised head a picture of assurance.

"He's rather — fascinating," she murmured.

The sharp eyes of her sister raked the girl. "He's an impudent, arrogant scoundrel," she differed.

CHAPTER EIGHTEEN: SOMMERS MEETS AN ACQUAINTANCE

Rome Siddall came into the Bar Z Y bunkhouse and began to pack his personal belongings. From the bunk where Bill Sommers was reading a dime novel that young man looked across at the puncher, his attention for the moment distracted from the

151

adventures of Deadwood Dick.

"Going somewheres, Rome?" he asked.

"You've said it, young fellow," Rome answered, an edge of anger in his voice. "I'm fired. Nick Haley gave me and Dugan our time."

Bill was surprised. Siddall and Dugan were top riders, entirely dependable, men who had been with the Bar ZY a good many years. That Haley was an irresponsible light-weight he knew, but getting rid of the best men on the ranch did not make sense.

"Give any reason?" Bill asked.

"Said it was time to make a change. Seems that Bob and me have been here too long and act uppity. Suits me. I hate to work for an outfit that's running down, as this will under Haley."

As Sommers rode the line he mulled this over, trying to figure out what was behind the move. When he returned to the bunk-house, he learned that a third cowboy had ridden down the road with his roll. The men discussed this guardedly. It might be the turn of any one of them to go next.

At supper three strangers sat down with them, replacements for the men who had just left. Ringold introduced them as Grogan, Darrow, and Bullen. The one called Bullen was a smiling little man as mild as

152

skim milk. Sommers nodded a greeting to Darrow, a tall, slim man with friendly manners.

"Glad to see you again," he said, omitting to mention that when they had met before the name of the man was Elza Lay.

Lay answered smilingly, not at all disturbed. "Didn't know you were in this neck of the woods, Bill." He remembered that at their last previous meeting Sommers had been on the dodge because of the too free use of a running-iron.

The shifty eyes of Ringold shuttled from Lay to Sommers and back. "You fellows know each other?" he asked.

"We're both drifters," Bill told him casually. He did not think it necessary to add that he identified Grogan too, since evidently the fellow did not remember having seen him in a saloon at Buffalo, Wyoming. Grogan then had been known as Kid Curry. The third stranger Sommers did not know. He was unaware that this amiable little chap, who certainly did not weigh a hundred and twenty pounds, was a desperate and ruthless killer by name Nate Winters.

Later that evening Ringold came to the bunkhouse and called to Sommers that he would like to see him. He walked with Bill as far as the outdoor blacksmith shop where

153

the ranch horses were shod.

"If you know what's good for you, Bill, you'll padlock yore lips about knowing who Darrow is," he ordered harshly.

Sommers stiffened at once. His steady eyes fastened to those of the foreman. "Don't tell me what I am or am not to say, Ben," he answered in a low voice. "I'll ride herd over my own talk."

That his approach had been wrong Ringold knew, but he was too stubborn to amend it now. "I'm telling you for yore own good," he snarled. "I don't know who these fellows are, but they look plenty tough to me. If they thought for a minute you were going to do any blabbing —"

"Are you speaking for them or for yoreself?" Sommers asked gently. "If for them, tell the gents to come and make their own threats. They are none of them shy. If for yoreself, get the blazes out of here."

"You can't talk thataway to me," Ringold cried angrily. "I'm boss of this outfit, and what I say goes. If you don't like it —"

"I don't," Sommers interrupted. "I get thirty dollars a month to prod the Bar Z Y longhorns along, but that doesn't include asking any two-bit foreman can I wipe my nose."

He turned sharply and walked away. Ringold glared at the back of the cowpuncher, fury boiling up in him. The foreman did not quite know what to do. It had not been his business to take this up with Sommers. If Elza Lay had wanted to do so, he could have done it himself. Maybe it would be better now to keep his mouth shut and let things ride.

But when he met Nate Winters a few minutes later, his rage exploded in speech. He warned the outlaw that Sommers might betray them.

"What makes you think so?" the little bandit asked.

"I thought it might be a good idea to tell him I wouldn't stand for any talking. He said he would do as he pleased."

Winters smiled. "Feeling his oats some, looks like. You keep outa this, Ringold. We'll take care of Mr. Sommers."

Lay and Curry were pitching horseshoes and two cowboys were watching them. Curry threw a ringer, collected half a dollar from Lay, and moved down with him to the end of the pitch where Winters had stopped. Out of a corner of his mouth the small outlaw said, "Meet me at the corral in ten minutes," then drifted into the bunkhouse. The other two outlaws finished their game.

When Winters sauntered down to the corral, his companions were seated on the top rail of the fence smoking.

"What's up, Nate?" Elza Lay asked.

Winters told them what he had heard from the foreman.

"I think Ben is way off his base," Lay said. "When Bill was a kid he and I worked for the Broken Arrow. We were sidekicks for two-three weeks during the round-up. Bill is no squealer."

"There's a thousand-dollar reward out for us," Kid Curry mentioned, his thin lips twisted to a sneer. "Maybe he thinks he could use that thousand."

Lay shook his head. "No," he answered with sharp decision. "Bill wouldn't do that, not unless he's changed a lot since I knew him."

"You can't ever tell what a guy will do for dough," Winters murmured softly. "Maybe we had better nip in the bud any intentions Mr. Sommers has."

"That would be plumb foolish," Lay protested. "The last thing we want to do is to call attention to ourselves while we're here lying low. A killing now would point a finger right at us. I tell you Bill Sommers is all right. Another thing is that there isn't any thousand dollars reward out for us. The reward is for the guys who held up the

156

express at Wilcox. It can't be proved we did it. We were masked. All the clothes we wore were burned at our first campfire — all except our boots. We can't be identified. No use in getting goosy every time we see a fellow that knows one of us. Tell you what, I'll talk with Bill and feel him out."

Kid Curry amended that suggestion. "We'll all talk with him. Nate and I are interested in this much as you are, Elza."

"Well, don't get his back up to start off. Lemme put it to him kinda easy."

Standing in the doorway of the bunkhouse, Lay asked Sommers if he would come out and take a look at his horse. He added that the animal was lame. It looked as if he had been badly shod.

"Sure," Bill answered.

He knew this was an excuse. It flashed through his mind that it might be well to reach under the pillow of his cot and get the forty-five lying there. But he discarded the idea. Better not show any evidence of suspicion. In any case, if he needed it, the gun would do him no good. He would be dead before he could use it.

"The boys want to have a little talk with you, Bill," the outlaw said, as he steered the cowboy down to the corral. "Ringold told Nate something you said that didn't go down very good."

"Ringold is an interfering fool," Sommers replied.

"My opinion too," Lay assented. "But go easy in what you say. The boys are kinda touchy."

In answer to a question Bill told them what he had said to Ringold. He added that no bully-puss foreman could give him orders about what he was to say. Any man with a lick of sense ought to know without having it rammed down his throat when it was necessary to have no information on a subject.

The cowboy felt their hard eyes boring into his.

"Last time I saw you, Bill, the story was that you were on the dodge," Lay said. "You know how it is, give a dog a bad name and hang him. We weren't within a hundred miles of Wilcox when that train was held up, but everybody who ever had a drink with Butch Cassidy had to run for cover to keep from being arrested and framed. We don't have to tell you every stick-up is blamed on him and his friends. So we're lying low for a little while."

"Fine with me," Sommers told him. "I don't give a cuss who robbed that train."

"You told Ringold you would turn us in if

you felt like it," Winters said, his voice deceptively gentle.

"Wrong. I told him to mind his own business." The gaze of Sommers held to Winters coolly and steadily. "If I was thinking of running to a sheriff, would I be dumb enough to blat it to Ringold, who wouldn't have hired you boys unless he was more or less friendly to you?"

"I wouldn't think so," Lay assented.

"Unless you are one of those lunkheads who have to tell all they know," Curry put in acidly.

"Elza has told you I was on the run last time he saw me. What gives you the idea that I am so hot for Mr. Law now?"

"A thousand dollars isn't hay," Curry jeered.

"Isn't it? I lost a thousand one night at poker and didn't cry about it. I don't sell men for money." Sommers went on, with an easy smile: "And I haven't anything to sell anyhow, except that I have met an old friend who used to share the same tarp with me. Seems to me you ought to be having yore powwow with Ringold, who is fussing around stirring up trouble where there isn't any."

"You talk a good story, fellow," Winters answered, grinning at him. "Darned if I don't pretty nearly believe you."

"He'd better be all right," growled Curry. "If he's not it will be just too bad."

Sommers rolled and lit a cigarette. "I don't like to be threatened, Mr. Grogan," he said, his voice even and low. "And I don't scare easy. I've as much right here as you have. I'm minding my business, and that's more than you are doing right now. You can like it or not as you please, even if you are packing a gun and I'm not."

The cowpuncher turned and walked back to the bunkhouse. He lay down and picked up again the dime novel. But he was no longer interested in the hairbreadth escapes of Deadwood Dick. His mind was busy with the situation in which he had become involved. That these men were some of those who had robbed the express at Wilcox, he had no doubt. They had come here to lie hidden until the hunt died down. Ringold knew who they were. Probably Haley did not. Well, it was no affair of his. He had once known a man who lived to be nearly a hundred by keeping his mouth shut when he should. Already he had sounded off too much. What sense was there in ending his talk with the bandits on a note of defiance? Lay had given him a friendly tip to speak softly. Instead of which he had got bullheaded and made them sore. It would not take much now to spark their hostility into action.

Chapter Nineteen: Sommers Jumps Up a Camper

Bill Sommers was not happy about the Bar Z Y set-up. There was something going on that he did not understand. It was all very well to say that he was just a hired cowpoke whose obligations ceased when he swung from the saddle at the end of the day's work. But he knew this was not true. A puncher owed loyalty to his outfit out of proportion to the wages he received. He endured blizzards, rode out stampedes, swam bank-full rivers, and breathed the hot dust of the trail for twenty-four hours at a stretch when necessary. Though he complained as a matter of course, he was proud of the spread which employed him.

If Nick Haley had been a competent cowman, Bill would have dismissed from his mind the doubts that stabbed at him. But his opinion was that Haley did not know Ringold had turned the ranch over to outlaws as a refuge for them and perhaps as a base of operations for future depredations. He could get his time and leave. That would be the easy way out. It would also be safer, for he saw that Curry and Winters were watching him suspiciously. When he had wanted to go to town Saturday night with some of the other boys, an excuse had been found to keep him on the ranch. But he had a feeling that to leave now would be almost desertion.

Bill rode the huddled hills along the north boundary line, turning back stock inclined to wander into the bad lands beyond. A thin drift of smoke rose from a hollow between two slopes. The rider drew up. None of the Bar Z Y boys were supposed to be on this far range except him. He dismounted and trailed the bridle reins. Easing the gun in its holster without drawing the weapon, he moved silently toward the top of the rise, reaching it at a point where a clump of thick brush grew. Carefully he pushed aside the twigs to see better.

A man was washing some tin cups and plates in the sand beside a water hole. There was no longer any smoke, for he had put out the fire. He was whistling cheerfully as he worked. Thirty yards from him a picketed horse grazed. The camper stopped whistling. He sluiced half a bucket of water over the sand-washed dishes. His back was toward the watcher. Without turning, he called up a drawling invitation.

"Better come down from where you're roostin' up there."

Sommers descended to the water hole. "Thought you were in a steel-barred hotel up in Wyoming," he said.

"I like the climate here better," Jack Lovell answered.

"Should think you might find it too hot," Sommers mentioned casually.

The camper did not follow that opening. "I'm lucky in my visitor," he said. "I wasn't sure whether he would come down from the bushes or send a messenger."

"You're packing a six-gun, and there is a rifle handy. Why didn't you reach for one?"

"Too far from the bushes for my forty-five, and if the gent had been hostile and I had started for the Winchester, he would have blown me off the map before I reached it."

"So you give him an invite to plug you in the back." Sommers's gaze ranged over Lovell in keen appraisal. He thought it had been a long time since he had met a man so cool of nerve as this one.

"Nothing else to do. If he had a rifle and wanted to collect me, I was his meat."

The Bar Z Y man noticed that the camper had washed two cups and two plates. He read the evidence of a second horse picketed in the draw, though no horse was now there.

"Aren't you a little careless?" he asked.

"Of my campfire? The answer is yes. I thought this was miles off yore range. Got in last night after dark."

"You must have eyes in the back of yore head. I didn't make any noise. How did you know I was in the brush?"

"My bronc. He lifted his head and quit grazing."

Sommers did not ask Lovell how he had escaped or what he was doing here. Those came within the list of forbidden questions. Nor did he inquire who and where his companion was.

He said, "I'm startin' back for the Bar Z Y ranch house if you're headin' that way."

Jack shook his head. "I wouldn't want to impose on its hospitality," he answered dryly. "Mr. Ringold has taken a little dislike to me."

"I thought maybe he had got over it, since he has thrown in with yore friends."

"My friends?"

The cowpuncher backed away from the lead he had opened. "Just a guess. Likely I'm wrong. None of my business anyhow." He lifted a hand in farewell.

"One moment, please," Lovell interposed.

164

"About those friends of mine. You mean the guys who held up the U.P. express with me?"

"Don't put words in my mouth," Sommers said coldly. "I didn't mention any train stick-up. If one was held up, I don't know who did it and I don't care. I've said that before. Do I have to keep repeating it like a parrot?"

"You haven't said it to me."

"All right. I'm telling you now."

"How many of these alleged friends are around?"

"I wouldn't know."

"Maybe you can tell me how I can get in touch with them."

"No."

Lovell knew he had come to an impasse. "Okay," he said. "One more question, and there's no dynamite in it. Is that bowlegged Casanova Nick Haley running the ranch?"

"Yes." Sommers turned to walk up the slope and pulled up in his stride. "What's that?"

From the brush above came the sounds of somebody moving hurriedly through the bushes, followed by the slap of galloping hoofs.

The two men in the hollow ran to the rim. A rider was urging his mount over the top of the next hill fold. He was quirting the big sorrel furiously. For an instant man and beast were silhouetted against the sky line, then were gone. But both Sommers and Lovell recognized the big-barreled gelding with the white-stockinged legs.

"Was Ringold riding with you?" Jack asked.

"He must have been spying on me," Sommers answered. "The fool thinks I'm selling him out. Now he'll be sure of it."

Without another word he walked to the dip where he had left his horse. Lovell watched him ride away.

Jack did not quite understand this. Something had evidently occurred to make Sommers less friendly toward him than he had been. It probably had to do with the train hold-up. The bandits were somewhere in the neighborhood and Ben Ringold had lined up with them. So much was clear from what the cowboy had blurted out and later tried to cover up. They might have a hide-out in some of the hills back of the Bar Z Y.

The line rider would no doubt report that he had met Lovell by chance. In any case Ringold would start a hunt for him. As soon as Lloyd Parker returned from Live Oaks, where he had gone to buy supplies, they must move out of this locality. On the Circle 72 range was a pocket between two hogbacks that would do nicely for a camp. It had water and grass, was away from the usual run of travel, and access to it was difficult. An added attraction was that he could slip down to the ranch house some evening and renew his acquaintance with Esther Young. He still remembered the biting scorn with which she had repudiated him. It would be a pleasure to watch her eat her words.

CHAPTER TWENTY:
SELF-INVITED GUESTS AT CIRCLE 72

Lucy was curled in a window-seat of the big living-room reading *Innocents Abroad*. Her sister sat at a desk figuring the ranch expense account for the month. Both had been too absorbed for talk.

A rallying voice broke the stillness. "May I disturb this quakeress meeting?"

Rudholt's big body filled the doorway. He was smiling at them cheerfully, as one assured of his welcome.

A ripple of laughter broke over Lucy's mobile face. "Another business visit?" she inquired saucily.

"Business and pleasure too, I hope."

"Afraid you have come to the wrong place, Mr. Rudholt," Esther said stiffly. "We are not in the market either to buy or sell, nor are we at home socially."

"I'm sure you are mistaken." He moved into the room and took a chair. "I come bearing gifts tonight — gifts of news. If you are not interested I miss my guess. First, your cousin has discharged from the Bar Z Y three of its best riders — Siddall, Dugan, and Elson."

Esther stared at the man incredulously. "You must be wrong. Nick wouldn't do that."

"But he did. Siddall and Dugan are now working for me at the Flying R."

"Why?" Esther asked. "They are top hands, steady and competent. Siddall and Dugan have been on the ranch a dozen years. Nick must have given a reason."

"The reason he gave is that they have been there too long. In their place he has hired three strangers who have just come down the trail — tough customers. There is something shady about them, Dugan thinks."

Esther frowned, trying to make sense of this. "What can Nick be thinking of? I don't understand why he did it."

There was a touch of complacence in his

smile. "I told you what was going to happen. This is the first move. Nick isn't boss at the Bar ZY. He just thinks he is. The man using him for a cat's-paw has moved the ranch headquarters to the courthouse."

The girl at the desk was appalled. If somebody was deliberately trying to wreck the big ranch he had made a good beginning. Her mind searched for some other explanation and could not find one. Nick, of course, was no party to such a scheme. He was being used by a man who knew how to flatter his vanity skillfully. It could not be Ringold. He was another tool. Krock was at the bottom of this.

"You may be right, though I don't like to think so," she said. "Nobody who wished the ranch well would throw out three of its best men. I'll have to see Nick at once."

"Don't see him until you have a plan made — some way of putting a squeeze on him."

"I don't want to put a squeeze on him," Esther replied, annoyed at such advice. "He is our cousin and part owner of the Bar ZY. It is to his interest as much as ours to keep the ranch in tiptop shape."

"You'll find he thinks he is doing that," Rudholt answered dryly. "His idea is that he is cutting out dry rot and making the spread a better-paying concern."

Dad Cantrell walked into the room, Jack Lovell at his heels.

"Here's this no-account rooster back again," he piped. "Crowin' jest as loud as ever."

Lucy jumped to her feet. "My goodness! it's our train robber." Her eyes sparkled with excitement. "Maybe he has come to hold up the ranch."

"He claims they found he didn't do it and turned him loose," the old man explained.

Esther's eyes held to those of her former employee. A pulse beat fast in her throat. "I hope that is true," she said quietly.

"It's my story," Lovell answered, smiling at her.

This was not the way he had arranged in his mind their meeting. He had meant to tell her why he had been forced at the time of their earlier acquaintance to carry the stigma of a law-breaker, but with Rudholt present he could not do that. For it might still be necessary to fall back upon his evil reputation to get the evidence he wanted.

Rudholt's arrogant eyes were scornful. "You're still just a puncher riding the chuck line?" he jeered.

"Unless you can think up a better line for me, Mr. Rudholt," Jack flung back.

"I could suggest one," the cattleman retorted promptly. "A story more credible. I suppose you have just come down the trail from Utah?"

"Yes."

"Naturally you did not travel it alone. You no doubt had friends."

"You think so?"

"Other cowpunchers on the loose. I understand that three of them have just got jobs at the Bar Z Y. Maybe you expect to join your friends there."

"One with so vivid an imagination has to guess wrong sometimes," Lovell replied.

Esther interrupted. "Have you any proof of your innocence, Mr. Lovell?" she asked bluntly. "I am tired of evasion."

"Isn't it evidence that I am free?" he wanted to know. "Bandits under suspicion are not turned loose."

"They have been known to escape," Rudholt said. "With the help of other criminals."

"Mr. Rudholt's faith in his fellow man is unshakable," Lovell drawled ironically.

A wave of color beat through the tan in Esther's cheeks. "I don't know why you have come back, Mr. Lovell," she said firmly. "But I must make it clear that this ranch is no Robbers' Roost. I do not care to condone lawbreaking. When you have cleared your name we shall be very glad to welcome you to the Circle 72. Until then you must excuse us."

Lovell's sardonic gaze rested for a long moment on Rudholt. The young woman interpreted correctly the slight smile on his lips. It asked, without words, how long it had been since the owner of the Flying R had white-washed his reputation for rustling, violence, and fraudulent entry of land claims. The insolence of the drifter's criticism annoyed her none the less because she recognized it as just, and felt exactly the same way about Rudholt. For Jack Lovell was beyond the pale, or at least had offered no proof that he was not. He should be abashed and shamefaced. Instead he was facing her with a raffish insouciance that seemed to imply no explanation was necessary.

"If you've got anything to say for yoreself, fellow, you'd better spit it out," Cantrell snapped.

"No defense," returned Lovell. "Or maybe I had better put it, defense reserved."

Lucy asked impulsively, "Why do you have to be so — so stuffy?"

"Mr. Lovell knows his own business best, dear," her sister said quietly. "We must not embarrass him with awkward questions."

172

She walked to the door and opened it.

At the threshold Lovell turned and gave Esther a long, steady look. "I'll be back," he told her.

Rudholt broke the silence his departure left. "Strange how impudent these scalawags get," he commented. "Some of them ought to be horsewhipped."

Her eyes rested thoughtfully on the cattleman. "Do you think so, Mr. Rudholt?"

Cantrell strangled what threatened to be a whoop of glee. He left the room hurriedly with his wrinkled hand over his mouth.

Chapter Twenty-One: Bill Makes His Own Break

Sommers did not return to the Bar Z Y by the usual route. He made a wide circle and came to the house by the back way through the south pasture. It was possible somebody might be waiting for him in the bushes along the creek. If so, he wanted to disappoint the expectant gunman. Since he was a realist, Bill knew he was in for trouble. If he could, he would talk himself out of it. His job was to persuade the outlaws that he had jumped up Lovell by chance. The fact that the Green River man was himself a fugitive might tip the balance in his favor.

He slipped down a draw, rode past the corral, and grounded the reins in front of the bunkhouse. There was a chance he might have to leave in a hurry, and he wanted a saddled horse handy.

There were three men in the bunkhouse. In front of a cracked mirror a redheaded cowpuncher was shaving. He was going to a dance fifteen miles distant. The other two were Elza Lay and the man who was passing by the name of Bullen. They were playing pitch, but at sight of Bill they lost interest in the game. He thought they showed some surprise when he came into the room. Perhaps they had expected his journey home to be interrupted by a bullet whistling from the brush.

The little man laid the cards dealt him face down on the table. He spoke in a voice gentle as a kitten's purr. "Have a nice ride?"

Sommers grinned, not very successfully. His smile was set and frozen. "A cowpoke forks a bronc only to get somewheres," he said.

"And did you get somewhere this mo'ning, Mr. Sommers?" Winters inquired mildly. The half-hooded deadly eyes of the pint-size bandit never left the face of the cowboy.

"Rode the north boundary," Bill answered.

"Funny thing. I jumped up a guy I know. He was camping there."

Sommers hoped his voice was easy and casual, with no rasp of strain in it. He spoke of the meeting because he knew Ringold must already have reported it.

"That was sure funny," Winters agreed. "Shows what a small world it is. Who was the guy?"

"That bird Lovell, the one who nearly got lynched for killing Zach Young."

"So it was Lovell you met. That's just jim dandy. An old friend of yours, I reckon." There was a thread of bleak cruelty in the suave, ironic voice of the bandit.

"No friend at all. Never met him but once before he came hell-for-leather south on the dodge."

"Told you he was on the dodge, did he?"

Winters rose from his seat carelessly and began riffling the pack of cards, his gaze not lifting from the face of Sommers. Lay moved from the table to the head of his bunk. There was an anxious frown on his face. It was plain he did not want any part of this. Winters was in no hurry because he felt sure that the killing of this run-of-the-mill cowboy raised no problem. He could take his time with no risk. But Lay counted Bill a man as good as dead.

The cowboy sized the situation up accurately. He could expect no help from Lay. In case of a showdown he would have to back his partner.

"No need for him to tell me. A deputy United States Marshal took him up the trail several weeks ago claiming he was in that U.P. train robbery. Lovell must have broke loose somehow." Sommers realized he was making no impression on the warped mind of the killer, but he had to carry on as if he believed he was gaining ground.

"A regular Billy the Kid this Lovell," Winters jeered. "It would of scared me to meet him. Did he make you feel jumpy?"

"No. He may be a bandit. I wouldn't know about that. But he is no crazy killer. You might like him."

"You think I'd like him. Maybe we would lie under the same tarp and tell each other windies." The outlaw's laugh was not pleasant. "Pity you didn't bring him back with you. I'd kinda like to meet him — once." The ice-cold eyes of Winters narrowed. "Strange he came back to the place where fifty gents are waiting for a chance to hang him."

"Does seem queer. I couldn't guess why."

"Different here. I could."

The cowboy who was shaving stopped

scraping his chin. It had come to him that this friendly little chat covered a sinister menace. Razor in hand, he turned startled eyes on first one and then the other of the men.

"So you figure he broke loose," Winters went on, almost in a murmur. "Who was the marshal that took him?"

"He registered at the Live Oaks hotel as Lloyd Parker."

Bill knew it would be soon now. His one chance was that Winters was underestimating him.

"Sure enough?" Winters let the cards slip through his fingers to the table. "We get another laugh there, Mr. Sommers. For Lovell and Parker have just come down the trail together like buddies."

Sommers's stare held genuine astonishment. "I don't get it. If Parker is a marshal —"

"Why, then Lovell must be one too," Winters cut in. "As you know damned well, you two-timing spy."

The right arm of the cowboy swept up without stopping. On the way his fingers had closed on the butt of a revolver.

"One move and I'll drill you!" he cried.

Winters had been caught flatfooted. The draw had been both swift and unexpected, betrayed by no warning from the eyes. Like a fool, he had waited too long.

"Ease over this way, Elza," Sommers ordered. "With yore hands reaching for the roof. . . . That's right. No monkey business or I'll plug you both. Jim, collect the hardware from these gents . . . Good. Fling the guns out of that back window."

The startled eyes of the man with the half-scraped face stood out like baseballs. He laid the razor down and did as he was told.

From the corner of Winters's thin lips snarling words dripped. "I'm gonna kill you for this," he promised, in the midst of them.

Sommers backed to the door, rammed the revolver into its holster, turned, and caught up the reins of the mustang. He vaulted to the saddle and jumped the pony to a gallop. Before he had gone a dozen yards, he dragged his mount up and swung it round. Kid Curry and Ringold were jogging down the lane at a road gait. A bullet zipped past Bill's shoulder.

There was no way of escape left except across the pasture. He had no time to open the gate.

"Take it, Blaze!" Bill cried, and set the horse for the jump.

Blaze sailed over with inches to spare. The crash of the rifles boomed behind the man and horse. Crouched low in the saddle, Bill kept going.

Chapter Twenty-Two: A Girl Makes an Apology

Sommers spent the night at a dry camp on the desert. The Circle 72 riders were at breakfast when he dropped in on them and drew up at the table. After he had eaten, he looked up Dad Cantrell and asked if he could tell him where to find Jack Lovell.

The old man snapped back a question. "What you want with him?"

"I want to borrow a match," Sommers answered curtly.

"Hmp!" grunted the old-timer. "Tellin' me it's none of my doggoned business. All right. You go find him."

Bill's eyes narrowed thoughtfully. "Believe I'll have a talk with the little boss," he said. "Maybe I know something she would like to hear."

"There she is right now," Cantrell said, tossing his head toward the house.

"Come along with me, old-timer," Sommers invited. "What I've got to say is no secret."

Esther nodded a good morning and asked him how things were going at the big ranch.

Bluntly Sommers told her not so well. "I might be biased because I left with guns smoking at me," he added.

That brought out the whole story — of his suspicions, the threat of the outlaws, his meeting with Lovell, and the adventure at the bunkhouse. To his surprise the impressive part of the narrative to Miss Young was the disclosure that Lovell was a United States Marshal. Her eyes lit with pleasure. The information seemed to warm her through and through.

"Are you sure?" she asked.

"I'm sure Winters thinks so enough to want to kill me for talking with him," he replied. "And it's the only explanation of Lovell that looks reasonable. His rep up north is that of a tough young fellow but straight."

"Knew it all the time," Cantrell broke out jubilantly. "Told you so. Stood to reason Gabe Lovell's son wouldn't be a dirty crook."

It was not quite true that Dad's faith in Lovell had never wavered, but Esther knew he had always hoped the young man would come out clean. So she gave him full credit for all he claimed.

"I'm the one who mistrusted him," she said humbly, with deep gratitude that she had been proved wrong.

Cantrell veered around like a weathercock. "Heck, what else could you do? He was playing it so you couldn't figure him anything but a crook. I don't get it. What crazy idea was in the fellow's nut?"

"If he is really a law officer, it must have been planned between him and Mr. Parker for him to pass as a bad man to get in with the outlaws," Esther guessed. "He was in a difficult position and couldn't set us straight."

"My idea is to get in touch with him and let him know the bandit bunch are at the Bar Z Y," Sommers said. "If he and Parker are looking for them, I thought some of throwing in with the marshals. These scalawags played their hand mighty bad with me. I would of kept my mouth shut, but they wouldn't have it that way."

"I don't know where you can find Mr. Lovell," Esther said. "He was here last night, and I told him not to come back. He must be camped not too far away."

"He wouldn't be where I saw him yesterday, on account of Ringold having seen him there," Sommers decided. "He'll be where there is water, in some place not easily found."

Cantrell slapped a band on his thigh. "I'll

bet I know where he is. At that water hole above Dutchman's Flat. When he and I were there one day, he mentioned what a good hide-out it would make."

"Why don't you two go and see?" Esther suggested. "If you find them, bring them back here. They can make this ranch their headquarters. Tell him it is important for him to see me."

She did not want to make the invitation too urgent. It would not do to let Jack Lovell guess how deep an emotion was involved in this right-about face. She did not know whether he would return after her cavalier dismissal of him. He might punish her with a curt refusal. She reflected ruefully that ever since their first meeting she had been insulting him to his face and secretly denying to herself that he could be a villain.

All day she went through the routine of the ranch activities with only a surface interest. Her mind was disturbed. She scourged herself for her deep interest. Why should it matter to her whether this gay, turbulent fellow, so careless and so strong, came back into her life? He had never given her a second thought. It was humiliating to know that she, who had been so sufficient to herself, so indifferent to what others thought of her, was eager to see again one who did not want her.

The four riders came in at sunset. As Cantrell had guessed, the officers had been camped in the hill pocket above Dutchman's Flat. With very little persuasion they had accepted the invitation to stay at the Circle 72. Here they would be able to pick up information about the movements of the outlaws. Esther discovered that they were not prepared to make any arrests. It was clear from Sommers's story that the new Bar Z Y riders were the men they wanted, and that Ringold was tied up with them, but the evidence to support this conviction was still too slight to stand up in court. They were waiting for a break. It might come soon. The Hole-in-the-Wall bunch were wild and undisciplined, likely to go on a jamboree. While drunk, they might talk. Or word might reach Parker from the north that proof had been found clinching the hold-up on the Cassidy gang. If so, the officers would be on hand to round up the train robbers.

As they were finishing supper, Esther said, in a voice she hoped was even and casual, "Like to speak with you a minute, Mr. Lovell."

That they might be alone, she led the way to a small side porch. It was one of those

Arizona nights when the air is velvet-soft and the distant range stands up a thin saw-toothed line against the starry sky. There was silence between them while she tried to find the words that would give her apology the right shade of importance. They would not come, and she blurted out what was in her mind impulsively.

"I've been a fool, Mr. Lovell, and I have insulted you grossly. What can I say?"

He tilted an eyebrow at her whimsically. "You've already said it."

"I know so much. I'm always right." In her low voice was self-scorn. "Yet all the time I was sure you couldn't be what they said."

"Not sure," he corrected, his smile warm and understanding. "I had to leave you in doubt, to play the part given me. Every time you were ready to believe in me I jolted your faith again. I hated to do it after you had saved my life once — maybe twice. The balance tips in your favor so much I can never thank you enough."

He sat on the porch railing, his face in the moonlight, lean and strong-jawed. Beneath the tan was a rich bloom. She noticed the line of golden down on his cheek just above where the end of his razor had swept. How could she ever have mistaken his careless assurance for villainy?

"I'm glad you have forgiven me," she said.

"If I had anything to forgive," he amended. "We're friends now?"

"Yes."

He rose from where he sat and took her hands in his, looking down at her warm, vivid face. A pulse was beating in her throat. He thought her unsure humility charming. The feminine perfume of her rose to his nostrils like heady wine. He kissed her, then abruptly turned and walked away.

CHAPTER TWENTY-THREE: A MAN TALKS TOO MUCH

Parker and Lovell spent a good deal of their time in Live Oaks. The little town was full of gossip, and the marshals were of opinion that any valuable tips about the bandits would more likely reach them there than in the country. By this time it was generally known that Lovell was a law officer who had been sent down under cover to help break up the trade in stolen cattle. This did not make him any more popular, but it lifted from him any suspicion that he might be the murderer of Zach Young.

The deputies were stabling their horses at the corral when Jim Roberts mentioned that

Pud Lyman wanted to see them. "I was up at the courthouse seeing Colonel Krock about getting an extension on my mortgage when the old man dropped in," the owner of the wagon yard explained. "Seems he thinks he knows something about the Zach Young killing and feels he ought to tell you. He must of already talked it over with Krock, because the colonel laughed at him and told the old coot what he knew didn't amount to a hill of beans. Pud had his fishing-rod along. Krock advised him to go get himself some nice trout. If he still felt the same way when he got back, Krock would bring him to you-all for a powwow."

"Pud did not tell you what it was he knew?" Parker asked.

"No. Looked like the colonel kinda hushed him up."

There was something queer about this that disturbed Lovell. Pud Lyman was a shiftless old fellow who had lived a fairly long life without ever having done much work. He was a horse-trader and spent most of his time loafing around the barns. Occasionally when pressed for money he had done odd jobs around the stables. Nobody in town was a better fisherman. It might be that what he knew concerning the Young murder was unimportant. But one certainty was that if he had any real evidence, Colonel Krock would not bring him with it to the marshals.

"Did the old man go upstream or down?" Jack inquired.

Roberts did not know. It had been six or seven hours since Pud had left the courthouse. He ought to be getting back soon.

The marshals walked down Rincon Street. Krock came out of the courthouse, caught sight of them, and moved forward to the sidewalk. Lovell he ignored, but for Parker his smile was warm and friendly.

He said, "Like to see you a moment, sir — alone."

Lovell sauntered on and left them.

"An old loafer named Pud Lyman thinks he knows something about the killing of Zach Young," the lawyer said. "I don't know what it is. He hints around and won't come to the point. My own opinion is that he just wants to make himself important. He is out fishing now, but when he returns I would like to bring him around to see you on the off chance he has some information of value. Will you be in town for a couple of hours yet?"

Parker said he would, and after the colonel had walked up the street repeated to Jack what the judge had said. Suspicions still trooped through Lovell's mind. He guessed the colonel had spoken to Parker about Lyman because he wanted to forestall anything Roberts might have reported. From a barefoot boy on the street he learned that Pud had gone downstream in the morning.

"Aren't you making too much of this?" Parker asked.

"I hope so." Jack's anxiety was written on his troubled face. "But I don't like any part of it. The old man ought to be back by now. They say he never fishes more than three or four hours. Let's walk down the creek to meet him."

A path through the brush ran close to the bank and they followed it. They had traveled nearly two miles when dusk began to fall. Jack grew more uneasy. He was convinced some evil had befallen the old man, and he could guess what it was.

They found him lying face down among the riffles close to the bank. Pud Lyman had been shot three times through the back of the head. The first bullet would have been enough, but there had probably been some sign of life in the prostrate body and the panicky murderer had sent two more smashing into his victim.

Roped muscles stood out in Lovell's jaws. He said in a low voice, "Just the way he killed Zach Young."

Parker nodded. "Ringold's work, you think?"

"Ringold pulled the trigger. Another man ordered it." Jack continued bitterly, after a short pause: "So Krock was going to bring Lyman around to tell you his story. He'll be shocked to find out Providence has interfered."

"You feel sure Krock was responsible?" Parker asked. "He has the reputation of being a very responsible citizen. We must not let personal prejudices run away with our judgments."

"Look at the facts, Lloyd. Go back to the beginning. Zach Young made Krock because he found him useful. But Krock is ambitious. He did not intend to stay anybody's tool. There came a time when Zach had to be got out of the way. Maybe he had found out Krock and Ringold were pulling off some crooked work. Or perhaps Krock had it done because he knew that with the old man gone he could get control of the Bar Z Y."

"That is guesswork, Jack."

"It is no guess that Krock now manages the Bar Z Y, that he fired three good honest cowboys to make place for outlaws. Why did he do that, or permit it done, if you want to put it that way? Because he is hand in glove with them, because something rotten is being cooked up."

"I'll concede something is wrong about that," Parker said.

"Zach was the big mogul around here. Now he has been rubbed out, Krock intends to take his place. But Pud Lyman throws a monkey wrench into his plan. The old man makes a mistake that costs him his life. He goes to that fine respectable citizen, Colonel Krock, and tells him his conscience is worrying him about concealing what he knows about Young's death. Krock plays for time — promises to bring him around to see us this evening, after Pud has returned from fishing. Unfortunately for Krock, Roberts was present when the old man came to the judge's office. That, of course, is why the colonel spoke to you about it. But I would bet my best horse against two bits that he spoke to somebody else first."

"To Ringold."

"To Ringold if he was in town. But he had to work fast. Lyman must be got out of the way before he came back from fishing. If it was not Ringold that Krock saw, it was one of his bandit friends. My choice is Ringold."

The killer had left no visible evidence of his identity. Along the edge of the creek the ground was too hard and rocky for footprints. A horse had been tied in the bushes a hundred yards distant, but there was no way of telling what horse.

After the officers had laid the dead man on the mossy bank, they covered the dead with his own handkerchief. A wagon would have to be sent from Live Oaks to bring in the body.

On the way back to town, they agreed that Parker had better make inquiries at the Blue Moon as to who had been in that day from the Bar Z Y. It would be time enough after getting this information to notify Sheriff Houck of the murder.

From a bartender at the saloon, Parker learned that Ringold and Bullen had been the only two riders from the big ranch. Colonel Krock had come in and spoken to the foreman. They had left together. About two hours later, Ringold had returned, drank two quick ones, and departed hurriedly. When somebody had asked him why he was in such a rush to get back to the ranch, he had told the man sourly to mind his own business.

By patient investigation the marshals found a man who had seen Ringold fording the creek below the town a few minutes after the foreman had left Krock. The man,

Moss Conway, was fishing, and at the moment was making his way through brush from one hole to another, so he felt sure the Bar Z Y rider had not seen him.

"Looked like Ben was kinda anxious not to be noticed the way he scurried into the willows close to the creek instead of taking the path. But I wouldn't know why," he said.

He would have a guess why when he heard of Lyman's death, Lovell thought. Parker warned Conway to tell nobody else that he had seen Ringold fording the creek. One man today had talked too much, and would never talk again.

The story of Conway placed Ringold within a mile of the scene of the crime about the hour when it must have occurred. He was heading down the stream toward the spot. The officers had no doubt that he had caught sight of Lyman fishing, tied his horse, crept forward, and shot him without warning. But they had nothing but presumptive evidence to support this opinion. It hung on the assumption that Ringold had killed Zach Young, that Krock was an accessory to the murder, and that therefore it had been necessary to eliminate Lyman before he told what he knew.

Darkness had fallen long before Houck set out to bring back the body of the dead fisherman. News of the murder had spread through the town and the sidewalks of Rincon Street held half a dozen groups discussing the crime.

As the marshals were untying their horses from the rack in front of the post office, Conway hurried across the street to talk with them. He was plainly disturbed in mind.

"You don't think that Ringold could of — could of had anything to do with this, do you?" he asked.

Lovell's gaze held the eyes of Conway fast. "Leave us to worry about that. Remember just one thing. Pud knew too much — and he talked. Keep that fixed in your head, and *padlock your tongue* if you want to live."

"But, good God, I don't want —"

Parker's voice, heavy and overbearing, rode down Conway's frightened protest. "This town is gossipy as an old maid. It will talk about this killing for a month. We've told a dozen other guys to go to Houck if they want information. Now beat it."

This outbreak surprised Lovell, until he turned and saw Krock moving along the walk toward them.

Krock said, "Gentlemen, this is terrible, a tragedy beyond understanding."

The lips of Lovell, above his clenched

teeth, were tight as a trap. He let Parker answer.

"Murder is always understandable when one has the key, Colonel," the marshal said quietly. "Somebody could not afford to let Lyman live until he talked with us."

"Good Heavens, do you think that was it?" The face of Krock was a map of shocked surprise. "I hope not. If you are right, I fear I am to blame. I should have brought him to you at once. But how could I tell? The old man was such a fuss-budget I presumed he was making a mountain out of a mole-hill."

"Don't let this distress you, Colonel," Parker said, and made him a promise. "The guilty will be discovered and punished."

"I hope so. I devoutly hope so." After this pious wish the judge asked a question. "Have you any idea who did it?"

For the first time Lovell spoke. His grim face was hard as granite. "We know who did it, and we know who was responsible for it."

Krock looked at him without batting an eye. "You know so many things that aren't true, Mr. Lovell," he said. "So much that is dangerous to know."

Without another word he turned and walked away, outraged dignity in his straight back and firm tread. But for one instant there had flashed in his face a challenge born of rage, hatred, and perhaps fear.

CHAPTER TWENTY-FOUR: NICK AND ESTHER DISAGREE

A letter to Lloyd Parker from his chief confirmed the opinion of Jack Lovell that Colonel Krock was involved in nefarious practices. A deputy had been sent to Steamboat Springs, Routt County, Colorado, to investigate the sale of cattle driven up the trail and switched into this sparsely settled region. Sheriff Kern of Routt County had suspected that stolen stock was being sold cheap to the ranchmen. Following his hunch, he had written to Zach Young that a number of Bar Z Y stuff were on this range and asked if they had been driven north after a legitimate sale. The answer that came was from Young's lawyer Krock. It stated that Young had been killed but that the title of the drover was good. Since some doubt had arisen as to Krock's honesty, Parker's chief thought he had better check up on this.

Parker did not have to leave his chair to get the information, since he was in the parlor of the Circle 72. Esther Young had kept the books for the big ranch and she was quite sure no Bar Z Y herd had gone up the trail legally that year.

Dad Cantrell slammed a fist down on the arm of his chair. "That cinches it. That letter will put Krock in the pen. We've got him where the wool is short." The old man's voice was shrill with excitement.

"I wouldn't be too sure of that," Lovell differed. "When Krock gets in a jam, he'll make medicine fast. He is wary as a panther. You'll see he has left himself an out, probably claim he never wrote to Sheriff Kern — and get away with it."

"But if he signed it —"

"Any one of his tools could have written his name, in which case he could claim a forgery."

"I wouldn't believe anything he said if he swore it on a stack of Bibles high as his head."

"I don't suppose you'll be on the jury, Dad," Lucy said. "You know how unhappy he can look when he is shaking his head over other people's sins."

None of those present doubted Krock's guilt, but they were aware that with the general public his reputation for Christian probity was still high.

Jerry Young rode to the Bar Z Y with a

note from Esther to Nick Haley asking him to come and talk with her on a matter of great importance. Haley was annoyed. He did not care about going to see Esther just to be scolded, since he guessed that she wanted to upbraid him for the discharge of Dugan, Siddall, and Elson. On the other hand, Esther might be out with the men and he would have a chance to meet Lucy alone, an opportunity that came rarely of late. He told Jerry that he was very busy, but he would ride over as soon as he could.

Lucy was in the sitting-room when Nick walked in on her. She knitted her brows in thought and said, "Haven't I met you somewhere before?"

He answered, "The name is Haley. Every day has been a year since we saw each other last century."

"Dear me," she replied. "You must be tottering with age."

"If you have missed me as I have you —" Nick concluded his sentence with a sigh.

"It has been dull," she admitted. "I haven't had a good fight since you were here."

"Doesn't your great friend Ford Rudholt fight with you?" he asked.

Lucy slanted a smile at him. So he was jealous. She approved that in men. It made acquaintance with them more spicy.

"Mr. Rudholt comes here on business," she said demurely.

"That's bunk. He comes to see you — or Esther."

"If I only knew which," she murmured sadly.

"You've got no right seeing that fellow. He has been our enemy for years."

"I'm teaching my class in Sunday School that we must forgive our enemies," she told him. "And I must set them a good example."

"When I went to Sunday School I was taught that evil communications corrupt good manners," he retorted. "This fellow was a cow thief before you were born."

"If you feel so deeply about thieves, why do you employ them at the Bar Z Y?" she asked.

"What do you mean?" he asked indignantly. "There isn't a thief on the place."

"I hope you are right," she answered. "The story I hear is that your three new riders are outlaws."

"It's not true," he flung back hotly. "Why, Colonel Krock himself told me he knew them and that they were all right."

"Oh, if Colonel Krock said so." Lucy was ready to drop the subject. Maybe she ought never to have opened it.

"Where did you hear such crazy talk?" he

demanded, and answered himself. "From that fellow Sommers, of course. He tried to hold up some of the boys in the bunkhouse and was driven off the ranch."

So that was the version of the bunkhouse quarrel that had been told Nick and that he had swallowed. Lucy did not accept it as true. She liked Sommers.

Esther came into the room, and her cousin snapped at her a sharp question. "What do you mean by taking on that man Sommers after he made so much trouble at the Bar Z Y?"

"Did he make trouble there?" Esther asked.

"Drew a gun on some of the boys. He's still at it — telling lies about them."

"What lies?"

"Dirty lies about their being outlaws."

"That's what I want to talk with you about, Nick. I think they are outlaws of the worst type."

"You're off your chump," Haley barked angrily. "Just because you don't want me running the ranch, anything I do is wrong. These fellows are good cowhands."

"Don't you think Dugan and Siddall were top men — and Elson too for that matter?"

"They had got too big for their boots. When I'm bossing an outfit, I won't stand for any of the men making cracks about me in the bunkhouse."

A pair of high-heeled boots clumped up the porch steps. Esther glanced out of the window and called to their owner, "Jerry, would you mind asking Mr. Lovell and Mr. Parker to step this way?"

Jerry returned with Parker. "Jack has gone to town," he said.

"Mr. Parker, I wish you would tell my cousin why you feel sure that the new riders at the Bar Z Y are bad men," Esther said.

The marshal was not pleased at the request. He did not want to say anything that might lead the outlaws to slip away from their present quarters. "I'm not sure," he replied. "They might be outlaws. I can't prove it, and I'm not going to ask them."

"Bill Sommers says he knows two of them, and that they belong to the Hole-in-the-Wall gang." Jerry blurted.

"What Sommers says doesn't count," Haley retorted. "He's a trouble-maker and tried to gun two of them. We ran him off the place."

"That's not his story," Jerry answered. "He says they were fixing to kill him."

"Isn't it your personal opinion, Mr. Parker, that these men belong to the gang that held up the Union Pacific train in Wyoming?" Esther insisted.

"I don't know who held up that train, Miss Young," the marshal replied blandly. "I don't think anybody does except the men themselves."

Esther was annoyed that her witness had failed her, but she guessed he had a reason for hedging. "I'll take Bill Sommers's word as to who these men are," she told her cousin.

"And I won't," he flung back at her.

Yet Haley took back with him to the Bar Z Y a worried mind. There might be something to what Esther had said. He would have a talk with Ben Ringold.

That talk he never had.

Chapter Twenty-Five: Jack Lovell Walks Warily

A thin drizzle was falling as Jack Lovell dropped down the long hill to Live Oaks. It had begun a quarter of a mile back, but since he was so near town he did not stop to untie the slicker from the back of the saddle. He did, however, after a look at the lowering sky, turn in at the stable instead of tying in front of the post office.

Roberts knew of no developments in the Lyman murder case. Houck was still making inquiries, but if he had discovered anything of importance, he was not divulging what it was. Jack smiled cynically. He guessed that Houck was not a happy man these days, with two unsolved murders on his hands and an election looming up in a few months.

The corral man mentioned, his voice casual as if it were of no importance, that Ringold and one of the new hands at the Bar Z Y had ridden into town an hour ago.

"Which of the new men?" Lovell asked.

"The fellow they call Grogan."

The officer made no comment, but he eased the gun in its holster to make sure of a quick draw. Grogan was the man Bill Sommers had identified as Kid Curry, one of the most desperate of the Hole-in-the-Wall gang, a fellow both mean and trigger-tempered. No doubt they had already been in conference with Krock, who would surely have inflamed them against him. It was not likely they would bother him openly in town, but frontier marshals on a man-hunt lived longer when they were prepared for the unexpected.

Lovell walked along the boardwalk through the misty rain, all his senses keyed to quick response. His easy bearing and quick, confident step suggested no uneasiness, no expectation of impending trouble. He thought as he passed the Blue Moon that it was a fifty-fifty chance the Bar Z Y men were standing at the bar within twenty feet of him. He did not stop to investigate. There would be no fight unless one was forced on him. Parker and he were not yet ready to make a move, though he felt that a crisis was not far distant.

At the post office he met Krock as the colonel was turning away from the window with his mail.

"Good morning, Mr. Lovell," the lawyer said, his voice honeyed with good will.

The man's urbanity startled Jack. He understood the reason for it. Five or six people within hearing would be prepared to testify later to the colonel's suave friendliness. The trap had been set for him. It would be sprung soon, and Krock would regret the tragedy blandly.

Lovell's thoughts shuttled from one possibility to another. It might be a blast through a window as he passed down the street, but he did not think so. The killing would either be done in the open with a semblance of fair play or from the brush where no evidence would be left to put a finger on the murderer. If Krock had his way, it would be the latter, but he was working with trigger-fingered tools irritable and undisciplined.

The marshal's half-shuttered eyes watched Krock's smiling progress toward the door. He had a pleasant, cheerful word for every man he passed. No candidate for office could have built up favorable opinion more sedulously.

Lovell sauntered back up the street, his lean body apparently relaxed, but his chill gaze covering every foot of the way in front of him. He was prepared for anything except a shot from a building. That he could not guard against. He turned in at the Tip Top Restaurant and sat down at a table in a corner from which he could watch both the front door and entrance from the kitchen.

Jim Wong shuffled up to him and poured water into a glass. "You like loast beef?" he asked.

On a notebook which he took from his pocket Lovell wrote a few lines. He tore out the page and folded it.

"Call in that kid across the street — the one bouncing the ball — and ask him to give this note to Sheriff Houck." Jack handed the folded paper and a quarter to Wong.

When Houck arrived fifteen minutes later, he found the marshal finishing a dinner of roast beef, potatoes, cabbage, cornbread, and coffee.

"Well, I'm here," the sheriff said, plainly annoyed. He still did not like Lovell. The officer had disappointed him by not turning out a killer and a bandit. Also, he resented the trick played on him in the concealment of the marshal's true status. He should have been taken into the confidence of the two Government men.

"Sit down and have dinner with me," Lovell suggested.

"I've eaten," Houck said shortly.

"Then sit down and drink a cup of coffee. I've got something to tell you."

Houck sat down reluctantly. "No coffee. What do you want to say?"

Jack explained that he had been sent down the trail the first time in the role of a fugitive under explicit orders not to let anybody know his real standing. The idea had been for him to gain an entrée into the cattle-rustling gang. This had not proved feasible on account of the discovery of his real name. He told Houck the whole story, with the conclusions to which he and Parker had come. The only omission he made was his expectation of a personal attack within a few hours.

The sheriff did not like any part of the

story. For him personally it meant nothing but trouble. Krock had endorsed his candidacy for re-election. Everything would have gone smoothly, in spite of some criticism of his failure to discover the murderers of Young and Lyman, if these marshals had not interfered to throw a bombshell into his campaign.

Houck did not know what to do. Krock was now the big man of the community. He controlled not only the bank and the Bar Z Y; he was personally very influential. But if these officers had uncovered evidence implicating him both in theft and murder, Krock might be due for a ruinous collapse, in which case his support would prove a liability.

"What do you want me to do?" Houck asked sourly.

"Nothing just now. Let things ride as they are. Don't let Krock know that you suspect him. As yet we have not evidence enough to convict. If you pick up anything more, get in touch with us. We want to co-operate with you."

Lovell was not looking at the sheriff. Two men passing along the sidewalk had stopped to look into the restaurant. They were there for only a moment, and then were on their way again. The men were Ringold and Curry.

The sheriff had his back to them and did not see the Bar Z Y men. He was feeling more comfortable. He could still play along with Krock, and if an explosion came, escape condemnation by showing that he was working with the marshals. He was glad Lovell had not asked him to help in arresting the outlaws at the ranch. That part of his job which involved personal risk did not appeal to him.

"I can't think you are right about Krock," he said. "But I'll keep an eye on him, at the same time staying friendly."

Jack Lovell did not leave the restaurant with Houck. He did not want his enemies to get the impression that he was relying on the sheriff for protection. When he had finished his dinner, he went out by way of the back door. Curry and Ringold might have left town with intent to waylay him on the way back to the Circle 72. The foreman would favor that idea. But Kid Curry was a bold and confident killer, afraid of no man, and if he was in drink might insist on having the battle here and now. If so, Jack did not intend to let him set the scene for it.

CHAPTER TWENTY-SIX: THE GUNS BARK

Lovell passed along the alley back of Rincon Street as far as Holbrook's store. Through the back door he walked into it. The post office was in the front part of the building and half a dozen men stood around the window receiving or reading their mail. Jim Roberts was one of them.

He joined Lovell. In a low voice he said, "Ringold and that bird Grogan have been making war talk at the Blue Moon. They have been drinking a good deal."

"Where are they now?" the marshal asked.

"Down the street a ways. They are watching the stable so you can't get yore horse out without being seen."

"Are they packing rifles?"

"No. Six-guns."

"Only the two of them?"

"So far. If you want it that way, I'll bring a pony to the lower end of town and you can cross the creek and light out without being seen."

"No," Lovell answered. "If they're looking for me, I will be waiting at the gate. I don't want a fight, but I can't run away from one."

Roberts hesitated. "I'm no gunman, but if I could help any way —" The sentence broke off uncertainly.

"You can. I'm going down to Fry's saddle shop to wait there. I'll be standing at the entrance. Since I haven't eyes in the back of my head, I can't look two ways at once. They might find out I'm there and come in the back door. If they do, let me know."

"How?"

"A half-finished saddle is resting on a block near the door. Knock it off by accident if they show up."

Roberts promised that he would. He was getting into this deeper than he had intended, but he knew that only a weakling dodged risks when an obligation called to him.

"Don't mix up in the trouble," Lovell told him. "Duck back of the counter soon as you knock the saddle over. Chances are they will come at me from in front and you won't need to warn me."

"Good luck," Roberts said. He thought the marshal would need luck if the guns began to smoke, with the odds two to one against him.

Again Lovell took the alley path and went into the saddle shop from the back. The saddler looked up from the chair where he was working and nodded a greeting. He was a small thin man in spectacles. The Adam's apple in his throat stood out prominently.

"Like to rent yore place for half an hour," Lovell said.

The proprietor stared at him. "What you mean rent it?"

"I need a place to welcome some gents who are going to call on me. This one suits me." The marshal laid a twenty-dollar gold piece on the workbench. "All you have to do is walk out and come back after we have had our little talk."

Surprise and suspicion both showed in the man's bright, round eyes. There must be a catch in this. "I could stay here and you could talk in the back of the store," he said.

"Know who I am?" Lovell asked.

"A United States Marshal, they say."

"Right. The fellows who are coming to see me are hard characters. There may be trouble. I don't want you shot up."

The Adam's apple moved up and down, a barometer of emotion. "Creeping jeepers! You don't have to meet them here," the shopkeeper protested. He waved a hand excitedly toward the street. "There's a million miles of outdoors."

"Better not wait to argue," Lovell suggested. "They may be here any minute."

The barometer jerked up and down violently. Swiftly the saddler made up his mind.

This was outrageous. Nobody had a right to do this to him. But he was up against six foot of fact with cool, hard eyes laying down the law to him. He snatched up the gold piece and scuttled out of the back door like a frightened hen pursued by a hound. On the way out he passed Roberts entering.

"Fry seems to be in a hurry," the corral keeper said.

"He's just remembered an appointment," Lovell replied.

Jack had chosen this store because the front door was set back from an entryway that might offer protection if necessary. He stood there negligently leaning against one side of the frame, apparently interested idly in the drift of pedestrians passing to and fro. The rain was still falling from a heavy sky in a fine drizzle. Three cowboys came whooping up the street, flung themselves from their mounts, tied in front of Pete's place, and bowlegged into the saloon. A woman in a sunbonnet carrying a basket came out of a grocery store and headed homeward. Two boys stopped to spin their tops on the sidewalk.

"Some other place, boys," Lovell told them brusquely, with a gesture that waved them on their way.

Two men came into sight from a lane

between stores. They were Kid Curry and Ben Ringold. After the foreman had crossed to the other side of the road, they moved toward him. Jack knew what that meant. They were going to come at him from different directions. He guessed that somebody had told them where he was stationed. The Bar Z Y men walked deliberately, with no haste. The marshal noticed that Ringold hung back. *His feet are dragging,* Jack thought. *He does not like this.* Curry would be the more dangerous of the two. The man from Wyoming was a hard, tough hombre who had been often tried in battle.

Neither of them had yet drawn their weapons. They were still too far away for accurate gunplay with a six-shooter.

From the store next door Rudholt came out to the sidewalk. He stood for a moment undecided whether to turn right or left, then swung right. Recognizing Lovell, he stopped to rally him.

"Have you made up your mind yet, Mr. Lovell, whether you are outlaw or officer?" he asked.

The cattleman was standing in front of Jack, his back to the Bar Z Y men. Lovell's gaze went past Rudholt's shoulder to the gunmen. For the moment they had stopped, waiting for the ranchman to step aside. They did not want to give their victim the chance of having a shield while they had none.

"I'm an officer tonight," Lovell said. "I don't want to hurry you, Mr. Rudholt, but I think you are interfering with the plans of two gentlemen who have business with me."

Rudholt glanced at the two men frozen in their tracks and understood the situation without any further words. He said, "Excuse me," and stepped out of the firing-zone, moving with an unhurried, even stride. Before he reached Curry, he swerved into a saloon.

"End of the trail, fellow," the bandit jeered at Lovell, and came forward slowly on the balls of his feet, each step balanced and light.

The forty-five had jumped to his hand. The crash of it went booming down the street tunnel. A splinter of wood ripped from the planking back of Jack. Before the echo of the shot had died, Ringold's gun was in action.

Lovell moved deeper into the entry and was for the moment out of Curry's line of fire. He felt the jump of the gun as he flung his first bullet at Ringold. The slap of Curry's running feet came to the marshal. *I have to work fast,* Lovell thought. A second bullet from the foreman's forty-five struck the door jamb. Jack fired again at Ringold, deliberately, and knew instantly that the foreman would trouble him no more. The slug tore into the man's body as his finger was closing on the trigger. The barrel of the revolver dropped sharply down and the charge plowed into the street flinging up a spurt of yellow dust.

Ringold staggered forward, his face twisted with agony. The knees of the man buckled and his head dropped. His figure went down in a huddled heap.

Lovell gave him no more thought. There was another job to do. He waited, poised, for the instant when Curry's stocky body would come into sight. It did not come. The sound of the footsteps had ceased. Jack came out from cover cautiously. What he saw was hardly believable. Kid Curry lay face down on the sidewalk. Looking down at him was Rudholt, revolver in hand.

"You shot him!" Lovell cried in astonishment.

"Pistol-whipped him as he passed," the cattleman corrected. "Better gather his hardware while he is out."

"Yes," agreed the marshal, and did so. He looked up at Rudholt, a question in his eyes.

"Don't ask me why I did it," Rudholt answered cynically. "I don't know."

From out of stores and saloons men poured. Houck bent over the body of the foreman. "Ben is dead," he said. "What about the other fellow?"

"Just knocked out," Lovell replied. "Handcuff him, Sheriff, and lock him up."

"Wait a minute," Houck protested. "How did this happen? Who saw the start of it?"

"They were asking for it," Rudholt announced. "Both of them fired before Lovell. By the way, I knocked out this one. Very likely I saved his life."

Roberts told what he knew. Others had heard the men making threats in the Blue Moon. There was no doubt that Lovell had acted in self-defense.

"This man is Kid Curry, suspected of being one of the bandits who held up the express at Wilcox," Lovell told the sheriff. "Keep him in your calaboose, Mr. Houck, and you may pull down a nice reward."

Houck handcuffed the prostrate man, and as soon as he was able to walk took him cursing to jail.

Chapter Twenty-Seven: Lucy Helps and Regrets

As Lovell walked down Rincon Street, he knew he was the focus of attention. Already

215

the rumor had spread that the foreman was guilty of killing Young and Lyman, that his companion was the notorious Kid Curry. A group of barefoot boys, big-eyed with awe, trailed after him a dozen yards in the rear. Jack did not like this at all. The last thing he wanted was notoriety as a killer. Bad as Ben Ringold had been, he found no satisfaction in having destroyed him. It was a dreadful thing to have blotted out a life that God had created.

Roberts had his horse saddled for him.

"Well, you didn't need me after all," the corral owner said. "It came out fine. I'm mighty pleased."

"I'm obliged, Jim," the marshal replied. "Don't tell anybody you were posted at the back of the shop to warn me. These fellows might do you a meanness."

"I'll sure keep that under my hat," Roberts answered. He chuckled. "Did you see Krock out on the courthouse steps explaining to the boys how shocked he was to find Ringold had deceived him? He was certainly deploring to beat the band."

"I reckon he was shocked all right," the marshal agreed. "He didn't figure it would come out this way. Tough on him, after he had prepared a nice smooth line regretting I was such a tough hombre I had practically forced these two reluctant gents to get rid of me in self-defense."

"Better be careful, if it's true what they are saying that the Hole-in-the-Wall gang are in this neighborhood. I'd stick close to the ranch if I was you."

When Lovell reached the Circle 72, he was surprised to find that the story of the fight had already been brought to the ranch by a wandering cowboy on the chuck line. Since he was a stranger, the maverick rider was not sure how many and who had been killed. Jerry and Parker were saddling two horses, on which Esther and the marshal were preparing to start for town to find out what had occurred.

Esther had changed hurriedly to riding-clothes and come out to the porch ready for the trip. At sight of Jack her hand caught the railing with a grip so tight that the knuckles stood out white. As the long, lean body swung lightly from the saddle and moved toward the porch, her gaze held fast to the man. The small, firm breasts outlined against the dress lifted in a long, deep breath of relief.

"We thought maybe — we were afraid —"

Esther's sentence broke down, almost in a sob. Emotion had driven the color from her face.

"You've heard," Lovell said.

"That somebody was killed. We weren't sure who."

"Ringold. They forced it on me. It had to be one of us."

Jerry gave a whoop and dropped the cinch he had started to tighten. "There he is, by gum!" He broke for the house on a run. "We were scared they had got you, Jack," he cried.

Parker joined them.

"He killed Ringold," Esther said.

"How come?" Parker asked.

In half a dozen sentences Lovell told them the facts, leaving the name of Roberts out of his story. The welcome intrusion of Rudholt surprised them all.

"Maybe he saved yore life," Jerry said.

"Mine or Kid Curry's," Lovell agreed. "Likely both."

"You must stay here on the ranch and not go to town as long as that bandit gang is at the Bar Z Y," Esther commented sharply.

"Lloyd and I can ask them to send us bulletins about their movements," Lovell said with a dry smile. "And we can explain to our boss that the new motto of the force is safety first."

"Does he want you to go around killing men — or getting killed?" Esther demanded.

"He wants us to do our job, Miss Young," Parker answered mildly. "Sixty United States Marshals were killed in ten years dragging varmints out of the Indian Territory to the court at Fort Smith."

"But several hundred are still enjoying right good health," Lovell added cheerfully. "Neither Lloyd nor I figure on turning up our toes for forty years yet."

Dad Cantrell rode into the yard and turned his horse over to a boy at the stable. He listened to exciting news and hurried to the house.

"What's this I hear about somebody getting killed?" he shouted in his shrill treble. Without waiting for an answer he slapped at Lovell a question: "You know anything about it?"

"Yes," Jack admitted.

"Bet you were mixed up in it somehow. You're the doggonedest fellow to be around where trouble is at. Well, make up yore mind. Was you? Or wasn't you?"

"Mr. Lovell was attacked by this bad man Kid Curry and Ben Ringold," Jerry explained. "He killed Ringold, and they hauled Curry off to the calaboose."

Cantrell glared at Lovell. "Knew you were in it up to yore neck. Most every time you hit Live Oaks there's a job for an undertaker." His voice calmed down to a lower pitch. "Serves that skunk Ringold right. Ought to have been rubbed out years ago. Meanest fellow I ever did know. Tell me about it."

After a moment of hesitation, Lovell retold the account of the fight. He finished with a curt injunction to Cantrell. "Tell the boys at the bunkhouse how it was. I don't mean to talk about this any more. The subject is closed, except for my official report."

This was a blow to Jerry. He wanted to ask a lot of questions. Now he would have to wait until he went to town to satisfy his curiosity.

"You done fine, boy," the old foreman told Lovell. "Wish you'd of got Curry too. He's p'ison mean. You want to look out for him or he'll plug you in the back."

"Thank goodness, Sheriff Houck has him safe in jail," Esther said.

Cantrell flung a disgusted look at her. "For how long? Do you figure that wolf is gonna sit quiet in that shack and read his Bible? He'll be out and on the warpath inside of three days."

Parker agreed it was likely. Curry's companions at the Bar Z Y would attempt a rescue and would probably succeed. Hogan alone could not defend the jail against a surprise attack.

"I've been wondering about those birds," Cantrell said. "If they belong to the Hole-in-the-Wall gang, where's Butch Cassidy at?"

"After a train or bank hold-up the robbers always separate and scatter, each one holing up at his own private hide-out — one at Hot Springs, Arkansas, say, and another at St. Joe, Missouri, maybe. Butch is living quietly and comfortably under another name, likely in some city where he can go to the races and have a good time."

The point that was puzzling Parker he did not mention, though he and Lovell had discussed it often. Why were three of the bandits still hanging together, especially now that they knew their location had been discovered? The only logical answer to that was that they expected to strike again soon, at some point not too far from where they were now. A contact with the Bar Z Y had been established by the marshals. All they could do was to be ready for the outlaws' move when it came.

Lucy had ridden across to a neighboring ranch to see a girl friend. After her return, Esther gave her the news, with the injunction not to talk about it with Lovell. This did not mean, the girl decided, that she was not to talk around it. After supper she maneuvered Jack into the orchard back of the house to help her pick a basket of peaches.

"Are you going to be a man-hunter forever?" she asked him. "I mean until somebody shoots faster than you do."

He slanted a derisive, inquiring look at her. "What's on yore mind now?" he drawled.

"I was thinking you're sort of nice. I kinda like you."

"That goes double. I like you."

"But, of course, if you're going to spend your life dodging bullets, no girl would want to get really interested in you."

"You're breaking my heart," he told her.

"I know all about that," she said, and made a face at him. "All the same, you ought to settle down and get married."

"Are you proposing to me?" Lovell asked.

"No. In a month or so I'm going up to Denver to the Wolcott School. I don't intend to get engaged for at least another year. But there are other lovely girls around." She added, reproof in her voice, "Far too good for you."

"I'm sure of it. That's the trouble. I'm not worthy." He achieved a note of dire humility in his voice.

"For a man you're not so bad," she said thoughtfully.

"And the refining influence of a good woman will, of course, do wonders," he chirped up cheerfully. Jack had no idea what she was getting at, but it promised to be entertaining.

"You're an awful dud," she deplored. "Maybe it's not worth trying to pound sense into your head."

"Oh, don't give up," he begged. "The friendship of a good mature woman like you —"

She broke in abruptly. "Cross your heart and swear never to breathe a word of what I'm going to say."

"Cross my heart," he promised.

"Well, I don't know whether you are just blind as a bat or haven't enough gumption to know what's good for you." She hesitated a moment before blurting out, "The best girl in the world is in love with you and you act as if you didn't know she was on earth."

Lovell knew now what she meant. More than once he had half-guessed at this himself, and then had pushed it from his mind as absurd.

"You're probably way off," he said.

"I'm not. I've seen her looking at you when she thought nobody was looking.

She's got it bad. She never was this way before about a man. I don't know why I'm telling you, unless it's because I want you to do something about it or pull your freight from here as quick as you can."

He remembered the surprise he had felt when he kissed Esther on the side porch. The girl's lips had been warm and passionate, not cool and indifferent. Since then both Esther and he had been a little embarrassed and self-conscious when together. There was some current flowing from one to the other that drew them close. He was never with her without being aware of an emotional tug. And he did not want it that way. According to the standard of the ranch country she was rich. He owned nothing but a hundred and sixty acres on the Green River and a small bunch of stock. As soon as this job was finished, he had better get out.

"You're entirely wrong," he told Lucy bluntly. "I don't know who you have in mind, but whoever it is she has no interest in me."

Lucy looked at him, anger in her eyes, then turned and walked fast out of the orchard. She would never forgive herself for this, she felt. Nor would Esther forgive her if she knew.

CHAPTER TWENTY-EIGHT:
KID CURRY IS PLENTY SORE

The battle on Rincon Street and the rumors arising from it were very disturbing to Nick Haley. The death of Ringold did not worry him. His foreman had begun to treat him with a scarcely veiled insolence annoying to his vanity, and he had become pretty sure the fellow was tied up with a group of rustlers. But the charges Esther had made against his new riders now had the backing of the marshal, Lovell. Moreover, he felt in the atmosphere at the ranch a sense of danger. The older employees were drawing aloof from the new men. They were uneasy in mind and were very careful of what they said. Haley himself shared in this distrust. When Bullen and Grogan slighted their work, he did not have the boldness either to reprove or discharge them. Yet he realized that it was risky to allow bandits to hang out at the Bar Z Y.

Colonel Krock had got him into this mess. It was up to him to find a safe way out of the difficulty.

Krock had troubles of his own in plenty. The power he had built up so carefully was collapsing, and if he did not move warily he would be ruined in its fall. His thoughts dodged this way and that like a hunted fox seeking safety. He could not even by sleep get away for an hour from his peril. But he had to keep a smiling front in public, since he had built himself up into the leading citizen who could do no wrong. He had to remain the suave, wise counselor.

With finger tips drumming gently on the desk in front of him, he listened to Haley's reproaches.

"I am too trusting," he admitted. "Ringold deceived me completely. If these men are outlaws, I fear he must have known it. But we have no proof that they are, Nick. Lovell says the man in jail is Kid Curry. That is probably false. It is still strongly fixed in my mind that Lovell is one of the bandits who held up the train at Wilcox. Think what an advantage it would be for this band of desperadoes to get a confederate into such a position. He could tip them off as to when the trains would carry gold shipments and as to ways of avoiding the pursuit. Mind, I don't say that Lovell was in the actual hold-up, but I think he planned it and shared in the plunder."

This brought no comfort to Haley. It was only a guess. He was convinced that his new riders were bad men, even if they were not train robbers. Already they had tried to kill

Sommers and Lovell. His practical problem was to get them off the ranch without angering them.

"They are dangerous," he told the judge. "I don't want them around. Instead of working, they sit around and play cards. If I don't get rid of them, some of the other men will quit. I wouldn't want to have trouble with a bunch of mean, bullheaded gunmen. You've got to fix it so they will leave."

Krock had good reason to believe they were not going to stay long. He could not tell Haley why he thought so, but he could and did suggest a fictional background for his opinion.

"One of these men came in to see me day before yesterday about getting a divorce from his wife. The fellow named Bullen. He said they were all moving on early next week. Fiddle-footed men of their sort never stay long in one place. My advice would be for you to stick it a few days longer and let them leave of their own accord."

Nick consented grumblingly. If they were going to hit the trail shortly, he could put up with them.

As Nick walked past the jail, Amos Hogan opened the door and called to him. "Want to see you a minute," he said.

"What about?" Nick asked.

The jailer beckoned him across the street. "One of my boarders would like to talk with you, Nick."

"Grogan?" snapped Haley.

"Right, first crack."

The ranchman had no desire to talk with the prisoner. This was going to be something unpleasant he was almost sure. But he could not refuse.

"All right," he said grumpily.

Hogan took him upstairs to the cell where Curry had been put. "Give you ten minutes," he said, and left them alone.

"Get me out of here," the bandit ordered harshly. A threat glittered in the hard, cold eyes.

"How can I get you out?" Nick asked.

"I'm one of yore men, ain't I? Use yore pull. Go to Krock and tell him to spring me *muy pronto* if he knows what's good for him. I don't give a damn how you and he do it, but — get me out."

"I'll see him and ask him to do what he can. He knows the law and —"

"To blazes with the law! Tell him to drag me from this cell sudden — if he doesn't want to be put in one himself."

Nick said he would — at once.

"Tell him I want to see him here inside of

228

ten minutes. And something else. Soon as you get back to the ranch, ask Winters and Lay — I mean Bullen and Darrow — what they think they are doing while I rot here. Tell them I'm plenty sore."

"I'll do that," Nick promised.

He returned to the courthouse and gave the message to the judge.

Krock showed annoyance. "A lawyer does some trifling legal service for a man and he expects to be got out of any sort of scrape his folly has led him into." He rose from the desk. "I suppose I might as well see him."

On the way back to the ranch, Haley wondered about the relation between Krock and these desperadoes. The explanation given by him was not good enough. The prisoner had talked as if the judge would not dare refuse to do as he was told, and Krock had lost no time in starting for the jail. That was not like Krock. He usually kept clients waiting, probably to give them a due sense of the value of his time. It looked as if these scoundrels had got something on the colonel.

Winters and Lay were pitching horseshoes in front of the bunkhouse when Haley arrived. He unsaddled at the stable and walked across the yard to them.

"I saw Grogan when I was in town," he said.

"Did you drap into the calaboose to cheer him up?" Lay asked.

"He must have been looking out of the window while I was passing. He had Hogan call me."

Winters threw a ringer. "I'll bet he's raising Cain."

"He had me go to Krock about getting him out. And he said for me to tell you fellows he was sore you weren't doing anything about it."

Lay exchanged a look with Winters and laughed. "He never could learn to wait. That fool attack on Lovell was just like him. He'll be out in plenty of time."

"Pick up any news while you were in town?" Winters asked casually.

"No-o. They're still talking about the killing of Ringold. It's claimed he killed old Pud Lyman to keep him from telling what he knew about the murder of Uncle Zach. Seems Lyman saw him come out of the livery stable about the time my uncle was shot."

"I never did like Ben," remarked Lay. "Couldn't trust him far as you could throw a bull by the tail. He must of been pretty well liquored up before Grogan deviled him

230

into standing up to Lovell."

Haley left them to their game. They ought to have been still riding circle with the other boys, but it was not worth while asking them why they had knocked off work and come back to the house. One of them would probably be insolent, and it would be humiliating to have to ignore it.

CHAPTER TWENTY-NINE: A JAIL BREAK

Sheriff Houck sat with his feet on the desk reading an advertisement in the newspaper which said he would be a candidate for re-election at the ensuing election. The office door opened and he looked over his shoulder to see Elza Lay and Nate Winters walk into the room. The small gunman closed the door behind him.

Though Houck was vaguely uneasy, his professional heartiness did not desert him. "Nice to see you boys," he said. "Anything I can do for you?"

"We'd like to have a little talk with Grogan, Sheriff," Lay said.

"Sure," answered Houck. "Any time you like. Tomorrow morning, say. Set the hour."

"We'll set it now, Mr. Houck," Winters said mildly. "Account of us being in a kind of a hurry and not being able to come to town tomorrow."

The man's gentle smile deceived the sheriff. "Wish I could oblige you. But the fact is we've got a rule —"

Winters interrupted, his voice still soft and purring. "You hard of hearing? I said now."

The objection of the officer collapsed. He noticed that the smile on Winters's face did not reach the hard eyes. A cold wind seemed to blow through Houck's thick body. He felt as if a giant fist were twisting his stomach into a tight ball. For something Parker had once told him came to his mind — that this little man was one of the deadliest killers he had ever met.

"I was gonna say," the sheriff continued, "that o' course I would stretch a point to oblige you."

"Nice of you," Lay said amiably. "We'll drift along the street chatting kind of friendly. When a man acts reasonable he sometimes lives to be a hundred."

The manner of the good-looking outlaw was pleasantly reassuring, but Houck was aware of the reverse side of the statement. When a man was not reasonable, he did not live to be a hundred.

As they moved along Rincon Street toward the jail, the sheriff did not find that friendly chat came easily. He let Lay carry the burden of the conversation and contributed only an occasional "Yes" or "No" from a chalk-dry throat. His reason told him that they would not kill him. There would be no object in that, but he did not know the pint-size bandit well enough to be sure of his reaction if any unforeseen difficulty should arise.

Houck exchanged an unhappy greeting with Dad Cantrell, who came out of the Blue Moon just as they passed. The spry old foreman of the Circle 72 stopped them a moment to inquire how Houck's campaign was progressing. The question was automatic. His speculative eye ranged over the sheriff's companions. Politics, he remembered, made strange bedfellows, but these transients did not have votes here.

"I'm in a sort of rush right now, Dad," Houck said, sensing the impatience of Winters. "Any other time I'd be right glad to have a talk with you."

Cantrell watched them cross the street and stop at the jail. He did not quite get this. The sheriff was plainly worried, and there had been a suggestion in his manner of one acting under a constraint.

"Who is that old cuss that stopped us?" Winters asked.

"Dad Cantrell. Works for the Circle 72. Foreman."

Before they reached the jail, Lay explained what they would do. "We'll scrouge up against the wall where we won't be seen and you'll call to Hogan. You won't have any trouble if you make it good, Sheriff."

"It had better be good," warned Winters. "If you've got any crazy idea of making trouble, shake it out of yore head right now. Get funny, and I'll pump a slug into yore belly."

Houck had no intention of trying to raise an alarm and took pains to make this very clear to them.

At the sheriff's call the jailer came to an upstairs window. He told Houck he would be down in a moment. The door presently opened and Hogan found a forty-five pushed into his midriff.

"Reach for the roof," Winters snapped.

The jailer flung a startled glance of inquiry at his superior officer.

"Do like they say," the sheriff told him. "They've got the dead wood on us."

Hogan's arms went up. "I got only four bits on me," he said.

"Take it easy," Lay told him. "We're not two-bit holdups."

Covered by the guns of the outlaws, Hogan led the way to the cell of Kid Curry. He threw open the door and the prisoner came out.

Curry slammed his fist hard against the chin of the jailer and Hogan's head tilted back against the steel-barred door. While he hung there helpless, the furious desperado flung another jolt into his stomach. The knees of Hogan buckled and he sank to the floor. The released man kicked him twice in the ribs.

"Cut it out, Kid," Lay cried, and pushed between him and his victim.

"What d'you mean letting me lie cooped up here three days?" Curry demanded angrily.

"Keep yore shirt on," Lay said, trying to appease him. "We'll explain everything later." He looked down at the prostrate body of the unconscious jailer. "Why make more trouble by bumping off this poor guy?"

"I'll learn him to keep me behind bars. The fellow ain't hurt a bit. He's just foxing."

"No, he's out cold," Winters said. "His head slammed against the iron mighty hard. It's done now. Let's get out of here quick."

They tied up Houck and gagged him with his own handkerchief, then dragged the two men into the cell and left them locked inside. In the darkness they slipped across the street to the hitch rack where they had left three saddled horses. Abreast of one another they galloped up the street. From the shadow of an alley, Dad Cantrell watched their hurried departure from town.

He lost no time in giving the alarm, but it was more than half an hour before anybody could get into the building. The outlaws had flung the keys of the jail into the creek, and by the time those of Houck were brought from his office to unlock the cell, it was past midnight.

The condition of Hogan was serious. The shock of the blow when his head struck the iron door had brought about a concussion that might prove fatal.

Houck made a lot of to-do organizing the posse of pursuit, but in spite of his bustling about, the sun was up when he led a group of heavily armed riders out of town to arrest the outlaws. At the Bar Z Y he learned that the three men he wanted had left the ranch several hours before. He followed them as far as the county line. His jurisdiction ended there, and he returned to Live Oaks with the sense of a hard duty well performed. There was some doubt in his mind whether his constituents would accept that point of view, but he hoped they would realize he had been a zealous officer.

CHAPTER THIRTY:
RUDHOLT MENTIONS
INTENTIONS

When Cantrell turned from watching the dust of the disappearing outlaws to shout out the news of a jail break, the first man he met was Bedford Rudholt, who had just swung to a saddle to start home.

Rudholt took energetic charge of those engaged in liberating the two imprisoned officers and getting Hogan to a bed at the hotel, but he declined to serve on the sheriff's posse. It was his opinion that the pursuit would turn out to be a bluff put on for the sake of appearances. He said as much to Cantrell, who agreed with that a hundred percent.

The old man said he was going to hustle back to the Circle 72 to let Parker and Lovell know what had occurred. Rudholt surprised him by deciding to go with him.

"What for?" Cantrell asked bluntly. He had no liking for the cattleman and as usual took no trouble to conceal the fact.

"If they are going to organize a posse, I might ride with them," Rudholt answered.

He added a cynical comment, "You know how strong I've always been for law."

Cantrell snorted indignantly. This man's brazen effrontery had been familiar to the old cowboy ever since Rudholt had appeared on the scene and settled at the entrance to Buck Canyon. In those days Dad had been all for the big ranch. The youngster's cool challenge to Zach Young's arrogant claim of sole right to the open Hardscrabble range had annoyed him personally as it had other riders of the Bar Z Y outfit. He had done his best to make life unbearable for the boyish upstart in the expectation of driving him away from his homestead. Rudholt had not only stuck it out; he had retaliated blow for blow. A week after a haystack in his pasture had been burned, eight calves of the Bar Z Y had disappeared. Young was convinced they were carrying Rudholt's Flying R brand, but though he had raked the hills he had been unable to find them.

Every attack on the nester had been met by a counterattack. Under his leadership the other nesters had rallied, and in the end he had emerged as a cattleman of importance in his own right. Cantrell still held his old-time grudge against the man, but it was mixed now with a feeling akin to admiration. The fellow had what it took to survive on the frontier. Moreover, Dad had grown tolerant enough to realize that Zach Young had not been appointed God's vice-regent over Hardscrabble for his own gain. Other settlers had a right to live and run cows there. Bedford Rudholt had come to the top because he was as lawless and ruthless as the old man he had been fighting.

What just now disturbed Cantrell was a worry over Rudholt's intentions regarding his young mistresses. Esther could look out for herself, and from what he had heard her say was apparently in no danger of becoming too interested. But Lucy was of softer stuff. He had seen her with Rudholt several times, and he had noticed how the man's eyes followed her. She was leading him on, perhaps excited by her sense of power over a man so strong and self-reliant. But it would be dangerously easy for her to go too far. You could not play with Rudholt safely any more than you could with a half-grown tiger. But there was nothing Cantrell could do about it. No need to warn Esther. He knew she was watching the situation closely, making her plans to end it. In a few weeks Lucy would be heading for school in Denver. Probably there she would forget about Rudholt.

All lights were out at the Circle 72 when the two men reached the ranch, but Cantrell aroused the marshals from sleep to give them the news. The rescue of Curry was not entirely unexpected to them. Their lookout man at the Bar Z Y had notified them that the outlaws had shown signs of departure in the near future. They had bought at Live Oaks a fresh supply of ammunition. Their mounts had been newly shod. Through Haley they had obtained at the ranch a packload of supplies for a trip of some length. Since they would not leave without making an attempt to free their companion, and since they had succeeded in the jail break and could not now stay at the Bar Z Y without danger of arrest, it followed that they would be on the move before daybreak. How far they would go the marshals could only guess. If they wanted only to find another hide-out, they would probably ride into the bad lands adjacent to the ranch and camp in some one of the tangle of canyons there. If they were ready for another robbery, they would leave the neighborhood entirely.

Parker did not want a large, unwieldy posse. In addition to Lovell he took only Rudholt, Bill Sommers, and a lanky cowboy known as Lucky, whose name was Harry Love.

Dad Cantrell helped Esther choose and sack the provisions for the trip. The sound of their voices in the kitchen awakened Lucy. She went to the door, still drowsy from sleep, and inquired what was afoot. When she found out, she dressed hurriedly, not to miss her share of the commotion. Through her window came the shouts of the men getting ready.

She stepped out to the porch. A man was sitting on the edge of it testing a Winchester. At sight of him a glow of excitement beat through her.

"Business or pleasure this time?" she asked lightly.

Rudholt looked round, put the rifle down, and joined her. "My duty as a good citizen," he explained, and took her hands in his. "Already virtue is finding its reward."

She freed her hands and backed to the wall, a ripple of laughter on her uptilted face. "Dear me, I thought only little boys expected lollipops for behaving well," she told him.

Esther appeared in the doorway. "I think Dad needs you in the kitchen to help him pack, Lucy." To Rudholt she said, after her sister had gone: "Lucy is not quite seventeen. She will be leaving for school in a few weeks. Please do not put any nonsense in her head."

"You talk plain, Miss Esther," he replied, his smile mocking her. "So shall I. My intentions are honorable."

Her eyes met his steadily. "You have no right to any intentions whatever as to my sister. I must ask you not to come here again."

"Afraid I can't accept your decree of banishment," he retorted coolly. "I'm not an easy man to get rid of, as your uncle Zach Young might have told you. He spent twenty years and considerable lead trying it."

"You mean you'll come here after being told you're not wanted?" Esther demanded angrily.

"It depends on who tells me I'm not wanted," he said, quite unruffled. "You rule in a limited monarchy, Your Highness, and your subjects have rights."

"If you think because Lucy is silly enough to flirt with you a little —"

"My thoughts are my private concern," he interrupted. "When I get ready to tell you about them, I'll let you know."

Before she could answer, Jerry came out of the night to the porch leading a pack horse from the stable. Cantrell brought the supplies from the kitchen and arranged them on the sawbuck saddle. He threw the diamond hitch himself. It was the opinion of the old man that none of the younger generation were skillful enough to pack a camp outfit properly.

The posse rode across the hills to the Bar Z Y. Before they reached the ranch, the gray light of dawn had sifted into the sky. They tied a quarter of a mile from the house and came on foot to the house by way of the pasture. Lovell and Sommers crept forward to the blacksmith shop.

Out of the bunkhouse the cowboy Sid came half-dressed. He walked to the pump and stretched in a lazy yawn.

"Hold it!" a low voice ordered.

Sid grew rigid, his arms still flexed. "Who says so?" he flung back resentfully.

"Take it easy. Nobody is going to harm you." Lovell added an explanation. "This is a legal posse come to make an arrest."

Sid grinned derisively at him. He was going to enjoy this. "Go right ahead and make it," he said. "Who is the guy you want?"

"We want three. They call themselves Bullen, Grogan, and Darrow."

"Now isn't that just too bad! They left an hour ago. Said they couldn't stick around waitin' for you all day. Looks like you were careful to get here late."

"Which way did they go?"

"I didn't notice," the cowboy drawled insolently.

Other riders of the Bar Z Y were less hostile. From them the marshals learned that the outlaws had ridden toward the east. This did not prove anything, since they might double back and cut across to the bad lands. But the leaders of the posse decided to follow the given lead. It would take them across the Navajo Reservation. If the men they wanted had gone that way, the trail could be picked up, as somebody probably would have seen them. There would be nothing lost, even if the bandits had turned aside. It was already too late to cut them off from the bad lands in case that proved to be their destination.

At Indian Wells they learned from a Navajo boy that three riders had passed a few hours earlier. From his father they had got information about the road to Gallup. The lad had noticed that one of the riders was small, another tall, and the third stockily built. Vague though his description was, it fitted the outlaws the posse was hunting.

It was long past sunset when Parker and his party reached the Black River. They camped there for the night and reached Gallup next morning. At the Bill Green Corral they learned that the bandits had stopped in town the previous evening long enough to eat supper and then had headed north after asking several questions about the Hog Back Mountains. After verifying this, Parker took the trail in pursuit. His party forded the Chaco River and followed the foothills below the east slope of the Chusca Mountains. They saw a sheepherder and later a nester hunting strays. Neither of them had seen anything of the Hole-in-the-Wall men, nor had a small ranchman at whose place they spent the night.

"They've fooled us," Parker said. "Fact is, I didn't half-believe they were really going north. It wasn't reasonable."

"No," Rudholt agreed. "If they were just looking for a hide-out, they didn't have to come this far. Of course they might be going to Cortez or Durango, up in Colorado. We had to make sure."

The posse scouted across country for a few miles and drew a blank. Nobody they met had seen three strangers on horseback. Late that night six weary horses reached Gallup again. At the hotel Lovell talked with a ranchman who had just driven in from the Campbell's Pass country. On the road he had passed three horsemen whose appearance tallied with that of the outlaws.

Between Gallup and Santa Fe news of the travelers ahead reached them more than once. With fresh horses they had taken at Santa Fe the road for Taos. On remounts Parker's men followed them up the long, steep canyon road to the pueblo town, a stretch of nearly seventy miles.

Here a surprise awaited the marshals. At Taos three more men had joined the bandit party and the group had taken the Cimarron Trail. Somewhere along that route the posse lost track of them. They might have cut across to Springer or to Maxwell. They could have pushed north to Raton and across the pass to Trinidad. To Parker the latter seemed more likely. He put it to a vote. They turned the heads of their horses toward Raton.

That they had lost touch with the outlaws was particularly disturbing in view of the addition to the band they were pursuing, for it stood out like a signpost that this meeting had come about by appointment and that another train or bank robbery was about to occur.

CHAPTER THIRTY-ONE:
CUTTING A LONG TRAIL

After leaving Taos, the first night camp of Parker's party was on the Cimarron River. Before daybreak they were in the saddle again. It was after dark when they drew into Raton weary from the long ride across the desert. The little town was humming with excitement.

"Looks like they're having the Fourth of July just one week late," drawled Sommers. "Never did see so many guys before milling around in this burg."

They drew up at a tie rack in front of the leading store. Before they had swung from their saddles, an old cowhand flung at them the reason for the excitement.

"If you boys blowed in with the tumbleweeds right now, mebbe you ain't heard the Ketchum gang has done held up the Colorado Southern express at Folsom," he said. "They got twenty thousand dollars."

Lovell glanced at Parker and laughed dryly. "We're late again for the dance, Lloyd."

A self-satisfied man dressed like a tinhorn gambler corrected the cowboy. "Thirty-five thousand."

"Tell us," Parker said.

The tinhorn and the cowboy started to explain at the same time, but the range rider was outtalked and gave up.

"They stuck up the train at the water tank," the gambler said. "Cut the engine and the express car from the rest of the train and ran 'em up the track a ways. Blew the express car open with dynamite. There were five or six of them, and they made a clean getaway. I reckon there will be a mess of posses out after them, but none of them will get anywhere. Trouble with our sheriffs is that they are gun-shy. No guts, I say. They won't mix it with a bunch of wolves like these ruffians. My idea would be —"

The man stopped, a startled look in his bulbous eyes. He had become aware that this travel-stained group of horsemen carried both rifles and revolvers. The dried sweat on the shoulders of the mounts showed that they had been pushed far and fast. Into his mind the thought had popped that these were probably the bandits. He turned and bolted into the store like a frightened rabbit diving into its warren.

The old cowboy said, "What in tophet dried him up so sudden?"

"He's got the notion we're the train robbers," Rudholt told him. "We'll never learn what his idea was."

The cowboy rubbed his lank, unshaven chin. "By gorry, you may be right at that, but I'm declaring right now I haven't lost any hold-ups. What they pull off is all right with me." His faded eyes brightened. "Not buttin' in or anything, I'll just mention that Sheriff Farr of Huerfano County drapped in over the pass from Trinidad about an hour ago with his posse."

"Good," Parker replied. "We want to meet him. Where is he now?"

"Up to the hotel eating supper."

"Exactly what we want to do," Bill Sommers said.

The ranch hand watched them ride up to the hotel and tie. He was disappointed. That he had met and talked with the robbers would have been something to brag about later.

Farr was a fine example of the Western sheriff, a big bronzed man, keen-eyed and quiet. He said at once that he would like to co-operate with Parker's posse. After the late arrivals had eaten, Farr, Parker, Lovell, and Rudholt adjourned to the sheriff's room to map out a plan of action. From such information as Farr had, the three bandits who had joined Kid Curry's party at Taos were members of what was known as the Ketchum gang. Originally they had come from Utah. Since all their hide-outs had been in the mountain country, it was unlikely that the robbers would travel south into desert terrain not known to them, nor would they venture eastward to the Texas plains. A ranchman looking after a sick cow had seen half a dozen riders passing in the moonlight at a distance. They had been heading west. Both Sam Ketchum and his brother "Black Jack" knew the wild Cimarron country as Farr did the streets of Trinidad. The sheriff was of opinion that the outlaws would make for this district and lie low until the heat of the chase had spent itself. It was likely that they had cached supplies enough to last them for several weeks, either in the Cimarron Canyon or forty miles back of it in the Sangre de Cristo Range.

Since Farr was a Colorado officer and there might be a question raised as to his authority in New Mexico, it was agreed that Lovell should join his posse, which was to comb the Cimarron terrain while Parker pushed directly into the Sangre de Cristos. Two of the sheriff's men were shifted to the marshal's group and the cowboy Lucky transferred to that of Farr. Lucky had worked on a ranch in the river region and might prove useful as a guide.

They camped on the edge of town, ate breakfast while it was still dark, and were on the back trail across the desert before the sun was up. At Cimarron the posses of Parker and Farr went separate ways.

Chapter Thirty-Two:
The Battle in the Park

In Turkey Canyon, a few miles north of Cimarron, Farr's posse came on a campfire that had been cold not more than a few hours. It was at a place where the gulch had widened to a small park. There were trout in the stream and grass sufficient for the half-dozen horses that had been picketed here.

"We're hot," the sheriff said. "Looks like they figure they have shaken off any pursuit. That is, if these are the parties we want."

Lovell picked up a piece of string from the dead ashes. Attached to the string was a blob of sealing wax run out of its original shape by heat. He handed it to Farr. That this had been part of a seal stamped on a package of money was an easy guess. The bandits had divided their plunder here.

The tracks of the horses showed that the train robbers had ridden south.

"They're holed up in Cimarron Canyon

right now," Lucky said. "Making their brags how easy they got away."

A redheaded deputy from Trinidad did not feel so sure of that. "If I was in the boots of one of them, I'd be rattling my hocks for somewhere a hundred miles from here. Even the Sangre de Cristos would be too near for me."

"Why? Nobody ever has bothered them here. They wouldn't expect anybody to find them now, seeing their trail was lost fifty miles back. Except for a lucky guess we wouldn't be here."

The posse passed through the village of Cimarron and took the canyon road. Farr was careful not to let his men get bunched, though he did not expect to run into the fugitives in the floor of the canyon. The camp would be located far up some gulch that was an offshoot of the main ravine.

A memory of a long-forgotten ride after strays flashed to Lucky's mind. He and another cowpuncher had circled well up to the divide above the rim of the canyon, and below the timber had come upon a mountain park through which a creek meandered on its way to the river. One slope was meadow land lush with grass in which were strewn columbines, Indian paintbrush, and a dozen other kinds of wild flowers. The ground rose more sharply on the far side of the stream, to a rugged hillside sown with great boulders fallen from the cliff above. This pocket in the rugged lip of the gorge would make an ideal hide-out for men who wanted to be let alone.

"Think you can find this park again?" Farr asked.

Lucky thought perhaps he could. A slab of rock shaped like a crouching bear stood at the lower entrance to the runway up which they had ridden. When they found the rock, it did not look much like any animal to Lovell, but if Lucky was satisfied he was. They went up a waterway formed by the angle between two hills. At the foot of it they had to push a path through a tight grove of young aspens, but as they advanced the going became easier.

High above the floor of the main canyon the riders came to the apex of two draws that ran together. Lucky viewed one and then the other, uncertain which to take.

The redhead grinned at Lovell. "If and when we get to this hide-out park of Lucky's, betcha it turns out we draw only a busted flush."

Jack shrugged his shoulders. "I wouldn't bet. We're gambling on a one-to-ten shot."

"Dogged if I know which to try," Lucky

said doubtfully.

"Take yore time," Farr encouraged. "Like Lovell says, we're playin' for a lucky break. We'll get it — or we won't. Chances are against us."

Lucky chose the left draw. It brought them by way of a steep trough to a wooded ridge. They stopped to breathe their winded mounts.

Farr swung from the saddle and moved forward toward the far edge of the ridge. His eyes swept the saucer-shaped pocket below. A drift of smoke lifted lazily from a campfire beside a creek. Half a dozen men were grouped there eating supper.

The sheriff walked back to his companions. "We've found them, boys," he said quietly. "Get off yore horses and tie them. We'll do this job afoot."

A timbered hill spur ran down to the park, and on the left side of this was an arroyo that would conceal the approach until they came to the lip of the valley.

"Whatever else you do, boys, don't bunch," Farr warned. "These fellows are going to fight, even if we take them by surprise. Take every bit of cover you can find and don't start crowding close. They will scatter into the rocks. Get them while they are running if you can. Chances are they'll see us soon as we come out of the arroyo."

"Do we smoke up right away?" the red-head asked.

"No. It's almost certain these are the fellows we want, but we must know for sure they are not ranch hands on a cow hunt. I'll yell to them and find out."

They crept down the draw, Farr and Lovell in the lead. As it opened into the park, the men worked through the brush to find separate cover in the scrub-oak thicket. The sheriff waited for them to get placed.

One of the campers rose and walked to the creek carrying an empty pail to get water. He moved with a touch of easy, indolent swagger. Lovell recognized that lean, lithe body. It belonged to Elza Lay.

Farr rose from the oak bushes where he had been crouching.

"Throw up yore hands!" he ordered.

Lay's rifle was at the fire forty yards away, but he did not hesitate an instant. The pail dropped from his hand as it slid to a belly-gun in his waistband. He whirled, flung a shot at the sheriff, and raced for his Winchester, a target for several marksmen. A bullet tore into his shoulder. Already his companions had jumped to their feet. Three of them waded through the creek and made for the boulder field. Kid Curry and Nate Winters crouched in the water back of the bank and returned the fire of the posse. Lay joined them. One of the running bandits dropped his rifle. His arm fell limply to his side. With his left hand he picked up the gun and continued his flight. Later the officers learned that this was Sam Ketchum.

Farr laid down his rifle, took a handkerchief from his pocket, and started to bandage a bleeding wrist. The marshal wormed his way through the foliage to him.

"Hit bad?" Lovell asked.

"Just above the wrist," the sheriff answered. "The fellow with the pail got me first crack."

Lovell bound up the wounded arm. "It's not bleeding too bad," he said. "That was Elza Lay. You'd better get back into the arroyo and let us finish this."

"No. It's my left arm, anyhow. Where do we go from here?"

"What say we work around the edge of the park and get closer to the boulder field? There's a clump of pines over that way would give us protection."

Farr agreed to that. The message was relayed to the others. Two men were left to fire occasional shots while the others fell back from the park and made a detour.

"We've scored two hits to one," Farr told his men. "And my wound isn't as serious as theirs. Don't expose yourselves, and we'll do fine."

They came up to the park through the pines and found themselves much closer to the boulder field. One of the outlaws gave a shout of warning as the officers appeared. Fire from the rocks centered on them. While Lucky was shifting from a small pine to a larger one, a bullet tore into his side. He straightened from his crouch, stood erect, then sank to the ground. Snipers from the rocks fired several times at him. Spits of sand spurted where the bullets landed.

Sheriff Farr was the nearest to him. He laid down his rifle. "I'll bring him in!" he cried, and ran out along the ridge to the wounded cowboy.

Gunfire focused on him. He stumbled, as a man does who has lost his footing, went down, and did not rise again.

"We'd better light outa here quick," the redhead shouted to Lovell. "They'll get the whole caboodle of us." He had volunteered for the adventure of the chase, but he was shaken by the swift tragedy overtaking them. Clerking in a grocery store had not fitted him for this kind of work.

"Stay where you are and keep firing," the

257

marshal ordered. "Don't pull in yore horns, Red. They won't rush us. I'm going to get Farr."

Lovell propped his Winchester against the tree-trunk that shielded him. He ran fast, his body close to the ground. The rifles crashed, flinging slugs at him. A blow smashed into his shoulder. It did not stop him. He reached the sheriff.

"No use," Farr told him. "I'm done for."

Jack picked up the officer, flung him across his shoulder, and made for the shelter of the pines. That thirty yards seemed to him a mile before he reached cover.

He gave the unwounded men orders. "We'll have to pull out. Carry Farr back to the others and get to the horses. Don't wait for me. I'll get Lucky."

The guns from the rocks sounded again as Lovell ran along the hill brow. He wondered how they could help hitting him. Small puffs of smoke billowed out here and there in the boulder field. One of the bandits shouted, "Get him! Get him!"

As he stooped to pick the cowboy up, he saw that Lucky was dead. A second bullet had struck him in the head. His luck had run out at last.

Lovell reached the pines again, recovered his rifle, and followed the other deputies.

His impulse was to hurry, but he curbed the urge. He must not get too close to the men carrying the sheriff. The outlaws might follow. If so, he must hold them back long enough for the others to reach the horses.

He was aware for the first time of the pain in his shoulder. With surprise he saw that his shirt was being dyed a soggy red. When he had time he would have one of the boys bind up the wound.

In front of him he caught sight of the deputies moving slowly up a slope. No use wishing they would go faster. They could not, with the load they were carrying. From a screen of brush he looked down into the park. Two men were helping a third mount a horse. Lovell hoped that meant their minds were occupied with thoughts of escape and not attack.

CHAPTER THIRTY-THREE: WINTERS SACKS HIS SADDLE

The firing from the pines had died down before Lovell disappeared over the brow of the hill. Kid Curry drew at once the correct deduction. Discouraged by its losses, the posse was drawing off from the pursuit.

"We've got 'em on the run!" he shouted to his companions. "Come on, fellows. We'll clean up on them."

"Don't get on the prod," advised Black Jack Ketchum. "We're in bad shape ourselves, with Sam and Elza both toting two wounds. Thing for us to do is to belly through the brush right damn now. We'll have to go slow. The boys sure will have to take it easy."

"I'll not go till I've bumped off that fellow Lovell," answered Curry stubbornly. "I'll never have a better chance. We've got him wounded. Who wants to throw in with me?"

"Why, I'd as lief side you," Winters volunteered. "I don't like that guy myself. The rest of you better get started. Before you know it, the Kid and I will maybe be along with Lovell's scalp."

The two bad men worked up the slope by way of a gully. It would not do to walk into a trap. The water run brought them to the edge of the pines. Cautiously they advanced, scanning every foot of the way. No sign of the posse could be seen except the sprawled body of young Harry Love and the rifles of Farr and the dead man. That the officers intended to give up the fight was evident.

"If we can reach 'em before they get mounted, we can collect Mr. Buttinski Lovell and one or two of his friends," Curry said.

"Might do," Winters agreed. "Teach 'em to leave us alone."

They caught sight of several sheriff's men on a knoll three hundred yards away. No use shooting at that distance and giving warning. Better take them by surprise later when they were bunched.

The officers disappeared over the brow and were gone. The outlaws trailing them quickened their pace. Now that they had located their prey, there was no need of caution just now. Thick brush concealed them as they moved through it.

The thick brush also betrayed their presence. Lovell heard the snapping of the branches fifty yards back of him. That he could not escape a fight he knew. He had reached a place where the shinnery had thinned and was scarcely knee-high. This was no good tract on which to meet them, since they would see him before they came into the open. He turned back into the heavier chaparral, tiptoeing swiftly and with as little rustle as possible.

In his mind there was a faint doubt. The men toward whom he was moving might just conceivably be the two Farr had left to create a diversion while the others attacked. He had to wait and find out, thus losing the advantage of a surprise.

The marshal stopped to listen. No sound broke the stillness. Whoever the men were, they had heard him and were prepared. Very quietly Lovell laid his rifle on the ground and drew from its holster the revolver at his side. A Winchester was too unwieldy for use at close quarters in such a thicket.

The long silence tried his nerves. He felt sure now that they were enemies waiting for him to move and betray his exact position. There might be three or four of them. The pit of his stomach twisted into a tight, cold ball. This looked like the end of the trail for him. But he could perhaps delay the outlaws long enough for his companions to escape.

A bullet from a rifle whistled through the leaves close to the marshal's head. Out of the brush men came, trampling it down, guns flaming. The forty-five in Lovell's hand jumped as he returned the fire. There were two of them, one large, clumsy, heavy-shouldered, the other small and neatly put together. Kid Curry and Nate Winters, two of the worst killers in the whole bandit belt.

The roar of rifles. The flash of a spitting revolver. Lanes of crossfire flung by crouched men pumping death.

Lovell zigzagged forward. With six-gun against rifles the shorter the distance the better. He was lost anyhow, for a slug had crashed into his side. From Nate Winters's rifle. A wave of sickness went through him. The hammer of his gun still fell, more slowly now.

The big man dropped his weapon with an oath, clutching at his torn and bleeding hand. For an instant, as Lovell shifted position, the mesquite branches interfered with the aim of Winters. The marshal's bullet caught him in the throat. He reeled, stumbled, and plunged to the ground, ripping away limbs from the mesquite as he crashed.

In the time it takes the heart to beat twice, the tide of battle had turned. Without waiting to recover his rifle, Kid Curry bolted through the brush. The sound of his body thrashing through the chaparral grew fainter.

Winters was dead. One close look at him told Lovell that. The luck had broken against him at last and he had sacked his saddle for good.

Pain went through Lovell in waves. He felt sick and tired and a hundred years old. The memory of something his mother had read him when a boy ran through his mind. Was it some poetry or a verse from the Bible? *There the wicked cease from troubling, and there the weary be at rest.*

He staggered into the open ground and sat down, an old man sick and broken. After a time — he did not know how long — he heard a man on horseback approaching and slowly gathered himself to his feet. The man was the redhead. The deputies had heard the firing and he had come back to find out what had occurred. He had not liked coming, but something stubborn in him had refused to let him leave without knowing what had become of the marshal.

Red helped Lovell to the saddle and walked beside him. They reached the wooded ridge where the horses had been left.

A hard-faced, heavy-set man moved forward to meet them. He was a professional gambler from Trinidad who had volunteered for the hunt.

"Farr has just cashed his checks," he said.

The marshal looked down at the strong face of the dead sheriff. He had fallen in the line of duty, as many a Western peace officer had done. It was men like Farr who brought law and order to the frontier.

"We better burn the wind outa here," a boyish deputy cried, in his voice a hint of panic. "Before they wipe us all out."

"Don't worry about that bunch of wolves," Lovell said. "They are skedaddlin' for the mountains."

The redhead explained that Lovell had killed Winters and wounded Kid Curry. From the brush above the park he had seen mounted men disappearing into the canyon that led to the Sangre de Cristos Trail.

They dressed Lovell's wounds as best they could, in the meantime discussing what was best to do with their casualties. The marshal decided it for them.

"We'll ride to Cimarron and send men back for the bodies of Farr and Lucky," he said.

The gambler looked at him with critical eyes. "Figure you can make it?" he asked doubtfully.

"We'll find that out later," Lovell answered.

For the marshal it was a dreadful ride. Every jolt, every uneven step of the horse, sent stabs of pain through his side. Waves of nausea flooded him. He clung desperately to the pommel to keep his balance. His body sagged, though no murmur came through his clenched teeth. The miles were interminable and the hours eons. He became lightheaded. A refrain beat through his mind, to accompany the agony and the weariness. *The wicked — cease — from troubling — the weary — be — at rest.*

One of the posse had galloped ahead, and when they reached Cimarron, the streets were filled with people. The wildest rumors were passing from mouth to mouth. Farr's posse had been trapped and practically wiped out. . . . The bandits were marching on the town to burn it and loot the bank. . . . Wounded men had been abandoned in the flight to escape. . . . All the women and children of the town were to be taken into the hills immediately.

Urgent questions were flung at the riders as they drew up in front of the hotel. Lovell's hands were clamped to the saddle horn and his shoulders bowed. The road was tilting up to meet the sky.

"It's been a massacre," the Trinidad gambler explained harshly. "They got Farr and Lucky. But what is left of them are scooting for the mountains. Cut the cackle. We have a wounded man with us."

He had swung from his horse and was helping to lift Lovell to the ground. The marshal slumped down into his arms heavily and was carried into the hotel unconscious.

CHAPTER THIRTY-FOUR:
A COLD TRAIL

A messenger rode into Parker's camp while the men were eating supper twenty-four hours after the battle in the park. His news was staggering. Farr's party had battled the outlaws, the sheriff and Lucky had been killed, and Lovell was so badly injured that he was not expected to live.

Parker rearranged his plans to meet this emergency. He put Rudholt in charge of the posse, with orders to keep a permanent camp near Eagle's Nest until further instructions came. He was to scout along the lower slopes of the range, keeping his men together and returning each night to the camp. The marshal himself saddled at once and rode to Cimarron. He reached there in the morning, saddle-sore and weary, his horse entirely spent.

There was still more than a flicker of life left in Lovell, though he was a very ill man. He had lost a great deal of blood, and Doctor Massey did not hold out much hope. The wound in his side was serious and might prove fatal. On the other hand, the doctor knew from experience that outdoor men of the saddle took a lot of killing. A clean life in the sun and the wind had toughened them so that they often made surprising recoveries from gunshot wounds.

The members of Farr's posse had left for Raton before the arrival of the marshal. At once he set about organizing another force to take up the hunt. This was a country where big game ranged and it was not difficult to find expert riflemen willing to serve.

Parker snatched three hours of sleep and started on the trail in midafternoon. An old trapper went with him as guide, a man who knew the location of the park where the battle had been fought.

They camped that night in the canyon, breakfasted early, and reached the scene of the fight while the day was still young. Extra men with pack horses had come with the posse to take back to Cimarron the bodies of the dead, but before they started on the return trip, Parker combed the rock field across the creek to make sure that Nate Winters was the only one of the bandits who had been killed.

A young posse-man named Danvers gave a shout of surprise. In the shadow of a big boulder he had come on a wounded man with a revolver in his hand. The rifle of Danvers covered the outlaw.

"Drop that gun," he ordered. "A big bunch of officers is here."

The weapon dropped from the fingers of the wounded man. "I'm too sick to fight," he said.

Danvers called to the marshal. "I've found one of 'em. He's alive."

The man was Sam Ketchum. He had been left behind because he was too badly hurt to travel. They dressed his wounds as well as they could and carried him to the ridge at the lip of the park.

Though Ketchum suffered from the jolting, he had to be taken down the gulch to the bed of the main canyon by horseback. Here the party broke up. One man stayed with the prisoner until a wagon could be brought to take him to town. The other extras carried the dead back to Cimarron. Parker and his men returned to the park and picked up the trail of the outlaws.

They had gone out through a break in the rock wall back of the boulder field. That they had at least one wounded man with them was clear, for the posse found a crimson-stained handkerchief in the gulch beside a stream. From the number of hoof marks in the sand, the old trapper was sure the fugitives had stopped here to give first aid to one of their men.

Before night the trail was lost. Somewhere in that tangle of huddled hills the fleeing men had disappeared. Though the marshal quartered over the rolling miles and searched a dozen canyon mouths for sign, he found no tracks of the desperate men.

They were somewhere in that rugged stretch which lies between Taos Pass and the Spanish Peaks, and they would be as hard to find as the proverbial needle in a haystack. In this high country, packed with ridges and gulches offering a hundred hiding-places, it would be sheer luck if pursuers found their prey. Farr had stumbled on the holed-in desperadoes, but Parker did not expect a near-miracle to repeat itself.

Three days later his weary riders drew in after dark to the camp at Eagle's Nest. Rudholt's posse had been no more successful than that of the marshal, except for one doubtful lead that might have no value. An hour earlier, Sommers had met a ranchman and fallen into talk with him. A wounded man accompanied by a friend had come to his place two days earlier. Their story was that they had been hunting and one had accidentally shot the other. But the rancher was not satisfied with this explanation, because the wounded man had been shot in two places. The unhurt hunter had ridden away, leaving his friend at the ranch. Both men had plenty of money and were prepared to pay well for the care of the injured one.

"It's a cinch the wounded man is Elza Lay," Sommers said. "We know he was wounded. They had to leave him somewhere."

"They might have left him in some gulch with a bullet hole in his head," Rudholt answered.

"No need to do that. They know Elza won't blab."

Parker was inclined to agree with Sommers. At any rate, the lead was worth investigating. Next day he rode up Dead Cow Creek with three deputies. He did not include Sommers among them, for he knew that Bill had once been a comrade of Lay and would not like to take part in his capture. The officers made a circuit to come on the homestead house from the rear. Mrs. Wood, the wife of the ranchman, was in the kitchen baking bread when the men tiptoed in without knocking.

She stared at them, startled at this interruption. "What do you want?" she demanded.

"We want to talk with your guest," Parker murmured.

She knew at once why they had come. "You are a sheriff," she said.

"A United States Marshal," he corrected.

"He's in the front bedroom." She was a young and comely woman with kind, lovely eyes. Just now the eyes looked troubled. "You won't hurt him, will you? He's a nice man, no matter what he has done."

"We won't hurt him unless he makes us."

The door of the bedroom was open. Very quietly Parker walked in. Lay was lying on the bed reading an old newspaper. He looked up, dropped the paper, and thrust his hand beneath the pillow.

"Don't you," warned the marshal, covering him.

Lay's fingers slid back into the open empty. "All right," he said. "I give up."

"Any of the rest of your gang around here?"

"No. I wouldn't have been either if I had been able to travel."

Parker set a guard over him while he continued to search the hills. Rudholt was no longer in the marshal's posse. He had taken a train to return to his ranch.

CHAPTER THIRTY-FIVE: RUDHOLT PLAYS BIG BROTHER

The latest word Esther had heard about Parker's posse was from Nick Haley, who had ridden across to tell her the officers were crossing the Navajo Reservation in pursuit of the outlaws. She knew of the train robbery at Folsom and that sheriffs were pursuing the bandits. But during the week since that first wire nothing but rumors had come through.

She was watching a ranch hand shoe a horse at the open-air blacksmith shop when Rudholt rode into the yard. Esther had told him not to come to the Circle 72 again, but she did not raise that point now. He was bringing news she wanted to hear.

"I'm back from the war without firing a shot," he told her. "Rode clear across New Mexico, sacked my saddle, and came home."

"You didn't catch the train robbers," she said, a question in her inflection.

"The posse I was in didn't. We split up. Lovell and Lucky joined Sheriff Farr's outfit. They ran into Curry's gang at Cimarron Canyon. There was a fight and several were killed."

The girl's heart stood still, then began to hammer fast. She waited, her fear-filled eyes on him.

"Farr was killed, and your boy Lucky," he continued. "Lovell is badly shot up. I don't know whether he can make the grade."

"Where is he?" she asked.

"He's at the hotel in Cimarron. Got hit trying to save Farr, and again while he was holding back the scoundrels to let his men reach their horses. He killed that ruffian Winters and wounded Curry."

"I must go to him," she said, her low, throaty voice almost a murmur.

Rudholt was surprised, but he made no protest. She had told him, though not in words, that nothing in life was so important to her as this.

"If you hurry we can make the train at Holbrook tonight," he replied. "I'll get you there."

Lucy helped her pack a small valise while Jerry harnessed a horse and hitched it to the buggy. Rudholt rode to town ahead of them. When they reached Live Oaks, he was waiting for Esther with a buckboard. The younger sister kissed Esther good-by, clinging to her as she whispered, "He'll be all right. I know he will."

They traveled over land that the centuries had rippled into waves, with sagebrush on either side of them far as the eye could see. The sun beat down upon them through the clear air flooding the earth with light. In the distance antelope flitted lightly through the sage. Sage chickens crossed the road and vanished in the brush. For hours the desert engulfed them, no sign of human life in the vast solitude.

Rudholt covered ground fast, but he did not have to give his mind entirely to driving. There were long silences, but he talked at times to divert her thoughts. His kindness surprised the girl. He might have been a solicitous older brother. He revealed a side of his nature quite new to her. Perhaps she had been too hard on him. After all, in those early years he had been fighting fire with fire. A scrupulous man could not have held his own against Zach Young's attacks. She had thought him callous. Now she was not so sure.

At Holbrook they had an hour to wait for the train. When he took her into a restaurant, she discovered that she was hungry. After supper they walked the station platform.

"You've put me in your debt again," she confessed.

He laughed. "A man owes his sister something."

Esther did not answer that directly, unless it touched the point to mention that Lucy was very young.

"Time will cure that," he guaranteed.

"If she has time — until she is out of

school next year, say," Esther suggested.

"You are fishing for a promise," he charged.

"Would it be too much — to let her find out what she really wants?"

He understood that there was an implied pledge on her part too. If he waited, she would not actively oppose his suit.

"I can talk turkey to you," he said. "I thought of this first because of the advantage it would be to tie together our ranches. I dare say that was selfish. You have to be selfish to get what you want. Life is like that. If I hadn't taken all I could get, I would still be a forty-dollar-a-month cowpuncher. But about Lucy I have changed my mind. I would want to marry her if she didn't have a nickel — if she was slinging hash at a Harvey House. The lovely little thing is in my blood as no other woman ever has been. I can't get along without her. If I were to tell you how I feel about her — well, let's cut that out. Anyhow, I think I will make her a better husband than any other man she would ever meet. This means a great deal to me. Because it does, I am willing to wait until next June. But before she goes to school, I must tell her where I stand. She does not need to bind herself."

Esther agreed to that. She felt happier

about this than she ever had before. He was strong, and his strength would protect Lucy.

His last words before he put her on the train were of comfort. "We outdoor men are tough," he said. "I have seen a cowboy with half a dozen bullets in him pull through. Lovell has led a clean, hard life in the sun and the wind. He'll have a far better chance than most men would."

At Albuquerque the conductor handed her a telegram. It said: *Rudholt asks me wire you condition Lovell. Patient much improved.*

It was signed, *Doctor Harvey Massey.*

Back of the magazine Esther broke down and cried for joy. The relief was tremendous.

CHAPTER THIRTY-SIX: A GIRL LEARNS TO LAUGH

Jack Lovell awakened from a long, deep sleep and did not believe what he saw. Esther Young sat in a chair by his bedside smiling at him. To clear his mind of fantasy, he looked out of the window at a woman hanging clothes on a line, then turned his head and squinted sun-wrinkled eyes at the illusion. The girl was still there. He reached out and put his fingers on a flesh-and-blood hand.

"It's really you," he said.

277

"It really is," she answered.

He wondered how he could ever have thought she was not beautiful. Her face had the fresh warmth of spring, young and tender and vivid. "This is marvelous," he told her. "I dreamed I was with you."

She felt a happy excitement drumming in her veins. From the moment Rudholt had told her about Lovell's wounds, she had known she must come to him, but it had been in her mind often during the journey that perhaps he would not want to see her, might think her a silly fool flinging herself at him. Now that fear was blown away. He had wanted her.

Esther lifted his head and arranged the pillow to make it more comfortable. The feminine perfume of her was like heady wine to his nostrils.

"In my dream I kissed you." His voice was low and drawling, but the eyes were eager. "Sick folks must be humored."

The lips that met his were warm and soft. He put his arms around her and held the young body close. "I reckon I'll have to be yore prince consort after all," he murmured.

"Not ever," she denied. "I'm tired of wearing Levis and dusty boots, of doing a man's job. You'll be boss of the Circle 72 now."

He built up the lost blood and strength

fast. Soon he could walk slowly to the porch on her arm. She read to him. They talked — of books and life and of each other. It was wonderful to feel their minds meet and make comfortable contacts. Esther found that she could talk nonsense with him and love it. They spilled together a lot of laughter over nothing.

On a sunny afternoon Lloyd Parker rode up to the hotel, four other men in his wake. One of them was Elza Lay, a prisoner, captured far up in the hills at a small ranch where his wounds had tied him. The outlaw sank wearily into an armchair next to the one where Lovell sat.

Lay grinned across at the man who had frolicked with him before he began to follow crooked trails.

"Glad you're going to make the riffle, Jack," he said. "I worried some about that."

"How about you, Elza?" He threw in an introduction. "Miss Young, this is Elza Lay. We used to ride together."

"Pleased to meet you, ma'am," Lay said. He replied to Lovell's question dryly. "I'll make out. By the time of the trial they will have me patched up fine. I get a queer notion in my nut sometimes, old-timer, that a fellow might do better going straight."

Parker came out of the hotel, into which

he had gone to arrange for bedrooms over-night. He took his prisoner inside and left him in charge of Bill Sommers, then re-turned to chat with his friends. In answer to questions he told them of the capture of Lay. The other outlaws were still at large.

Esther asked what the law would do with Lay.

"He'll probably be hanged," Parker re-plied. "His story is that he didn't kill either Lucky or Sheriff Farr. But that won't save him. He was one of the bandit outfit."

"Men who ride the outlaw trail die young," Lovell said. "Inside of a few years all this bunch of bad men will be rubbed out. Law catches up with all of them finally."

"If they know that, why do they keep on in their evil ways?" Esther wanted to know.

"Each one thinks he will be the exception, and there are practically no exceptions," Jack explained. "They are doomed, every one of them." (Lovell's prophecy was very nearly correct. At least twelve men who rode with the Cassidy and Ketchum gangs died with their boots on.)

The girl was puzzled, even though she had been brought up on the frontier West. "I don't understand it. This man Lay does not seem bad. He has a nice smile, and he acted so friendly, as if he held no grudge at Jack because he had been trying to capture him."

"Probably he doesn't. It's all in the game. Some of these outlaws were just wild cowboys who drank too much, not very different from other punchers who settled down to go straight all their lives. They got wrong ideas in their heads of getting rich quick by a short cut. First, they started rustling. From that they drifted into a stage or bank robbery, very likely after they had been on a spree. Once outside the law, it is hard to escape from the life they have chosen."

Jack agreed. "When I first met Lay, he was one of the most likable young fellows I ever knew. Reckless, maybe, but with nothing about him to suggest he would go bad. I once saw him dive into the Arkansas River and drag out a drowning man."

"He would do that now," Parker admitted, "but nonetheless he is a menace to society."

Lovell was both embarrassed and annoyed at the attention he was getting because he had killed a notorious bad man with a record. When he and Esther sauntered along the main street of Cimarron, all eyes centered on him. He was pointed out in a whisper to strangers. Once three barefoot youngsters stopped him to put a question.

"Mister, was it a Colt's forty-five you used

to kill Nate Winters?"

This was too much. The marshal told them if they did not light out in a hurry, he would paddle them where it would do most good.

Esther was amused. She had been serious all her life, but she was discovering how much fun it was to tease him.

"If you are going to be a public hero, you should wear long hair like Buffalo Bill," she told him.

"Don't ever use that word to me again," he ordered sternly.

"What word?" she asked innocently.

"You know the word."

"Yes, my lord. If I do you will give me the where-it-will-do-the-most-good treatment," she suggested demurely.

Her audacity shocked him. In the outdoor West young men held nice girls a bit in awe and treated them as if they were almost too good for human nature's daily food.

Parker and Lovell had more than one talk with the prisoner in an attempt to pry information from him. They pointed out that the rest of the gang would be captured soon and that any information he gave them would be likely to mitigate his sentence.

"You figure that if I sell out my friends they will hang me gently with a silk rope,"

Lay jeered.

"You might get a life sentence," Parker suggested.

"That would be nice," the outlaw said, his voice low and biting. "I could lie in a cell twenty years cussing myself for a yellow coyote who couldn't take what was coming to him."

"Look at it this way," Parker advised. "Curry is a killer, mean and vicious. You're not. He has been that way ever since he grew up. It's not fair he should escape and you take the rap. Give us a tip where we might find him. It would help you and nobody would know."

Lay's eyes, hard and steady, looked into those of the marshal. "I would know. What did I ever do to make you think I would throw down on my partners?"

"I knew you wouldn't, Elza," Lovell said. "But we had to give you the chance."

"You got three of us," Lay said bitterly. "Isn't that enough for one roundup?"

"It won't ever be enough until the last bandit is combed out of the chaparral," Parker told him.

Bill Sommers took the train with Jack and Esther for Holbrook. Parker was already in the field with a posse hunting for the rest of the Folsom bandits.

As the Santa Fe churned through New Mexico, Esther talked with Jack about Bedford Rudholt. She wanted reassurance as to his character in view of the fact that he might soon be a member of the family.

"He can be kind and gentle," she said. "Not many men would have been thoughtful enough to wire Doctor Massey asking him to send a telegram to Albuquerque letting me know how you were getting along."

He laughed. "I didn't think I would ever listen to you pleading a case for Rudholt. But really I don't think he would be a bad husband for Lucy. He would see she got a lot out of life. The man has character, though you have believed it not a good one. The cattle country has always been violent. Most good men have done things that can't be defended. Circumstances forced their hand. Rudholt was more right than your uncle in their fight. The law is on his side, though it doesn't say he could do all the wrongs he did. I think it would be safe to close the books on his past and open a new set."

"I'm afraid we shall have to," Esther said. "I never saw Lucy so interested in a man before."

The train began to slacken speed as it entered Gallup. Bill Sommers sang out at them as he passed down the car, "Thirty minutes for supper at the Harvey House."

They joined the line in the aisle waiting for the train to stop.

Chapter Thirty-Seven: The Plotter Squirms

Judge Krock said, in a murmur, "Five hundred dollars."

The ugly mouth of the little man beside him opened at one corner and words dripped out. "You didn't hear me right. I said a thousand."

Their heads were close, the fine silvery hair of the lawyer and the cropped bristles on the bullet head with the small bright eyes set too near together.

"Be fair, Winters," whispered Krock. "He killed your brother Nate. You came here to do the job. What you get from me is a pick-up. It's safe and easy if you're careful."

Dan Winters showed a set of bad teeth in a thin-lipped grin. "You do it, then. I'll give *you* five hundred." He added pointedly, "Ringold and Kid Curry did not find it so safe and easy — nor Nate."

"They didn't go at it right. Cut him down from the brush."

"Fine. You do it, since you know just how."

"No sense in talking that way," Krock protested peevishly. "I'm not a gunfighter. But you are. A good one. You have traveled a long way to fix this meddling fool. My five hundred is just lagniappe."

"Big words won't cut the price down. It's still a thousand."

Krock's eyes swept the doors of the courtroom. "Don't talk so loud," he warned. "Someone might walk in any minute."

"He couldn't hear a thousand any easier than he could five hundred," Winters jeered.

"Have it your own way, though it's a hold-up," Krock groaned.

"You bet I will. It's my hide I'm risking. Half now, half after it's done."

"Why now? You'll get the money when you have delivered."

"You don't have to tell me that. You wouldn't dare welsh." Malicious mirth glittered in the little eyes of the killer. "Still, good friends like us won't fuss over trifles. Just to bind the bargain we'll say half now."

The judge threw up his hands. "All right — all right." He took bills from his wallet and pushed them at the other man under the desk. "Count it later," he said.

"I'll count it now," Winters said, and did.

"Go out by the back door and keep close to the wall so you won't be seen in the dark," Krock told him.

The judge sat at the desk a long time after the killer had gone. He was not happy about this. He was not happy about anything these days. The world had gone sour on him. He had built so carefully, he thought, and the structure was tumbling down on him. This man Lovell was responsible for his troubles. He was back again, and Krock did not deceive himself. He meant to gather more evidence, until he had enough to destroy the colonel. The meddling fool had to be rubbed out. With him out of the way there would still be a chance to salvage something.

Early in the morning he drove out to the Circle 72. It was not a visit he expected to enjoy, but he had to save face, to keep up the pretense that there was no gulf between him and the Youngs. He knew that Esther had lost confidence in him. The relation between them would never again be a friendly one, but he must try to convey to the outside world his sense of sorrow that she so misjudged him, must make it appear that her mind had been poisoned against a good man and a dear friend.

Esther was busy in the kitchen when she heard the sound of wheels and looked through the window to see him drive into the yard. A heat of anger swept through her.

He had no right to come here. She washed the flour from her hands and went out to the porch to meet him.

His smile was sad and wistful. "I have come, my dear, to clear up any misunderstanding there may be between us," he said.

"There isn't any," she told him bluntly. "We understand each other perfectly."

"I'm afraid not," he differed, his voice mellifluous and forgiving. "Busybodies have been making trouble. We must get to the bottom of it and save our friendship."

She looked at him steadily, contempt in her clear eyes. Her hand swung open the screen door. "Come in," she said curtly, and followed him into the room.

Jack Lovell was lying on the lounge. He sat up, the book he had been reading still open. The lawyer's lids narrowed, an evil glitter in his eyes. He had not expected to meet the marshal. Almost instantly he recovered his suavity.

"I was distressed to hear that you were injured," he said. "I trust that you are recovering nicely."

A warning flashed through Lovell's mind. *Look out,* he thought, *the fox is building up a defense again to let him out after I have been killed.*

"I'm doing fine," he said. "Your concern

touches me."

Krock sighed. His manner was generously free of resentment. "Your judgment of me has always been prejudiced and unfair. I regret this, but there is nothing I can do about it."

"No," Lovell agreed. "My opinion is fixed." His eyes consulted Esther for a moment. "I'll lay a few cards on the table, Colonel Krock. You will know then why I am so obstinate. Before his death Zach Young discovered that you and his foreman, Ben Ringold, were at the head of a gang of rustlers looting his ranch and other spreads, pushing the stock north through unknown canyons to markets in Utah and Colorado. On the morning of his death he called on you at the courthouse and told you what he had learned and that he meant to break you."

Krock was watching Lovell closely. The marshal must be guessing. Lovell could not be sure of this. There was no way he could have found out. "This is all wrong," the lawyer said confidently. "There is no word of truth in it, except that he did call on me to talk over some business an hour before he was shot. We were partners and the best of friends. It is outrageous for you to make such assertions."

Lovell paid no attention to the lawyer's defense. "You got in touch with Ringold at once," he continued. "The case was urgent. A day's delay might ruin you. Ringold murdered Young as soon as he could get him alone."

Though Krock was frightened, he gave no outward evidence of it. He spread his hands, shaking his head in denial. "Talk — empty talk. You haven't a scintilla of proof. What you say is absurd and libelous."

"When Young found out he was being robbed, and by whom, he wrote a letter to Governor Brodie and asked him to send some of the Rangers to make a gather of the guilty men. In that letter he names you and his foreman as leaders of the thieves."

The heart of the lawyer died inside of him. The blandness went out of his face like the light from a blown candle. He looked haggard and old. "That is impossible," he answered. "If Governor Brodie received such a letter, why did he do nothing about it?"

"He never received it. After he had written the letter, Young evidently decided to have it out with you first. I gather he was an irascible and impulsive man. He couldn't wait. That haste destroyed him. He left the letter in the old work coat he was wearing.

Nick Haley discovered it yesterday and brought it over to us."

"It is a forgery!" Krock cried. "Written by my enemies to destroy me. Let me see it."

"You will see it when your case comes to trial," Lovell said. "When you set out to make easy money, you did not realize that to save yourself you would have to kill Young and that because you had killed him you would have to snuff the life out of poor Pud Lyman, nor that it would then be necessary to kill me. You have spun a tangled web and are caught in it yourself."

"Your whole silly fairy tale rests on a forged letter," Krock retorted. "It won't get anywhere."

"You wrote to Sheriff Kern of Routt County that the stock driven there had been sent up the trail by Zach Young," Lovell went on inexorably. "We can prove that isn't true."

"If such a letter exists, it is another forgery. I have had no correspondence with Sheriff Kern."

The marshal did not argue the point. His level voice pressed home more evidence. "Two of the Folsom train robbers have been captured. One of them has since died of his wounds. He left a signed confession. Your name is mentioned."

"The word of an admitted bandit is worth nothing against that of a responsible citizen," the harassed man cried. "The plain fact is that you want to prove me guilty because you are my enemy."

"I advise you not to put any hope on that, Colonel Krock," the marshal said. "You have come to the end of a long crooked trail."

Esther said, "I think there is nothing to be gained by any further talk, Colonel Krock."

Internally Krock was a small earthquake of fear, but his façade of dignified virtue remained unbroken. "I do not understand you any more, my child," he reproached. "All your life you have known me, a friend of your father and of your uncle. A stranger comes along and bewitches you. He flings vile accusations at me, and you believe them. My long and honorable record has no weight with you. Some day you will be bitterly sorry for having so misjudged me."

He shook his head sadly and walked out of the room.

After the lawyer had gone, the girl turned to Lovell. "Why did you tell him so much?" she asked.

"I want to force his hand. He is likely to make a move that will ruin him. The fellow knows he has his back to the wall."

Jack did not tell her that the next move would probably be another attempt on his life.

"What are you expecting him to do?" she demanded, holding his eyes fast to hers.

"I don't know. But whatever it is he'll have to do it fast. He won't sit still and wait while we pile up more evidence."

"No, he won't," she said. "He'll strike at you again because he feels you are at the bottom of his troubles. You know that very well."

He grinned at her. "Since you have warned me I'll be very very careful."

Esther let the subject drop. There would be no use in arguing with him. She had a talk with Bill Sommers.

When Jack strolled down to the end of the lane next day to look at the calves in the pasture, Bill was with him. When he took his first ride he found Bill jogging beside him, a forty-five on his hip and a Winchester across the saddle.

"Expecting to meet a bear?" Lovell asked.

"Or a wolf, maybe."

"That's why you are garnished with hardware?" the marshal drawled.

"I reckon."

"Just happened to come along with me, accidentally on purpose?"

"That's right," Sommers agreed.

"When you see Miss Esther, mention to her that I'm right glad to have you for a nurse to ride herd on me." The mirth died out of Lovell's face. "And for a fact, I am. I feel a lot more comfortable having you to side me. If I'm lucky, maybe they'll get you instead of me."

"That would be nice," Sommers said gravely. "For you."

Chapter Thirty-Eight: Bull Rattler From Bitter Creek

A stranger who called himself Dave Walters dropped into the livery stable to feed his horse. He had been in town two or three days and spent most of his time at the Cowboys' Resort drinking and gambling. Jim Roberts was mildly curious as to what he was doing here. Apparently he was not on the lookout for a job. Nor did he seem to have any other business at Live Oaks.

Jim had taken a dislike to him. It might be because he was a small man that he bragged and swaggered, to make sure nobody would think him insignificant. But there was something evil about him. He had bad teeth

294

back of a thin, crooked mouth and there were moments when his tawny, glittering eyes could be as savage as those of an angry tiger.

He took a bottle from his pocket, wiped off the top with the cuff of his coat, and offered Roberts a drink. The corral owner declined. He had given up snorting so early in the day, he said.

Walters helped himself to a long drink, corked the bottle, and put it back in his pocket. He lifted himself to the edge of the oat bin and watched Roberts oil a set of buggy harness.

"This is a hell of a town," he growled. "The men have no guts and the women no ginger."

Roberts took no audible exception to this outburst, unless it was one to suggest that probably then Walters would not be staying long.

The bleak eyes slid round and rested on the livery-stable keeper. "I'll go when I get good and ready," he snarled from his slitted mouth.

"I didn't mean it that way," Roberts explained. "My idea was that since you didn't like us you very likely wouldn't stay."

"You're right there. When I've finished what I came for, I'll pull my freight."

Roberts did not answer. After a long silence Walters mentioned that he used to know a fellow named Lovell and had been told the man was living around here.

"At the Circle 72 just now," Roberts answered. "I don't know as you would say he lives here. He's a Government man and likely won't be around long."

"What's he doing here?"

"I don't know."

"Come to town much?"

"Not just lately." Roberts went on to say that Lovell had been shot up by the men who robbed the C. & S. train at Folsom, but was recovering nicely from his wounds. He added that it was not more than six miles to the Circle 72 and that Walters could easily ride out there if Lovell was a friend of his.

"Did I say he was my friend?" Walters inquired sourly.

Sommers and Lovell rode up to the stable and dismounted. Roberts waited for a recognition, but none came. Evidently Walters did not know the marshal. The man had lied to him. That was a little strange. The corral owner decided against making any introductions.

The men from the Circle 72 walked uptown. Walters inquired who they were.

"Bill Sommers and Jack Lovell," replied the corral man.

There was a flash of malignant hatred in the yellow eyes of the stranger. "Which one was Lovell?" he asked.

"The one in the blue shirt. Thought you knew him."

The answer of Walters came a moment late. "Not the Lovell I knew."

Roberts did not quite like this. It might not mean a thing, but he decided to let Jack Lovell be a judge of that. A few minutes later he walked into the post office, saw Lovell, and drew him aside.

Jack took the information seriously. He was quite sure he had not before met Walters, but he had had an impression of a likeness to somebody else.

"Did you leave him at the stable?" Jack asked.

"No. He came with me far as the Cowboys' Resort and dropped in there."

"I'll have another look at him," Lovell said.

He and Sommers walked into the saloon and ordered beer. Walters was at the bar. When his gaze met that of Lovell, the marshal read in it an appalling fury. For an instant only. Then a shutter dropped over the eyes, a film which left them opaque and blank. It stood out like a newly painted wagon in the sagebrush that since they had met in the stable this stranger had learned who he was. The man's leathery face was sly and cruel, the features held together by a certain animal ruthlessness. He wore the gun in his belt low, well forward on the thigh.

"Hotter than Billy-be-damn," Sommers mentioned, speaking to Walters lightly.

"You fellows from the Circle 72, ain't you?" Walters said, clearly making an effort to keep the hostile rasp out of his voice.

"Rang the bell first shot," the puncher answered.

"Wonder if yore outfit could use another rider."

"You'd have to ask the boss about that. We're kinda full up, but she has an interest in the Bar Z Y. Two-three of the boys there quit lately. Might be a spot for you."

"She? I dunno as I want to work for a sissy woman-bossed outfit," sneered Walters. "Nice Sunday-school talk in the bunkhouse, I reckon."

"Too bad," Sommers regretted. "Looks like the Young ranches will have to worry along without you. We cain't rope and hogtie waddies to make 'em work, even when they are bull rattlers from Bitter Creek."

His voice, gently ironic, brought a dull flush to the face of Walters, who glared at him, struggled with a rising temper, and decided not to make an issue of the retort. The stranger knew he had asked for a sharp answer. No cowboy would let an outsider belittle the outfit for which he worked without resenting it. For Walters to start trouble now over nothing would be sheer folly. He did not want to give any warning before he struck.

He said sulkily, "No offense meant, gents."

They declined the drink he offered and left him at the bar. After they had swung to their saddles, Bill appraised the man in four words. "Ugly as galvanized sin."

"And dangerous," Lovell added.

"Remind you of anybody?"

"He does — in a way. The guy doesn't look a bit like Nate Winters, but there's something about him — the way he struts, maybe — the pointed ears — that makes me think of Nate."

"Might be," Sommers assented doubtfully. "Know anything about Nate's kin?"

"I can find out."

Before leaving town Lovell sent a telegram to the sheriff of Johnson County, Wyoming. He picked up the answer next day. It read: *Bud and Dan Winters brother of Nate. Bud okay. Dan bad reputation. Penitentiary record rustling. Killed man named Brand last year. Appearance small wiry brown eyes scar above right temple bad teeth. Left Buffalo week ago.* JOHN SANDERS.

"So Mr. Dan Winters changed his name to Dave Walters," Cantrell exclaimed, his voice high and excited. "That's right interesting. Whyfor do you reckon?"

They were in the big room at the ranch. After deliberation Lovell had decided to read the message from the Wyoming sheriff to them all. If Winters went gunning, he might by mistake get the wrong man. Better have everybody on the ranch warned.

Sommers looked at Jack and grinned. "Why, he wants to get him a man for breakfast."

"Y'betcha!" the old foreman piped up. "He's laying for Jack."

Lovell was of that opinion himself. "I think he'll be out here today asking for a job," he said, smiling at Esther.

No answering smile met his. She was plainly worried. "What are we to do?"

"Funny he didn't say anything about a job the first two days he was in town," Sommers contributed. "Not till after he found out Jack was staying here."

Dad Cantrell banged a fist on the table.

"We gotta run him out or string him up one," he exploded.

The marshal shook his head. "We can't do it. He has a legal right to be here. The law isn't a mind-reader. It can't move until a suspect has taken overt action."

"You mean until he has killed you," Esther interpreted, protest in her sharp voice.

"He isn't going to kill me," Lovell corrected gently. "He just thinks he is."

"If he shows up, I'll get the boys to give him a welcome he won't like," Cantrell promised.

Sommers had already talked the situation over with Lovell. He made a suggestion. "If Winters comes pretending he wants a job, why not let him have one? I can ride herd on him instead of on Jack. If he's here, we'll know where he is at."

Though Esther did not like the proposal, she agreed to it after Lovell had strongly supported it. The marshal held that under constant surveillance the man would have no opportunity to shoot from ambush.

When Winters rode up later, Esther reneged on her consent. The man's looks sent a shudder of dislike through her. His ugly lupine face exuded evil. She knew she would live in a torment of fear every hour he was on the place. Curtly she told him there was no job for him on the Circle 72. Lovell later smilingly agreed she had done right. If she was going to be unhappy about it, the man had better not be on the ranch.

CHAPTER THIRTY-NINE: SOMMERS SERVERS AN ULTIMATUM

Two men were lurking in the shadow of a doorway across the street from the court-house when Dan Winters slipped up the front steps into the building.

"Like we guessed, he's gone to report to his boss," Cantrell said.

"Looks like," Bill Sommers agreed.

They had come to town over the notch gap and reached Live Oaks fifteen minutes before Winters. From the time the Wyoming man had turned his horse into the corral, they had known where he was every minute of the time until now. He had spent a couple of hours at the Cowboys' Resort drinking and then had eaten supper at the Tip Top. Afterward he had taken a couple of quick ones at the Blue Moon. It was dark when the man came out of the back door of the saloon and moved down the alley toward the courthouse square.

The Circle 72 men followed Winters into the courthouse and trod softly up the stairs into the corridor which led to Krock's office. Listening at the door, they could make out a low murmur of voices, but nothing that was said. Presently they retreated to the end of the corridor and waited. They had to make sure that it was Winters who was talking with Krock.

When the door opened and Winters came out, it was half an hour later. His shadows followed down the dark street. Before he reached Rincon, he heard their quick footsteps and turned. Though expecting no trouble, it was the habit of his life not to let men walk back of him at night without checking up on them. A man cannot kill four times and not leave enemies in his wake.

Sommers observed that the man's fingers were hovering near the butt of the low-hung revolver. He said, in cheerful, idle talk, "How did you come out at the Circle 72?"

The vanity of the bad man would not let him acknowledge any rebuff. "She offered me a job and I turned it down," he lied. "Didn't like the layout."

"Too bad," Bill replied. "I'll bet you are a top rider."

"I can ride the worst of 'em straight up

and throw a loop farther than any man in this damn territory," the Wyoming man boasted. His hand had fallen away from the belt. These cowboys did not mean to make trouble, he had decided.

"Ever compete at one of those rodeos?" Bill asked.

"Kid stuff," the gunman jeered. "I wouldn't be caught dead at one of 'em. Let's go have a drink."

"Not just yet, Mr. Winters," Sommers answered, his voice grown chill and hard. "We thought we'd like a little talk with you."

Winters's body stiffened. He had been tricked into relaxing his vigilance. His eyes narrowed, as his thoughts stabbed fast. The old man he mentally brushed aside. Any time he could beat him to the draw. But Sommers had the advantage and he might be dangerous. His gun was not out, but a thumb was hitched in his belt not an inch from the butt of the six-shooter. The cowboy was standing at poised ease. The words had fallen from his lips cool and even. The fellow was not nervous. He acted like he was enjoying himself.

"What's yore game?" Winters demanded hoarsely.

"Nobody is going to start smokin' unless that's the way you want it," Sommers told him. "Keep yore shirt on, Mr. Winters."

"My name is Walters."

"Walters in Arizona, Winters in Wyoming." The voice of Sommers was still gentle and almost casual. "We hear you don't like Arizona. Why stay here?"

"I got a right to stay where I want to. What's eatin' you, fellow?"

"You won't like this part of the country," Sommers continued. "Yore brother Nate found it bad for his health. We're worried about yours. Try Wyoming again."

"You're not scaring me any. And I don't get the whyfor of this hurrahing."

Cantrell had agreed to let Bill do the talking, but now he broke out angrily. "You don't have to get it. All you have to do is to burn the wind *pronto.*"

"Of course you don't understand, Mr. Winters." Bill apologized. "My error. Arizona is great for law. It leans backward with righteousness. Up in Wyoming when you bump off a citizen, like you did Mr. Brand last year, folks figure maybe you're a leetle mite impulsive. In this territory they hang you to a live oak kinda sudden or cut you down in yore tracks like Lovell did Nate."

"Are you claimin' I've killed anybody here?" the bad man snarled.

"Not yet," Sommers told him sweetly.

"The point is you're not going to. Yore intentions are to dry-gulch Jack Lovell. It won't be that way. Try it, and you'll be a gone goose. Colonel Krock cain't help you. He's already a busted flush. And when you get in a jam he won't lift a hand for you. Like Dad Cantrell says, you'd better hit the trail for anywheres but here."

"And if I don't," jeered Winters.

"Why, I reckon there would be an open season on you. Some of us boys might take a hand."

"Come a-smokin' when you like," Winters broke out harshly. "I'm here tendin' to my own business. If you think you'd have any luck trying to run me out, hop to it."

The killer turned on his heel and swaggered away.

Bill watched him go, aware that the scene he and Cantrell had staged was not too successful. "Maybe when he thinks it over he'll light out," the young man said. "Anyhow he knows what he's up against. We had to throw a scare into him. He's got plenty of sand in his craw, but I'll bet he won't feel comfortable if he sticks around and tries to bushwhack Jack."

"We'd ought to of stopped his clock right here," Cantrell said savagely.

Bill knew that was just anger talking.

CHAPTER FORTY:
JACK LOVELL MAKES SURE

Sommers and Dad Cantrell reported to Lovell what they had learned about the relations of Winters and Colonel Krock. That these two had an understanding was clear, an intent to destroy the man they both hated. Both of the Circle 72 men were convinced of this. They told Jack of their talk with the Wyoming bad man.

"We put it plain to him," Sommers said. "He'll worry about it, but that won't keep him from going through. I expect he's a gun shark, and he's sure bullheaded. He doesn't figure to give you a break." The black-headed cowboy hesitated before offering a solution. He did not know how it would be received. "Some of us boys will take this off yore hands. We're not going to stand for a dry-gulching. We'll put him out of business for you."

Lovell shook his head. "No, Bill. I'm much obliged, but it must not be that way. We'll have to let him make his play. I'm a law officer and have to wait till he cuts loose."

"Hell's bells!" yelped the old foreman. "It will be too late then."

"I don't think so," the marshal disagreed. "My idea isn't to offer him chances. Perhaps he'll think better of it and hit the north trail."

His friends went away troubled in mind. This was all wrong, and they did not know how to set it right. Lovell stood for law and order, his enemy for everything that was bad in this frontier land. Yet the good had to wait, unable to make a move, until evil had struck.

Esther was unhappy when her lover was out of her sight. At night she lay awake hours and worried. She could see he was careful. He kept away from brush country. He submitted to having Sommers with him as a riding-companion. But the thought that a killer was lying in wait to destroy him was torture to her.

"Why don't you go to New Mexico and join Mr. Parker?" she asked him.

Lovell laughed. He understood perfectly what she had in mind, to get him far away from this killer lying in wait to ambush him. "I didn't make out so well when I was there before," he said.

She had read a letter received by Jack from Parker saying that he had lost touch with the bandit gang and adding the guess that the survivors were by this time back in Wyoming. He would be safe enough combing New Mexico hills, she thought.

"I don't think you ought to stay here just now," she said. "It makes me dreadfully uneasy."

"My orders are to stay and finish the first job we were sent to do," he mentioned. "I'm sorry, sweetheart, but you don't need to worry about me. I'll be all right."

"Why don't you resign? You are going to quit soon anyhow. We could get married and go to Denver on our honeymoon."

"That could not be too soon for me," he told her. "As soon as I have cleared up unfinished business here."

"Haven't you done your share?" she demanded resentfully. "You were nearly killed fighting the train robbers. There are other marshals besides you. Let them come and finish this."

"I'm not the one to decide that. My orders keep me here. Would you like me to write to my boss that there is a character hanging around making big talk and I'd like to be relieved because he has me scared?"

"I could ask Governor Brodie to send Rangers as Uncle Zach meant to do."

"No," he told her decisively. "You're not thinking straight, honey. This is *my* job. What would you think of a soldier who wanted to quit just before a battle? Not that I'm in any serious danger. We'll laugh about this later."

She gave up. Even before she began, she had known she could not win her point. She would have liked him less if she could. He was a man who would make his own fundamental decisions. What had attracted her first in him had been the cool, almost insolent insouciance with which he had faced enemies bent on destroying him, together with a physical magnetism that set excitement strumming in her veins. That he was a man tough and hard was clear, but the strength in him might be directed toward good or bad. That sardonic, reckless gleam in his eyes might be the outward token of an inner callousness. It was a deep satisfaction to her now to know he was entirely dependable.

He was a good stockman, and Esther tried to keep him busy on the ranch. Here he was comparatively safe. But he was still gathering evidence, and his duties took him far afield at times. Parker and he had thrown out lines among the old settlers along the creeks, honest men who had suspicions as to the identity of one or another of the rustlers with some tags of fact to back them. Two men of bad reputation had taken alarm and vanished from the country. The cowboy Sid had been discharged by Haley from the

Bar Z Y, but he was still hanging around Live Oaks. He had been seen on several occasions at the Cowboys' Resort whispering with Winters.

Bill Sommers rode with Lovell on all of his exploratory trips.

"Soon now," the marshal said to Bill. "I'm gathering up loose ends before I close in on Krock. He's the head of the rustler gang that was operating from here. When we get him the organization will break up."

They were riding to town by the notch gap. The trail down the gulch was hard on their mounts, but there was much less likelihood of an ambush.

"You've put the fear into them already," Bill said. "There hasn't been a raid on a ranch since you came."

"Krock has seen to that. He is a wary old scoundrel."

"I don't get him," Sommers answered. "He was sitting pretty, well enough off, highly respected. If he was a saddle tramp like Elza Lay, I could understand it, but Krock is a smart lawyer. How come he to start doing business with outlaws?"

They stopped at the entrance to the gulch trough that marked the steep descent to Live Oaks.

"I can guess, just as you can," Lovell

replied. "I may be wrong. First off, Krock is terribly ambitious. He wanted to be top dog. Always he had taken orders from Zach Young, and he hated it. Deep down, he felt he was a bigger man than Zach. His conceit is enormous. There is big money in cattle-rustling, and the physical geography of this country, slashed by canyons and gorges, makes ranch-raiding almost a hundred percent safe. He could get rich in two-three years and then quit. At the same time he would be milking Young's cow, as you might put it. Likely he got a kick from skating on thin ice, figuring he was smart enough to get away with it."

"I reckon he thinks now he would of been all right if he hadn't had reckless fools for partners," Sommers said.

"Yes," Lovell agreed. "But in spite of his smartness he was the biggest fool of all."

They slithered down the trough warily, keeping silent until they came to the exit from the canyon. At the livery stable they unsaddled. Jim Roberts had just come in from dinner. He told them that Winters and Sid Miller were playing poker in the Cowboys' Resort.

Lovell had come to town to talk with the owner of a small grocery. Information had reached him that Ringold had once been seen late at night loading a pack horse with supplies in front of this store. Since the Bar Z Y ran an account at Holbrook's and hauled the stuff to the ranch by wagon, the inference was that these goods were not to go there. The marshal jumped to the conclusion that their destination had been a cache far up some canyon on the route to Robbers' Roost.

Yenson took fright at the first approach. He was very taciturn. Under pressure he admitted that he had come and reopened the store about eleven o'clock one night to sell supplies to Ringold. The foreman had told him he had got into a poker game until after Holbrook had closed and that he did not want to return to the ranch without the groceries. He paid cash. That was all there was to it.

"Didn't it surprise you that Ringold paid cash for goods when you knew the ranch runs an account at Holbrook's?" Lovell asked.

"None of my business. The way it looked to me was that he was in a kind of jam for sitting in the game so long and would cook up some story later to get his money back from the ranch. All that interested me was that I was making a twenty-five-dollar sale."

"That the only time you ever sold goods

to him?"

"Yes." The answer had come after a just perceptible hesitation. "What difference does it make anyhow now? Ringold is dead and buried."

"Anybody with Ringold?"

"A fellow I didn't know. You can't drag me into trouble. My business is selling groceries."

The marshal explained that he had no intention of making Yenson any trouble.

As the two men from the Circle 72 walked back along Rincon Street, Lovell came to a decision to drop into the Cowboys' Resort.

"Okay with me," Sommers agreed.

"I'm going in alone, Bill."

"What's the big idea?"

"I don't want those rannikans to get the notion I need a nurse to ride herd on me in town. Out on the range where there is a chance of ambush, that is different."

"Miss Esther —"

"Don't worry about what Miss Esther says," Lovell interrupted. "She knows I'm bullheaded."

As the marshal pushed through the swing doors, his glance swept the room swiftly. There were two men at the bar, one asleep on a bench by the wall, and five near the back of the saloon playing poker. Two of those at the round table were Winters and Miller. A man glanced up, caught sight of the marshal, and murmured out of the corner of his mouth, "Gent dropping in to see us."

Winters slewed around his head, a king in his hand ready to discard. He pushed back his chair, as if to rise.

"Stay put, you fool," snarled Miller. "He's not calling for a show-down."

Arms hanging at length, Lovell moved toward the table, on his face a thin, satiric smile. The poised ease of the supple body showed an almost negligent indifference.

"What d'you want?" growled Winters.

The eyebrows of the marshal lifted, as if in polite surprise at the question. "If this is wishing day, I'd like a nice well-watered spread stocked with good whiteface stuff," he answered. "What would you like, Mr. Winters?"

"Walters," corrected the Wyoming man harshly.

"Excuse me — Walters. I'm always getting mixed on names. Don't let me interrupt your game."

A tide of rising anger purpled the face of Winters. He flung his cards on the table. "To hell with the game! If you've come in here to hurrah me you've picked the wrong

315

guy. I won't stand for it a minute."

"No call to get on the peck yet, Dan," warned Miller. "Cain't you see Mr. Lovell isn't lookin' for trouble?"

The bad man flung away the alias he had insisted upon. "He started lookin' for it when he killed my brother Nate. He's in it up to his hocks." A red-hot devil of fury glared out of Winters's eyes. He was near the explosion point, caution forgotten.

"If you are talking about Nate Winters, he gave me no choice," the marshal answered evenly. His hands had not changed position, but his eyes did not shift from those of the killer. Though his voice was low and even conciliatory, Lovell had never been more dangerous in his gusty lifetime. "He came at me with his gun smoking."

The eye can be a prince of deadly weapons. The urge to kill surged up in Winters like a flood of waters about to break a dam. Lovell still had made no motion toward the weapon at his hip. *I could drop him before he gets his gun out,* the outlaw thought. But there was a deterring doubt. The marshal was so cool, so sure. Even if he were hit fatally, there would be that half-second before the shock destroyed co-ordination. Better wait and follow the plan Krock had suggested. No use taking fool chances.

"Get out of here!" Winters cried hoarsely. "Before I fling a slug into yore belly."

Lovell gave the warning he had come in to say. His words fell gently, almost pleadingly. "Better leave this country, Winters. Don't wait until it's too late. Go tonight."

He turned and walked lightly out of the room. What he had already been convinced of, he knew now for sure. It was in the desperado's twisted mind to destroy him.

CHAPTER FORTY-ONE: COLONEL KROCK MAKES AN OFFER

Butler Krock sat behind his desk glooming at a firearms company calendar in front of him. His eyes saw it, but he was not aware of its presence. The net was closing in on him. He dared not run away. His only chance was to stay and fight. The weakness of his position was that he could not come out in the open and attack. He had to ignore, with a fixed, unhappy smile, the suspicious eyes of men who had always believed in him.

The fatal mistake he had made was in allowing Lovell to live after he had first recognized the danger in the man. It had not been for want of trying. The fellow seemed to have a charmed life. Ringold and Curry and Nate Winters had all failed. It was up to Dan Winters now, and not twenty-four hours ago the marshal had walked into a saloon and warned the desperado in public that he had better give up what he had in mind.

Krock rose heavily from the desk and walked out of the courthouse. He got into the buggy at the hitching-post and drove out of town. The road he took led to the Bar ZY.

Nick Haley greeted him very coldly. Against his wish, Nick had become convinced that Esther was right. There was a tie-up between the lawyer and the bandits, one more definite than that binding an attorney and his clients. He had been used as a tool by Krock, who had given him the place as manager to retain Ringold and get the outlaws onto the ranch.

The judge still presented a suave and benign surface. There was no evidence against him, he maintained, except the letter to Sheriff Kern of Routt County, Colorado, and the one written to Governor Brodie. Both of these were forgeries. It was clear that he had a bitter and relentless enemy trying to ruin him, but he was sure that in the end right would triumph.

"If this is what you came to tell me you might as well have stayed at home," Haley told him angrily. "You can't make a monkey of me any longer."

"I've never done that, Nick," the lawyer said, his voice unctuous with sad reproach. "I've always supported and helped you. No, I didn't come to justify myself, but to give up my stewardship. Since I am so badly misjudged, I can no longer be of assistance to you and your cousins. Send for Esther. I want to give you both my reasons in full for retiring, and at the same time to justify my conduct."

"We can go over to the Circle 72," Nick suggested.

Krock shook his silvery head. "No. I have been told I'm not welcome there. Never again shall I set foot on that ranch."

Haley wrote a note to his cousin and sent it by one of his riders. In it he explained the situation.

There was nobody at the Circle 72 ranch house except the three Youngs. The men were all away working the cattle. Jerry saddled for Esther.

"I could ride along with you, sis," he said. "Maybe I'd better." He had been greasing a wagon and was in dirty overalls.

"Why should you?" she asked. "When Jack comes back, tell him where I've gone."

As she rode across the brown hills to strike the road that led to the big ranch, her mind was full of conjectures. Krock must feel that he had his back to the wall if he was ready to give up such a source of power. Perhaps he wanted to make a bargain — the surrender of his trusteeship in exchange for a promise to drop the charges against him.

She discovered that apparently he did not have that in mind at all. The impression he conveyed was that of a man sorely hurt by the betrayal of old friends. He did it well, she had to admit, but it left her quite cold. She distrusted everything he said.

"If you mean this, Colonel Krock, you may take whatever legal steps are necessary to free yourself of any obligation," she said coldly.

"I need not tell you that this is a bitter blow to me," he answered. "The severance of a lifelong friendship is a grief that time can never obliterate."

"I'm sure it must be," she agreed shortly. "How long do you think it will be before we can terminate the present arrangement?"

"It will have to be approved by the courts, my dear. For the first time I am glad that your father and your uncle have passed on.

This would have made them both very un-happy."

Esther had a queer feeling of uneasy disbelief, as if this was a make-believe stage scene set by the lawyer with no reality back of it. He could not expect to convince either her or Nick of his integrity. Was he going through the performance only because it was the habit of his life to live behind a false front? Or was there some ulterior purpose she could not yet fathom?

From the porch of the house they watched him drive away.

"What's he covering up?" Esther asked her cousin.

"Blamed if I know," Nick answered. "The way things are crowding up on him, he's got a license to turn spooky. But I would have expected him to do a lot of horse-trading."

The girl nodded agreement. "He isn't the kind to give something for nothing."

Out of the incident both she and Nick found comfort in one way. They had been drawn together again in friendship. The old warm sense of kinship had been renewed in them.

CHAPTER FORTY-TWO:
GUNS IN THE DRY WASH

When Jack Lovell rode up to the barn, Jerry Young handed him a note that had just been delivered by a Mexican boy. Lovell read it.

"Know the kid who brought this?" he asked.

"I've seen him around. Name is Manuel Torres."

The marshal handed the note to Jerry. It was written on Bar Z Y stationery and was signed Nick Haley. The text of it was: *Krock is at the ranch making peace talk. Esther thinks it important for you to be here. Better fork a bronc and ride over pronto.*

"Sis got a note from Nick about two hours ago," Jerry explained. "She's over at the Bar Z Y now."

"Is that Nick's writing?"

Jerry examined the script. "Yeah, looks like it, anyhow." He looked up, startled. "Do you think — ?"

"No. It's all right. When Bill comes in, you might tell him where I've gone."

Though Jack had accepted the note as genuine, there was a faint doubt in his mind. Krock was full of guile. This might be a trick to lure him to an ambush. He did not take the most direct route to the Bar Z Y, but detoured to the right as far as the fenced pasture would let him. Since this was open hill country there were not many thickets where an assassin could hide. But the converse was also true, that he could not approach without being seen from a distance. The worst spot would be at Cow Creek, a waterway fringed with bushes.

His trained eyes searched every wash and draw, swept every slope and hilltop. The catch was that concealed enemies might see him without being seen themselves. If they were crouched among the willows on the bank of the creek, for instance, they could follow the dry bed to be nearer as he rode forward.

The untempered sun beat down on a dry Arizona from which heat radiated. Lovell started to lift his wide-brimmed Stetson with the intention of letting what breeze there was blow on his head. An unexpected force ripped through the crown. An explosion boomed. From the thick brush of the creek, smoke drifted skyward, nearly two hundred yards below him.

Before the crack of the rifle had died, before the first small lift of smoke had appeared, Lovell was out of the saddle and racing for the willows. He flew through greasewood, making the most of such cover as there was. A second bullet cut the brush in front of him. He plowed into the shrubbery and dived for the bed of the wash.

Temporarily at least he had saved his life by making the detour. The man or men waiting for him, after catching sight of their victim, had not been able to run up the creek bed in time to get an easy shot at him. Back of a bank jutting into the wash he found shelter.

His position was precarious. If there were several of the ambushers, some of them could circle around the hill and come at him from the rear. He considered making a bolt up the creek, but a slight bend in the stream's course would put him at their mercy for a hundred yards. Better stay where he was and see what developed.

He waited, heart pounding with excitement, his eyes sweeping each quadrant of the circle. They might come at him from any direction or from several sides at once. His horse was grazing fifty yards away. It might as well have been at Live Oaks.

That Krock had set this trap he felt sure. The note had been a decoy, Esther the bait. At this very moment he might be at the Bar Z Y, mouthing pious platitudes, nursing the hope that the man he hated was riding his last mile. An urbane and smiling villain with terrible and desperate thoughts seething inside of him.

A shot rang out. Lovell ducked instinctively before he realized that it had not been directed at him. Other shots followed — three, four, five of them, not bunched but with intervals between. Somebody else had moved into the battle area and was taking part. Reinforcements from Circle 72, Jack guessed.

He left the shelter of the bank bulge and moved down the sandy floor of the wash, sticking close to the bushes along the edge. Smoke from the brush in front of him rose and thinned out against the blue sky. Jack could not see the men in the thicket, but he fired twice to distract their attention from his friends.

He heard the hammering of another gun. Two men popped out of the willows and started to run across the wash. One of them was limping. They were making for two saddled horses grazing in a draw.

Farther down a man jumped from the bank to the sandy floor. The man was Bill Sommers. He took quick aim and fired. The foremost of the running men stumbled, wavered a few steps to the bank, and clawed at it. His head dropped into the bushes and he collapsed.

The limping man stopped and flung up his hands. "Don't kill me!" he cried. "I give up." He was the cowboy Sid Miller.

Jerry appeared on the bank, rifle in hand. "You all right, Jack?" he cried.

Lovell waved a hand, which instantly went back to his rifle. His gaze did not lift from the men who had been trapped in their own ambush. There were only two of them. He knew that because there were only two mounts.

Sommers called to the marshal. "I'll cover Sid if you'll check on the other fellow."

"All right. Better have Jerry collect his six-gun."

The other man lay face down against the bank, arms and legs sprawling. He had not moved since he had fallen. The dead man was Winters.

"Shot through the heart, I think," Lovell said. "He would have it. You and I both gave him a warning to get out in time, but he had not sense enough to take it."

"That's right," Bill agreed. "I had to do it."

Jerry was white and trembling. Bill dropped an arm around his shoulders. "It's all right, partner. We've all felt thataway. You stood up fine during the fight." Sommers explained to Lovell that it was Jerry who had wounded the big cowboy.

The marshal did not waste any time. He turned his attention to Miller. The man had grazed death and he was shaken. Now was the hour to work on him.

"Come clean," he ordered the cowboy harshly. "I'm going to know the truth. Who is back of this?"

"He told me he was just aiming to scare you," Miller pleaded. "I came along for the fun."

"You're going to prison for a long time, unless the boys at the ranch decide to hang you and save trouble. I'll do what I can for you if you act smart. The man who put you up to this will try to slide out of it. He won't lift a hand for you. Are you going to be fool enough to stand the gaff for him?"

"I dunno who you mean."

"All right." Lovell turned to Sommers. "Take him back to the ranch. Do what you like with him. I'm going on to the Bar Z Y to make sure Miss Esther is all right. See you later."

Sid moistened his dry lips. "Wait a minute." He swallowed twice. "I don't owe him a thing. If you'll see me through and speak up for me, I'll talk."

"I'll do what I can."

"I was a fool to come along. Winters hated you — Colonel Krock too. They fixed this up. I got nothing against you."

Bit by bit they got out of him the set-up of the rustler outfit. Krock was at the head of it, though he took no active hand in the stealing. Ringold had taken care of that end of the business as leader. The cowboy gave the names of others, including the two who had fled the country. He was in it himself, but he minimized his activities.

"Take him to the ranch and keep him locked up," Lovell said to Sommers. "Be sure he doesn't get any messages to town. We've got this rustler outfit sewed up at last and I don't want Krock to find out yet what has happened."

"He'll go to the pen sure as I'm a foot high," Sommers predicted.

"You boys got here in the nick of time to save my bacon," the marshal acknowledged. "I reckon you took them by surprise."

"We came down a draw and cut loose at them," explained the cowboy. "Jerry got Sid in the leg before they knew we were on the map."

"Soon as Bill got back to the ranch, I told him about the note," Jerry said. "It looked all right to us, but we figured we had better trail after you and make sure."

"You'll be wearing man-size boots soon, Jerry," Lovell told him. "I say thanks. Well, I'll be getting along. Better send for Doc White to look after Miller's leg. Maybe you'd better go yourself, Jerry. Don't tell even the doctor who has been hurt — or how it happened — until he reaches the ranch."

Lovell turned his horse's head toward the Bar Z Y.

Chapter Forty-Three: The Wages of Sin

When Jack Lovell walked into the rambling old ranch house he found Esther alone. Nick had gone down to the corral to look at a young horse badly cut up by barbwire. Jack closed the door behind him and looked down at her slim, beautifully poised figure. She had been at the piano picking out some music to take home.

Slowly she rose, her eyes fastened to his. No words were necessary to tell her that something important to their lives had occurred. A pulse of excitement beat in her throat. She waited, expectant, her breasts lifted by a quick intake of breath.

"It's all over," he said. "The trail ahead is clear for us at last. Dan Winters is dead."

"You killed him," she breathed.

"No. Bill Sommers did that. I walked into a deadfall at Cow Creek. Bill and Jerry came along and turned the tables on the ambushers. We captured Sid Miller. He came clean. His story will finish Krock."

She went into her lover's arms and clung to him as if she could not let him go.

They rode home beneath the stars, wrapped in the soft velvet Arizona night. In that semidarkness all the raw harshness of the landscape was blurred to beauty. The world was in tune with their love. They knew it would not be so always. Sometimes they would ride rough and dusty trails, but they would ride them together. This was their hour. Before the night was over, Jack would be snatched back into the harsh duty that had brought him to the territory.

Lovell and Sommers took the wounded man to Live Oaks in a wagon the bed of which was filled with hay. They turned him over to Sheriff Houck for safekeeping. In Houck's presence the prisoner signed a full confession.

Houck's perplexities were resolved for him. It was no longer necessary to balance Krock's power against the charges of the marshal.

"I'd better do the arresting," he said,

"since this offense is a local one."

Lovell understood that the sheriff wanted to save face, but he had no objection to this. "Sommers and I will go along, to make sure he doesn't try any funny business," the marshal replied. "You may have whatever credit there is in taking him."

They found Krock at the courthouse. As soon as his eyes fell on Lovell, he knew he was lost. Once more the man had escaped from the ambuscade prepared for him. The lawyer knew he would never have another chance. The pit of his stomach grew heavy and cold. He had come to the end of his last mile.

"You are under arrest for conspiracy to murder," the sheriff told him.

"So you've thrown in with my enemies to support a cooked-up story, Houck," the cornered man said. "I always knew you were a rat."

"It's no use, Krock," Lovell told him. "Dan Winters is dead and Miller has confessed everything."

The judge seemed to shrink physically. All the bland benevolence, the rich dignity, that had for so long supported his pretensions, had shriveled up. He had the hunted appearance of a trapped animal. The stark fear and fierceness in his eyes were wolfish.

"I presume you are going to refuse me bail," he said at last.

"That's right, Colonel," the sheriff said. "Maybe you can fix that up tomorrow."

"Yes — tomorrow." Krock rose, an old and broken man. He looked at his trembling, ink-stained fingers. "I would like to wash my hands before I go."

"Sure, Colonel," the sheriff answered. "Anything in reason."

Krock walked into the small adjoining lavatory and left the door open. Lovell's eyes did not lift from the man. But even he was not prepared for what followed.

Krock murmured something about soap and opened the small cupboard above the washstand as if to look for it. But it was not soap he took from the shelf. Swiftly he whirled and pumped two shots from the thirty-eight. One whipped past Lovell's shoulder. The second crashed into his own brain.

Chapter Forty-Four: Journey's End

The news that Krock was the leader of the rustler gang and had killed himself spread like wildfire to every ranch and mountain homestead in the district. Within twenty-four hours three men had departed in hurried flight. Two others were under arrest.

Jack Lovell's mission was finished. A letter of resignation was on its way to the office of the United States Marshal at Salt Lake. It had been understood at the time of his appointment that he had enlisted, not as a career man, but on special service.

One official duty remained. He was summoned as a witness to attend the trial of Elza Lay. Jack gave his testimony reluctantly. He managed to get into it the story of having seen the prisoner save a man's life once at the risk of losing his own. Lay made a good witness for himself. He admitted guilt and refused to implicate his partners in crime. There was no trace of bravado in his manner, no appeal for mercy. Without putting it into words, he acknowledged that since he had broken the law he must pay the penalty. His frank manliness had its weight with the jury. Instead of the death penalty he drew a twenty-year sentence.

After the trial Lay asked to see Lovell. They shook hands, both of them tall, strong men, sons of the frontier.

"When you and I frolicked around together years ago, we didn't have any idea it would end this way," Lay said, his smile wistful.

"No," Jack agreed. "I'm sorry."

"You're going to be a big man in the country, Jack," the convicted man said. "And I'm going to be shut away from decent folks. That's the way it should be. You had character and went straight. I took the easy crooked trail."

"You'll cut your time down for good behavior, Elza, and come out to live inside the law."

"Maybe," the outlaw answered. "*Adios*, old-timer."

Neither of them knew how true the prediction of Lovell was to turn out. Lay came out from the penitentiary six years later and lived as an honest ranchman in northwest Colorado for more than twenty years.

Parker walked to the station with Lovell to see him take the train for Arizona. They had faced peril together, but their comradeship had come to an end. They were to take different ways in life now.

"When I visit you, I reckon there will be a lot of little Lovells running around the ranch," the marshal said. "If you run out of names you might call one of the boys Lloyd."

"That's a thought," Jack agreed.

It was also a promise. Parker did visit the Bar Z Y nearly fifteen years later. The ranch was alive with healthy youngsters, boys and girls. One black-haired lad answered to the name of Lloyd. Parker thought he had never seen a more wholesome household. It might be, he guessed, because Jack and Esther were still so plainly in love with each other.